Soul Intent

a Soul Identity novel

Dennis Batchelder

NetLeaves

Soul Intent

Published 2009 by NetLeaves.

Library of Congress Control Number: 2009907927
ISBN   978-0-9798056-2-2
ISBN-10   0-9798056-2-7

Printed in the United States of America

For Irina

prologue

October 15, 1946
Nuremberg, Germany

ARCHIBALD MORGAN WITHDREW HIS hand from the prisoner's clammy grasp and wiped it on the sleeve of his brown robe. "The deposit has been made," he said.

The prisoner, a large man in a larger baggy uniform, licked his lips and spoke in a whisper. "Everything left was accepted? My gold and my papers?"

"All of it." Morgan dipped his hand into his pocket and pulled out a small sheet of flimsy paper. "Your depositary receipt."

The prisoner took it and used his finger to caress the listed items. "Sleep well, my little darlings." He handed the receipt back to Morgan. "Please destroy this. If the guards discovered it after they…" His voice trailed off.

"Neither of us would want that to happen." Morgan secreted the paper inside his robe. "Good luck, sir."

"I believe my luck has, how do you Americans put it? Run out." The man frowned. "Keep everything safe for my return." His voice rose in volume. "When I shall gaze upon the marble monument the Berliners erect in my memory."

The white-helmeted guard banged his stick on the door. The sound bounced off the stark walls. "Enough already with that monument crap," he said. "Keep the noise down, Nazi."

The prisoner bowed his head to the guard, then glanced at Morgan. "Since the verdict two weeks ago, they have become unbearably rude," he whispered.

As the guard let Morgan out of the cell, the prisoner called out, "I won't forget this, Archibald Morgan. I shall find you once I return, and I shall reward you for your good work."

The Soul Identity overseer shuddered at the thought. He shuffled as fast as he dared out of Nuremberg Prison's Cellblock C and almost tripped on his robe. He climbed the two flights of stairs, nodded at the soldier behind the desk, and escaped into the brisk October evening.

As far as Morgan was concerned, Reichsmarschall Hermann Goering's promises had fallen upon deaf ears. The Nazi general should rot in hell; his soul should never return.

He paused after he crossed the *platz* and stepped onto the sidewalk. Spotlights mounted on the Palais du Justice walls cast an array of sinister shadows in front of him. He had done his despicable duty. He alone had understood that the journey to a better world required distasteful compromises. Maybe someday Flora would also understand...

He shook his head. Enough. The journalists he had met in the Nuremberg Grand Hotel bar were giving four to one odds that the eleven condemned Nazis would hang before sunrise. He had finished the deposit just in time. His work was finally over—he could flee this war-torn country and return to his own battles in Sterling.

one

"THEY EXPLOIT PEOPLE WHO believe in reincarnation," Lester the reporter said. He glanced up at me, pen poised over his pad. "Did I get that right?"

"I didn't say that, Lester." If I squinted just right, the white streaks of scalp poking through his greasy combed-over hairdo looked like a bunch of tiny bananas.

Val sat next to me with her arms crossed. Her smile looked decidedly more forced than it did ten minutes ago, when this interview started.

The reporter gave me an oily smile. "I'm sorry, Mr. Waverly. Maybe you could repeat it for me."

"Soul Identity assists people who like the concepts behind reincarnation," I said. This was my fourth rendition.

He wrote that down again. "Got it. Exploits people who like the concepts behind reincarnation."

"I said assists. Not exploits." I pointed at him. "You put all kinds of words in my mouth last year, and it's not going to happen again. Either get it right, or get out."

He flashed that used-car salesman's smile again. "Assists. That's what I said."

Val uncrossed her arms and rubbed her palms on her tanned legs, just below her white shorts. "Let's just show him how it works, Scott," she said.

"You think that's wise?" I asked.

She shrugged. "We've got only twenty minutes until your picnic, and Lester seems tireless in his search for dirt." She smiled at him. "No offense."

He smiled back, showing off a gap between his front teeth. "None taken, Ms. Nikolskaya."

"Do you have a reader?" I asked her.

"I always have a reader." She dug into her purse and pulled out a yellow device about half the size of a matchbox car. It had a tiny lens on one end and a big button on its side.

"What's that?" Lester asked.

"A camera," I said. "Let Val take your picture, and we'll use it to explain how everything works."

Lester licked his palm and used it to smooth his hair. He sat up straight on the couch, sucked in his gut, and attempted to pull tight the gap in his shirt where his belly hair poked through. Then he smiled at Val. "Ready when you are."

She looked at him steadily. "I'm taking a picture of your eyes, Lester. It's not a portrait." She brought the reader to six inches in front of his right eye and clicked the button.

"My eyes?"

"Keep still." Val held the reader in front of his left eye and clicked again. "Okay, I'm done." She tossed me the reader. "Work your magic."

I caught it and beckoned to Lester. "Come with me as I uncover your soul." I followed that with the opening notes of Beethoven's Fifth: *Da-da-da-dum*.

The three of us walked out of my living room and into the office.

Lester headed for the windows. "You waste this scenery on your workplace?" He gestured at the panoramic view of the Chesapeake Bay. "Why not make this your living room?"

"Because this way we get to enjoy the view all day long." I flipped open the top of the reader, exposed its USB port, and plugged it into my laptop. "Now watch carefully."

I clicked on my latest Soul Identity icon. Images of two brown eyes appeared on opposite sides of the screen.

Lester stood next to me. "Those are my eyes?" he asked.

I nodded. "Pay attention."

The eye images cut away all but the two brown irises and pupils, then sprouted grid lines on their outside edges. The right iris rotated clockwise until it aligned with the left.

"You've improved your program," Val said. She stood behind my chair, her arms on my shoulders.

I leaned my head back and looked up at her. Her red hair caught the sunlight. "One hundred percent automated," I said.

She smiled, which upside-down looked like a frown.

"Is this some kind of way to steal my identity?" Lester asked.

I straightened up. "So far it's just a photo of your eyes. It's not yet your soul identity."

The two irises moved toward each other, but instead of colliding, the left slid over the right. The screen filled with an enlarged view of the resulting single image.

"Now it'll calculate the differences between your two irises," I said.

A few dozen arcs, whorls, lines, and starbursts glowed on the screen, and the overlapped irises faded to a very light brown. The computer beeped.

I pointed at the image. "And there you have it," I said to Lester. "That's your soul identity."

"Is it like a fingerprint?" he asked.

"If you mean, is it unique, then yes, it's the only one just like it in the whole wide world."

"At least for now," Val said. "But after you die, that identity will come back in somebody else's eyes."

He turned to her. "What does that mean?"

She smiled. "Your soul identity repeats. Before you were born, another person carried it in their eyes. And after you die, somebody else will get it."

He narrowed his eyes. "Can you prove this?"

She sighed. "It's a matter of faith, not proof."

He smiled and pulled out his pad. "So Soul Identity is tricking people into thinking they're reincarnated."

"Hold on a second," Val said. "It's faith, but there's some science behind it. We've read over fifty million sets of eyes, and we've never found two living people sharing the same soul identity."

He shrugged. "So?"

I spun in my chair to face him. "Lester, you're missing the point. These guys have been tracking soul identities for almost twenty-six hundred years. They have examples of identities repeating eight, ten, and even twelve times over the centuries. If you like reincarnation, you'll love Soul Identity."

"I still don't get it. What's there to love?" he asked.

"What they offer you," I said. "Are you married?"

He shook his head.

"Any kids?"

"Nope."

"So what happens to your wealth when you die?"

"I don't care. I'll be dead."

"But if you knew you were coming back in the future, wouldn't you want to give yourself a head start in your next life?" I asked. "Soul Identity can hold onto your money and memories until you reclaim them."

He scratched his head. "You're saying I could give my future life an unfair advantage? I could've used a leg up this time around."

"Check with the folks at Soul Identity," I said. "Maybe your previous soul carrier left you something."

"I can do that?"

He looked like somebody just told him he might have won the lottery. But I didn't want to raise his hopes, or his greed level, too high; if he found nothing in his soul line collection, he'd pen a nasty piece about us.

So I smiled and said, "Of course you can. The chances of having a recorded past are slim, but you can at least plan for a bright future."

Lester scratched his chin, and after a minute he nodded his head. "I'll do that."

Val handed him a card as she let him out the front door. "Give Madame Flora a call," she said. "She'll get you started."

As I straightened up the office for the party, I thought about how easy it was to seduce Lester with Soul Identity's promise.

Like everybody in the world, Lester's identity in his eyes will remain unique as long as he is alive, and then after he dies, somebody else will be born with it. That new person and Lester will share a *soul line*, and they each will take their turn being the *carrier* of the line. Soul Identity's first job is to keep these identities and soul lines connected—they maintain the bridges between Lester's past and future carriers.

Their second job is to be the world's largest bank. Once they calculate Lester's identity, they check to see if any previous carriers have left him any money, memories, and lessons in his *soul line collection*, stored in Soul Identity's *depositary*. Soul Identity invests the money on his soul line's behalf. They've been doing this for almost twenty-six hundred years. They have several million soul lines, and they're managing over two trillion dollars' worth of investments.

Over the past year, I've noticed quite a range in the way Soul Identity members think about their soul lines. Some become deeply religious: they attribute a grand plan to God, and they bask in the glory of how special they are. Others treat it as their proof of immortality. Neither of these approaches sits well with me. I prefer the way Val sees it—she hopes to pass on her memories and lessons to others who'd feel she was significant. This makes her relevant far into the future.

I sighed. I didn't think Lester was searching for relevancy. He probably was just gold digging.

two

MY PARENTS ARRIVED FIVE minutes after Lester bolted in search of his destiny. They wore shorts, our company polo shirts, and sandals. Dad carried a stack of red folders, and Mom wheeled a large cooler up to the front door.

She poked her head inside. "Yoo-hoo! You guys decent?"

"Of course we are," I said. I pulled the door open. "Come on in."

"Are the girls here?" she asked.

"Not yet," Val said. She reached for the handle on the cooler. "Let me take this to the kitchen."

Dad followed Mom inside. He dropped the red folders on his desk. He went to the refrigerator and helped himself to a beer. Then he and I headed out back.

"You got any bait?" he asked.

"It's all ready," I said. We walked out to the end of the dock, and I chopped two bloodworms in half. We baited, cast out, set the rods into their holders, and parked ourselves on the bench.

"Bluefish are running, I read online this morning," he said.

I grunted.

He drained his beer. "Something bugging you?"

I nodded. "Lester the reporter just left. He was back digging up dirt on Soul Identity."

"What'd he want, an anniversary story?"

"I can't believe it's been a year already."

Dad smiled. "His exposé was yellow journalism at its worst."

Last summer our tiny security company contracted with Soul Identity, and we helped save them from insolvency while we unraveled an insider attack. That took a little more than a week, and it took me a little less than a week to fall for Valentina Nikolskaya, the gorgeous redhead in charge of writing the software Soul Identity used.

At the time I had thought Soul Identity was some kind of wacky, New Age cult. But they're not. They don't force any religious accoutrements on top of their identification and depositary. They let people focus on spiritual questions without having to cater to any one group's thoughts on what the Almighty or the Everlasting is all about. Instead of acting like another religion, they foster personal spiritual thinking.

At least now they do. Some time in the last decade they had stopped paying attention to personal growth, and they left themselves open to a nasty insider attack. It came from someone they thought was a leader: Andre Feret. He started his own religion called WorldWideSouls, and he conned many Soul Identity members into transferring their deposits to his new church. Val and I helped to catch and expose him as a fraud. Now Feret rots at the bottom of a Venetian canal, WorldWideSouls languishes at a fraction of its former size, and Soul Identity flourishes as a place where spiritual thinking is encouraged.

Lester the reporter got involved because some of Feret's World-WideSouls goons had shot at my parents, Val, and me. We escaped on my boat, but while we were out of town in India, Iceland, and Italy, Lester's paper ran wild with speculations on a mob invasion of Kent Island. His exaggerated tales of mayhem brought in more work for our security consulting firm, but it also made my number one client nervous about our notoriety.

"If he writes any more dirt, Archie's gonna be pissed," I said. Archibald Morgan was Soul Identity's octogenarian executive overseer.

My cell phone rang, and I glanced at the caller ID. "Speak of the devil," I said as I thumbed the answer button. "Archie, we were just talking about you."

"Scott, I require your immediate services," Archie said. "Can you come to Sterling right away?"

I threw the call on speakerphone so Dad could hear. "We're in the middle of our company picnic, and then Val and I were going to celebrate our first year together with a week off somewhere." Not that I had planned anything yet, but I should have. "What's the emergency?"

"Our depositary has been robbed!" Archie's voice shrieked out of the phone.

Soul Identity's huge investment pool made its depositary quite a target. It explained why they preferred anonymity over notoriety.

"The whole depositary?" I asked, glancing over at Dad.

Heavy breathing over the phone.

"Archie?"

"I may have overstated the problem," he said.

I looked at Dad, and he shrugged. We waited until Archie continued.

"During the Nuremberg trials in 1946, I helped a Nazi general establish his soul line collection. Today I happened to look inside the account, and the items I helped him deposit are missing."

"Does the account have a current carrier?" I asked.

"It does not."

"Has anybody opened the collection since 1946?"

"The depositary has no records of any activity."

I scratched my head. "A soul line collection was broken into sometime in the last sixty-four years, and you want me to solve it?"

"I want you to find out who broke in and how they did it, and then make sure they cannot do it again," he said.

I glanced at Dad as I spoke into the phone. "You do realize how cold the trail could be."

A big sigh over the speaker. "Of course I do. But you must realize how important this is. Please come to Sterling, Scott. I need your help."

He did pay the bills, and a depositary break-in, no matter how long ago it happened, sounded interesting. "How about we fly up in the morning?" I asked.

"I will await your arrival," he said, the relief evident in his voice.

I disconnected and turned to Dad. "I never would have guessed that Soul Identity deposited Nazi money," I said.

"You'd better not tell Lester."

Val came down the dock. "Have you seen the girls?" she asked.

I cupped my hands around my eyes to reduce the glare bouncing off the water, and I tracked the closest boat heading south from the Bay Bridge. "That's them coming now."

"You let them use your boat?" Dad asked.

"They needed to get their diving credentials re-certified," I said. "They've been taking it out all week."

"Let's hope they sail better than they cook," he said. He got up and lowered the boatlift into the water.

While Dad readied the lift, I told Val about Archie's call. "He's acting kind of strange," I said. "I told him we'd fly up tomorrow."

She smiled. "I'd love to meet with my team again before our big launch."

"Then I'll book us a room at the guest house."

Rose and Marie waved to us and brought the boat close to the dock. Rose sat in the cockpit, and Marie stood at the bow, a coil of rope in her hands. The twins wore huge sunglasses and tiny bikinis. They each sported an official company baseball hat, their long dark hair pulled back into ponytails through the hats' fasteners.

"That's quite the summer uniform," Dad said. "What if we distributed a company calendar featuring the twins? It would be great advertising for the business."

Rose and Marie worked part-time with us, mostly on weekend assignments, as this fit into their freshman-year university schedule. Their exotic Gypsy beauty, happy laughter, and earnest acting made them perfect for their assignments.

Rose steered the boat into the slip, and Dad raised the boatlift.

Marie jumped onto the dock. "Sorry we're late, Scott," she said. "We had to drive Grandma to the airport this morning."

"She's taking a vacation?" I asked.

She shook her head. "Mr. Morgan asked her to come up to Sterling. Some problem with an old account from the forties that they both worked on."

Madame Flora, the twins' grandmother, operated a palm reading joint here on Kent Island. She recruited Soul Identity members, earning commissions when they matched existing soul lines. My parents and I met her and the twins last year as we started our Soul Identity work.

Madame Flora's involvement in Archie's current predicament didn't surprise me. The old Gypsy lady's entanglements with the organization appeared to run deep.

"Your grandmother's been working with Archie for a long time," I said.

Rose hopped onto the deck. "She told us she first met Mr. Morgan in Germany, right after World War II," she said.

"It's amazing how everybody's so connected," Val said to me.

"What did you girls make for the picnic?" Dad asked.

"Pasta salad," Rose said. "Only Marie forgot to peel the onions before she chopped them up."

"I was pulling out the little bits of onion paper all morning, bawling my eyes out," Marie said.

"And I soaked the pasta all night long, but it never did get soft," Rose said. "Good thing salad's supposed to be crunchy."

I looked down at the dock, biting my lip and trying not to laugh. Then Rose poked Marie, and the two burst out in giggles.

"What's the joke?" I asked.

"We know you guys never trust our cooking," Marie said. "We didn't really make a pasta salad. We ordered pizza."

And our fourth annual company picnic was a success. Rose and Marie whipped us all at badminton, Dad and I held court at the barbeque, and Mom and Val cooked up a storm. We sat out under a large maple and told stories about the adventures we had over the past year. When we all were full, Dad got us arranged into a semicircle and handed each of us a red folder.

"Why so formal?" I asked.

"It's our annual report," Mom said. "Your father worked on it most of the night."

Dad had us flip to the first page. "Look at the graph," he said. "Our business grew by seventeen hundred percent this year."

"Your Soul Identity work made up almost half the increase," Mom said. "But my testing business did even better."

Last fall Mom and the twins established a girls-only penetration testing service. The three went out on weekends to various banks and government facilities. They used low-tech hacking to break in, and they held seminars on making security improvements. Every now and then they'd invite Val, Dad, and me to join them on their escapades. Mom had made friends with a bunch of commercial insurance underwriters, and those guys fiercely promoted her services.

I flipped the page. "How about our costs, Dad?"

"That's even better news," he said. "Our profits are way up. Even after tripling our bonuses, paying taxes, and buying new equipment, our five person company has a little over a million dollars in cash reserves."

Smiles all around.

Val raised her hand. "Have you thought about donating to charity? It's a great way to give something back to the community."

I shrugged. "Honestly, no." I wasn't that thrilled with the idea, either. I looked around the circle. "What do you guys think?"

"It sounds like a good idea," Mom said, and everybody nodded.

"If we do this, it has to be a charity that actually uses the money wisely," I said. "Not some group that eats it up in administrative costs."

"You could give us each fifty grand, and let us choose where to donate it," Dad said.

Everybody nodded again.

"I know Grandma gives money to help the Roma in Croatia," Marie said. "That's where she grew up."

"Those Gypsies don't waste a dime," Rose said. "We spent the summer after our junior year over there, helping them build a community center."

"Rose and I will donate our portions to Grandma's fund," Marie said.

Rose nodded.

"I can support that," Mom said. She nudged Dad with her elbow. "So can you."

"It appears I can too," Dad said.

I looked at Val, and she nodded. "Let's make it unanimous," I said. I turned to the girls. "Find out from your Grandma where we should send the check."

"And see if you can get them to write us a press release," Dad said. "A quarter of a million should buy us some good will."

three

THE NEXT MORNING VAL and I caught the early flight from Baltimore to Providence. Ninety minutes later I drove the rental car up to the Soul Identity headquarters gates in Sterling, Massachusetts and whipped out my shiny gold membership card.

"It's my first time using this," I said to the guard.

After dragging my feet for almost a year, I had finally signed on as a full-fledged Soul Identity member. Bob, our local Soul Identity delivery person, dropped off my membership card and welcome package just last week.

Val reached out and straightened my collar. "But you're still wearing black."

"Because it pays so much more." At headquarters, employees wore green and contractors wore black. My agreement had Soul Identity paying my outrageously high contractor wages around the clock while I was on assignment. "And because I look better in black," I added.

"Don't you feel guilty, now that you're a member?"

Val and I had been having this conversation for the past few months. She felt I was taking advantage of the organization.

I thought they owed it to me. "I consider it hazard pay," I said. Last year Andre Feret's henchmen had blown up our guesthouse in Sterling, shot at us in Maryland, and almost suffocated us in India. Feret himself had threatened to kill us in Venice.

"Good point," she said. She leaned over and kissed my cheek. "Maybe this assignment will be nice and boring, and then you'll start wearing green to work."

"Let's hope not." I parked the car in the underground garage of the three-story, giant yellow clapboard building that was Soul Identity's world headquarters.

I punched the "3" on the elevator panel. James's stool stood empty and dusty in the corner, so I wiped it off, climbed on it, and shouted, "All aboard—next stop overseer floor and depositary!"

"You do sound like him," Val said. "I wonder if he's enjoying his retirement."

James had been Soul Identity's elevator operator until he retired and left for Florida last year. He had provided Val and me with some crucial help and comic relief as we fought against Feret's shenanigans.

"My guess is he got bored and took a job on the Disney train," I said.

We walked into Archie's office and saw him sitting around his coffee table with Berry, Ann, and Madame Flora. Berry, once my neighbor on Kent Island, was now Soul Identity's other overseer. Ann ran the depositary. Madame Flora, still a palm reader, was Rose and Marie's grandmother and the person who shot Feret. These four made up the organization's leadership.

After we greeted everybody, I looked at Ann. "So your impregnable depositary has finally cracked. Somebody broke in?"

"Back up, Scott," she said. She sat with her arms crossed and her forehead wrinkled by her scowl. "All our records are in order. There's been no break-in."

"But you know the gold is gone and the documents are missing," Archie said. His bowtie hung askew, and tufts of his usually neat and trim white hair pointed in all directions. "Tell them, Flora—you were there when we deposited it."

"I was there, but all I know is what you told me," Madame Flora said. "As you will recall, that wasn't much at all."

The two of them glared at each other.

After a minute of silence, Berry turned to face me. "These three have been going at it all morning. Mr. Morgan says somebody robbed a soul line collection, and Ann says there's no way anybody broke in. Flora's acting mysterious as usual." He let out a sigh and stood up. "Glad you made it, Scott. You can get to the bottom of this, and I can get back to my work."

Val patted me on the shoulder. "I'm going too—my team's waiting in the dungeon."

As the door closed behind them, I took Berry's chair and looked at Ann. "Whose soul line collection was it?" I asked.

"We've been waiting for you to get here so he'd start spilling the beans," she said.

Madame Flora gripped the arms of her chair, and I could see her wiry arm muscles straining against her wrinkled forearms. "There should be no bean-spilling," she said. "I strongly suggest that we let those sleeping dogs lie."

"Relax, Flora," Archie said. "Scott will perform his investigation with discretion." He looked at me.

"You have my word on it," I said.

Archie nodded. "Then I shall start at the point where I stepped off the Swiss ferry and entered post-war Germany."

four

ARCHIBALD MORGAN HOPPED ONTO the hot front seat of the green Willys-Overland Jeep. His green bowtie, white shirt, and green slacks were still spotless, but badly wrinkled, after three days of travel.

He rocked back and forth until the springs fit properly against his legs and back. The map showed a three hundred kilometer journey from the shores of Lake Bodensee to Nuremberg, and with Germany's vaunted autobahns still a mess, he expected the trip to last most of the day.

The driver tossed Morgan's luggage into the back of the Jeep. Then he buttoned the tarp and climbed behind the steering wheel. He wiped his brow, smoothed the wrinkles out of his green uniform, and jabbed the starter button. "We're all set, Mr. Morgan," he said. "Next stop, Nuremberg."

Morgan cocked his head at the driver. "It appears you worked for the railroads before the war."

"Assistant conductor on the Toledo—Cleveland line until forty-one, when I joined Soul Identity." The driver stuck out his hand. "First Sergeant James Little, Mr. Morgan."

Morgan looked at his hand. "First Sergeant?"

The driver's eyes widened. Then he shook his head and chuckled. "I've got to remember I'm back to deliveries now that the war's over. James Little, sir. My own line's got fifty-six years of service."

They shook hands.

"How long a drive is it, Mr. Little?" Morgan asked.

"It's James, sir," he said. "Four hours, if there's no truck accidents, so call it six to be safe."

"That is faster than I had hoped for."

James shook his head. "And then we have two more hours for the American checkpoint."

Morgan nodded. "We had better get going then."

"Yes sir." James pulled the Jeep onto the road and steered around the potholes. He reached behind the bench and brought out a dull green steel case the size of a lunchbox. A small brass padlock dangled from the front of it. "Mr. Morgan, this package arrived in the Nuremberg office yesterday afternoon."

Morgan took the case and examined it. It weighed only a pound or so. The wax seal covering the padlock's keyhole showed no signs of tampering, and he carefully peeled it off.

Morgan unknotted his bowtie, unbuttoned his collar, reached inside his shirt, and withdrew a key on a long chain necklace. He unlocked the padlock, then turned and used his body to shield the case from James. The hinges screeched as he opened the lid. He took a deep breath, then reached inside and pulled out a green velvet cloth bag.

A tap on his shoulder caused Morgan to whirl around and slam the lid shut. "Mr. Little, I must request privacy." His words cut through the stifling hot air.

James pulled back and frowned. "Sorry, Mr. Morgan. I'm supposed to watch you at all times."

Morgan narrowed his eyes. "Watch from a distance." He turned back to examine the contents.

five

"AND THAT WAS HOW my first European overseer assignment started," Archie said.

I thought about the last few wars we fought, and how long it took for the violence to quell even after we declared it over. "Germany must have been a mess in 1946," I said.

He nodded. "James told me that when he arrived in Nuremberg that June, the local resistance still strung telephone wires across the highways at night. They decapitated many of our soldiers before they were caught."

I remembered learning about Nuremberg in school. The Allies held the Nazi war crimes trials there because the city's courthouse was one of the few to survive the Allied bombings.

"Why would Soul Identity send an overseer to collect a deposit?" I asked. "Especially to such a dangerous place."

"The size of the deposit and the significance of the member," Archie said. He frowned. "Also, I was the youngest, and I suppose the most expendable, overseer."

That made sense. Now on to the driver. "Is First Sergeant Little also known as James the elevator man?"

Archie smiled. "The one and the same."

"After he was injured in Nuremberg," Madame Flora said, "Archibald let him run the elevator. He rode that little box-cage up and down until he retired last year."

Archie frowned. "Please, Flora, your out-of-sequence comments only serve to complicate my story."

I hoped she'd continue. Fortunately she appeared to agree with me.

"Complicate your story?" she asked. "You're about to bore us with your long road trip and introduce us to each pothole James drove you through." She pointed at him. "Maybe you're right—Scott can help us with a thorough investigation. I'll tell the next part."

six

FLORA STRADDLED THE WINDOW sill, sitting where the glass would have been if the house hadn't been bombed. She let her right leg dangle out over the patch of scorched earth below. Her left leg rested inside, her foot on top of the remaining glass shards she had plucked out of the frame.

While she waited, she leafed through the pages of an overseas January issue of Life Magazine that she had found at the last refugee camp. "Baba, you wouldn't believe what they're saying here," she said.

Baba sat on the dirty floor in the corner of the room with her head tucked tight against her chest. She had been dozing much more often since they reached Germany. Her heart just couldn't keep up, and even on this stifling hot summer day, she shivered in her sleep.

She'd just have to keep shivering until the overseer finally arrived and the suspicious housekeeper across the street let them inside the big house.

If the overseer actually did arrive. It had taken four weeks for Flora and her grandmother to stumble their way from the Istrian city of Umag to Nuremberg—and though Baba still claimed they would eventually make it to America, Flora remained convinced they were chasing yet another broken dream.

Just a week ago their last hope of finding Flora's father had been dashed at Dachau. The bearer of the dreaded news: a now-imprisoned concentration camp guard. He gleefully told them how a Nazi doctor and an SS officer had killed a hundred Jews and Gypsies to better understand how downed Luftwaffe pilots could survive a prolonged ice-water submersion. Apparently the method they used for Papa's resuscitation failed, and he was gone. Unfixable. Just like the glass pane in whose space she now sat.

When the prisoner leered as he told how he forced Gypsy women to have sex with the almost-frozen men, Flora hefted a discarded brick and smashed it in his face. His cheekbone broke; she heard the crack. She wanted to kill him, and she would have too, if the American soldiers hadn't pulled her away.

Baba's heart had given up that afternoon when the fate of her only son was confirmed. The two of them remained the only survivors of their Gypsy tribe. Baba spent every night telling Flora more of the old Roma stories. Knowing she would soon be the family's last surviving member, Flora struggled to swallow her anger, pay attention, and learn.

Where was the overseer, anyway? She leaned out and looked up and down the street. A family dressed in rags even more threadbare than hers and Baba's poked through the rubble of what must have been their former home. No overseer.

She turned back to the magazine. "Grim Europe Faces Winter of Misery," blared one article; the next read "Americans Are Losing the Victory." Flora couldn't understand why the Americans obsessed over finding and reporting bad news. Did they think they could just snap their fingers and make centuries of strife disappear overnight?

Now seventeen years old, Flora was born in a land overly familiar with strife. Istria suffered under Mussolini's forced Italianization program, which was the latest in a series of indignities inflicted upon the peninsula by her hungry European neighbors. Centuries ago during the Holy Roman Empire, the Venetians took control and remained Istria's overlords until Napoleon established his Italian Kingdom. Then the Austrians took charge, until they lost the Great War and Italy grabbed the reins. In 1943, after Mussolini's dismissal and Italy's capitulation, the new Italian Socialist Republic, Germany, and Croatia each claimed Istria. Finally Tito's Yugoslavian Army "freed" them last May.

During the early years of the war, Mussolini had successfully protected Jews and Gypsies from deportation. Life then was hard but bearable. But that was before *il Duce* capitulated—Flora vividly remembered her and Baba's return from a week-long food-gathering trip, when they discovered the rest of their family had been loaded on railroad cars and sent to Jasenovac, a Croatian concentration camp. Flora and Baba had been hiding in the forest ever since—even after the war ended—because apparently Tito's Yugoslavian Communists hated Gypsies just as much as Pavelic's Croatian Ustasi.

It was only by chance that the Soul Identity letter had reached them at all. A former Ustasi member had hiked into the forest to deliver it. He spent a month evading bands of Istrian freedom fighters and almost died when they shot and wounded him, but he eventually delivered the letter.

That set in motion the chain of events that brought the two of them to Nuremberg.

Baba kept the letter in a waterproof pouch pinned to her skirt, but Flora had read it to her so many times that she could recite the words from its blood-spattered pages.

22 March 1946
Soul Identity Headquarters
Sterling, Massachusetts, USA

Violca Drabarni
Soul Identity Reader
Umag, Istria, Yugoslavia

Dear Mrs. Drabarni:

We have an urgent need of your services in Nuremberg, Germany. A Nazi leader wishes to join Soul Identity and establish a soul line collection, and as his war crimes trial is already underway, it is important that we get him read and enrolled before his likely execution.

Since the war ended, we have found it impossible to locate a qualified reader in Germany. We have requested other European readers to help, but all have refused.

Therefore I am willing to make an extraordinary offer: if you travel to Nuremberg and perform the reading, and you assist in the enrollment and subsequent depositary transfers, Soul Identity will help you and two of your family members to immigrate to the United States. We expect the work in Nuremberg to last for as long as six months. We will provide you with a salary, room, and board during the assignment and for one year after arriving in America.

If you wish to avail yourself of this offer, you must be present in Nuremberg by 8 July 1946, when our overseer,

Archibald Morgan, arrives. Please contact me to accept these terms no later than 5 June 1946. I will provide you with more details at that time.

Sincerely,

Alexei Ivanov
Depositary Chief
Soul Identity

The Ustasi member gave them the letter in the middle of May, and Flora and Baba went through a mad scramble to contact Mr. Ivanov in time. They finally reached him on an dissident-controlled shortwave radio on the fourth of June, and Baba had accepted the offer.

Flora argued they should stay in the forest, but Baba held firm: the Roma were almost exterminated from Istria, and America would become their tribe's new homeland, their *amaro baro them*. Besides, traveling would give them a chance to locate Flora's father.

So Flora had given in, and she and Baba assembled their packs and set off on foot to the Jasenovac concentration camp. This led them to Dachau and the realization that only they from their tribe had survived.

They reached Nuremberg early this morning, two days after their last scraps of food ran out. They found the Soul Identity residence, but they could not convince the housekeeper to let them in, even after showing her the letter. "Wait for Mr. Little," she repeated as she closed the door.

Flora saw some movement at the end of the road. She leaned out the window and saw a Jeep with two men inside: the driver in a green uniform, and the passenger wearing a long sleeved white shirt and a green bowtie. Could it be them? The Jeep pulled in front of the Soul Identity residence, and the driver got out and unloaded the luggage.

"Mr. Morgan, I'm pleased to welcome you to our final stop, the Nuremberg Soul Identity residence," she heard the driver say.

"Thank you, Mr. Little," came the reply from the man wearing the bowtie.

The overseer had arrived.

seven

"THANK YOU, FLORA," ARCHIE said. He shook his head. "When you and your grandmother walked out of that bombed-out shell of a house across the street, I thought you were beggars."

"Until you arrived, we were beggars," Madame Flora said. "Half-starved and filthy."

I tried to picture Madame Flora as anything but a well-dressed, classy older lady. "Did you look like Rose and Marie do now?" I asked.

She shrugged. "I guess if the girls had to live with their own cooking and cleaning for a few years, then I'd have looked like them."

"From the moment I saw her, I thought Flora was…" Archie closed his eyes for a minute and frowned while we waited. "Striking," he said, opening his eyes and looking at me. "Flora was a striking and a most intense young lady."

Madame Flora shook her head and sighed.

"Which Nazi was joining?," I asked.

"The second-in-command, right up until almost the end of the war. Reichsmarschall Hermann Goering," Archie said.

"And you welcomed him with open arms," Madame Flora said. "What was it you told me? Nazi gold shines as bright as any other."

Archie sighed. "We have discussed this many times over the years, Flora. Soul Identity never discriminates against its members."

Apparently not even against Nazis. I wondered about the general problem of depositing stolen money. "Could I rob a bank and deposit the loot in my soul line collection?" I asked.

"You could try, Scott," Ann said. "People often attempt to deposit other people's money, and we usually catch them right away. But even if we don't, when you make your deposit, you first attest that the money belongs to you, and then you must agree that we're the sole arbiter on any claims against it."

Madame Flora crossed her arms and stared at Archie. "Archibald and I both knew Goering's gold was looted from the bodies and the belongings of the Jews and the Roma. Yet somehow it was deposited anyway."

Archie held up his hands. "You seem to have forgotten that we spent months cataloging and rejecting every piece of artwork and jewelry he sent us," he said. "I only deposited what we could not trace."

"The gold was traceable."

"No, it was not." He pointed at a brooch Ann wore on her green suit jacket. "May I borrow that piece?"

Ann unpinned the gold brooch and handed it to him.

Archie smiled as he took it. "The handiwork is beautiful," he said.

"Thanks," Ann said.

He held it out at arm's length, three tiny golden rosebuds with their stems entwined. He looked at Madame Flora. "How do we know where the gold in this brooch comes from?"

Madame Flora shrugged. "What does it matter?"

"Because," he said, "for all you know, it came from the fillings of dead people. This could even be made out of Nazi gold."

"That's disgusting," Ann said.

Archie nodded. "I agree—it is better not to think about it. Once you re-factor gold, it loses its provenance and becomes untraceable."

Madame Flora looked at Ann. "Where did you get that brooch?"

"It was a gift from my daughter," Ann said.

Madame Flora held out her hand. "If there's any chance at all that it's made out of Nazi gold, I want it back in the hands of its rightful owners. Give it here, Archibald."

As he was handing Ann's brooch to Madame Flora, Ann stood up and snatched it. "You two need to stop acting so ridiculous," she said as she fastened it back onto her jacket.

Archie shrugged. "Nevertheless, my point holds. Gold is untraceable."

Madame Flora glared at him. "Goering's gold and Ann's brooch are different, and you damn well know it." She twisted her body away from us, crossed her arms, and stared at the wall behind Archie's desk.

Ann turned to me. "These issues of provenance come up every now and again," she said. "Before we make the final deposit, we investigate all suspicious funds. I myself reject several transactions every year."

I had read many legends about Nazi treasures, including some scandals. I could easily imagine how an organization like Soul Identity had been involved.

But I had a hard time imagining how that organization could reach the Nazis in their prison cells. That took some serious clout.

"Wasn't Goering locked up tight during the Nuremberg trials?" I asked Archie.

"He was."

"So how did you read his identity?"

"We found a way," Madame Flora said, still staring at the wall.

"I'll need to hear that story," I said. "But first I want to know why Archie decided to open Goering's collection yesterday."

"I want to know that too," Madame Flora said.

Archie looked down at the coffee table.

I waited a minute for him to speak, and when he remained silent, I asked, "Did the new carrier show up?"

He shook his head. He glanced up at me, then back down at the table. "Yesterday was the sixty-fourth anniversary of that deposit," he said quietly. "I felt it was time to right an old wrong."

"So you admit you were wrong," Madame Flora said.

Archie stared at her for a long moment, then nodded. "Yes, Flora, I admit it."

He stood up and walked over to the window, then turned back to face us. "When our adventure with Mr. Feret ended last year, those old Nuremberg memories started haunting my dreams. Hermann Goering condoned and committed repugnant acts of evil. He looted treasuries and museums all over Europe. And I was the unlucky new overseer whose job it was to make him a member. I was the one who had to swallow my pride and do the dirty work."

Archie's voice rose in volume and he shook his finger at Madame Flora. "Contrary to what you may think, I despised that man, and I hated what I had to do. I could not wait to complete my task and return to Sterling."

He started coughing, and he bent over nearly double with his hands covering his face. After a minute he caught his breath, wiped his eyes, and sat back down.

"Back then," Madame Flora said, "you told me I was an idealistic child who should stay out of grownup problems. You may now say you hated what you did, but I hated you then for doing it."

Archie muttered something under his breath.

"What was that?" Madame Flora's voice was sharp.

He narrowed his eyes. "You did it too, right alongside me."

"You made me do it," she said, her mouth in a snarl. "Your threats against my grandmother left me no choice."

Another drawn-out period of silence.

"But that's all water under the bridge," Ann said. "You two have patched that up over the last six decades, haven't you?"

Archie and Madame Flora looked at each other, then eventually they both nodded.

"Good," I said. "Now quit your bickering and tell me how you got Goering enrolled."

"I'll tell it," Madame Flora said. "It's faster this way."

Archie smiled.

eight

August 1946
Nuremberg, Occupied Germany

"I STILL DON'T THINK we can do it," James said for what Flora thought was at least the fifth time that night. "The guards are right outside his door, peeking in every thirty seconds. His lights never dim, and thanks to Robert Ley strangling himself on the john last October, they won't let him sleep with his hands under the bedcovers. We can't sneak the old gal in to read him, and we sure as heck can't sneak Goering out."

"I am sure we will find a way," Archibald Morgan repeated.

It was a little past two in the morning. Mr. Morgan and James had been poring over a set of architectural blueprints of the Nuremberg Palais du Justice while Flora sat on the floor in the corner of the front room and watched them.

James ran his fingers through his close-cropped brown hair and glanced over at Flora. "How about another cuppa joe, hon?" He held out his chipped coffee cup.

Flora stood up and took the cup, then headed to the small kitchen in the back of the house. She took an American "K" ration breakfast package from the cupboard and slid out the inner wax carton. She emptied the coffee packet and sugar tablets into the cup and filled it with water from the kettle on the coal-fired stove.

As she stirred the coffee, Flora poked through the rest of the food in the package. No wonder the Allies won the war—the GIs consumed twice the calories of the Axis soldiers. Flora saved the gum for Baba, tucked the cigarettes in her skirt pocket, and left the biscuits, cereal bar, and ham and eggs for the housekeeper to bring to her family.

James was right—she had grown tired of the rations after only a month. When Flora and her grandmother first arrived in Nuremberg, he laughed at the way they exclaimed over the chocolate bars and canned meats. The Gypsies had wolfed down the food on that first day, barely noticing the two men gaping at them.

"Eat all you want," James had told them. "Soul Identity has rations a-plenty, and none of us will touch them."

Flora ran her hands over her hips. The bones no longer jutted out the way they did four weeks ago. Sitting was now less painful with some padding covering her pelvis and tailbone. And with her clean new clothes and shiny black hair, the soldiers around town were perking up and nudging each other as she ran her errands.

Even Baba had gained weight. She was back to her old self—except for her unrecovered heart.

Flora had spent the last month helping Mr. Morgan sort through Goering's paperwork. They completed the final documents that afternoon, which was why the overseer turned his attention to breaking into the prison.

Hermann Goering needed his soul identity read, but for that to happen, either Baba had to get to him inside the prison, or the Nazi had to get out.

It sure didn't seem like Goering would be getting out. The trials had uncovered so many evil deeds that Flora didn't think any Nazi deserved to live. James reminded her to keep an open mind, as only the prosecution had presented their case, but Flora's had been shut ever since she and Baba learned of her father's fate in Dachau.

Hating the Nazis only made her job harder. She rinsed the spoon with some hot water from the kettle. How did she let herself get roped into helping Goering join Soul Identity?

It must be her awe of the mighty organization Mr. Morgan worked for—awe of their vast funds, and their ability to obtain food in a city where many German inhabitants were still dying of starvation. How did they obtain their unlimited rations, anyway?

It was more than awe—it was the new clothes she wore, and it was the vitamins and medicine they supplied Baba. Flora had been seduced by the easy life. Every day she found herself drawn deeper into the comfort Soul Identity offered.

But she wasn't drawn into their plan—Goering's Last Shot, James called it—the Nazi leader's grasp at immortality by entrusting his memories and what remained of his fortune to Soul Identity's depositary, in the hope that one day his reincarnated soul would return in a fresh body to take up the Nazi mantle.

Flora shivered as she imagined a future Soul Identity member, excited to see what a previous soul line carrier had left for them, only to be burdened with Goering's evil Nazi machinations.

She knew what she wanted—what she needed—to do. She must destroy Goering's memories and return the money to its rightful owners, the Jewish and Gypsy survivors.

Mr. Morgan had pointed out that it wasn't that straightforward. "Our number one job is to protect our members," he declared. "Whether we agree with their philosophies or not, we must safeguard their collections until future carriers are found."

Would the depositary accept ill-gotten riches? Mr. Morgan said they wouldn't. He said their lengthy investigation into Hermann Goering's belongings was precisely because of this concern. "We will not accept goods to which others have a claim," he promised. "We will not be a knowing party in any theft."

So Flora had helped the overseer catalog and research Goering's treasures. The paintings and jewels were deemed too risky to deposit, and James arranged for them to be "discovered" by the OSS's Art Looting Investigation Unit. Those riches now sat in Munich, part of over one million other recovered works of art and gemstones slated to be returned to their rightful owners.

The gold, however, still lingered. All seventy-two bars of it.

Mr. Morgan unwrapped the bars last week, after they arrived as a special delivery from Goering's lawyer. Flora shrank from the hated German eagle and swastika stamped on the top of each bar, but she copied down the serial numbers and dates of each one.

A gold bar weighed four hundred troy ounces, exactly twelve and a half kilograms. At thirty-five dollars an ounce, the seventy-two bars were worth more than a million dollars.

At the trials, the prosecution showed how the Nazis pulled the gold teeth and fillings from the bodies of their concentration camp victims and sent them to the Reichsbank for re-smelting. Flora was convinced that her father's teeth made up part of Goering's gold now housed in the basement.

But Mr. Morgan had no such fears. After researching the serial numbers, he claimed it was impossible to identify the bullion's source, and therefore it would remain as part of Hermann Goering's wealth. So they had repacked the gold in sawdust, six bars to a keg. The gold and three boxes of Goering's papers sat locked in the basement, and as soon as the Nazi pig became a certified Soul Identity member, they would be transported to the depositary's Swiss facility.

The thought that the bad guys always seem to win was stuck in her head as Flora returned to the front room. "Your coffee, James," she said.

"Thanks, doll." James glanced up, then back at the drawing. "Just leave it on the desk," he said. "We're onto something here."

"You found a way to get Baba inside?" Despite her misgivings, the challenge of breaking into a prison intrigued her.

"No," Mr. Morgan said. "James is correct on that point—it is quite impossible."

"Then Mr. Goering cannot join Soul Identity?" she asked. Maybe the world still had some justice left in it.

Mr. Morgan frowned. "He will join. And you will help us."

"Haven't I helped enough?"

The overseer took a deep breath. "Miss Drabarni—"

"Flora," she said.

"Miss Drabarni." His words were cold. "You will continue to help us until Hermann Goering is a member and his remaining collection is safe in the depositary. I should not have to remind you that your grandmother is counting on you. Am I clear?"

She stared at him, unblinking, and forced herself to regain control before her tears betrayed her. "Yes, Mr. Morgan," she said without a tremble.

"Thank you, Flora." He spoke with a warmer voice. "Now, have you ever used a camera?"

nine

September 1946
Nuremberg, Occupied Germany

JAMES REACHED UP AND massaged his brow with his fingertips. "How many more pictures are you going to take?" he asked Flora.

She attached the new portrait lens onto the camera. "As many as it takes to get one that works," she answered.

Despite how the overseer had manipulated her, Flora had enjoyed the last month with her Kodak Six-16. The camera was a mechanical marvel, and she loved loading the film by turning the winding key slowly until the bubble indicator showed a '1'. She loved opening the front of the box and drawing down the bed until the lens and shutter clicked into position. She loved determining the f-stop and shutter speed, and revolving the lens mount to the right focus.

Most of all, Flora loved capturing moments within her photographs. Every time she looked through the view finder and pressed the exposure lever, she felt as if she was stopping time in its tracks and recording a piece of history.

And the photographs she'd taken! She started with buildings and landscapes. Mr. Morgan suggested she practice taking pictures in both bright sunlight and shadows, and she rambled all around Nuremberg's bombed-out ruins. Sometimes James came with her, and when he did, sometimes he let her drive the Jeep.

Flora loved going out in the early mornings, when the golden sun cast long shadows from the wreckage, before the weight of the day crept into the homeless Germans' faces.

Her black and white photographs covered the walls of her bedroom in the Soul Identity house. She had pictures of the ruins and the reconstruction, of stray cats and dogs, of fields and trees and soldiers and the homeless. And of children. Lots of children.

James helped her earn some money by selling framed copies of her photos to the American soldiers and VIPs who came to gawk at the Nazis on trial.

But with all of her picture-taking practice, she had been unable to capture a photograph of James's eyes detailed enough for Baba to calculate his soul identity.

For starters, Baba needed color. The war had destroyed the German photography laboratories, and Kodak only processed color film in the States. It had taken Soul Identity's best procurement team the entire month to pay for and establish a Kodak branch office in Nuremberg.

Then, the first ten rolls of the Kodachrome film produced fogged slides. Mr. Morgan found another source, and the images had cleared up.

Now the problem was the detail. To get close enough for clear eye images, the Six-16 needed a portrait lens, but the first lens arrived with a built-in diffusion filter. Its soft-focus effect left Baba unable to see any iris details. Mr. Morgan scrambled to order a replacement, and it just arrived yesterday.

She and Mr. Morgan planned to pose as a photographer and reporter so they could get into the Reichsmarschall's cell. She would have just one chance to capture a clean picture of the Nazi's eyes, because Goering's lawyer, Dr. Otto Stahmer, could only request a single meeting for any individual. Dr. Stahmer's message had come this morning: the Nuremberg Prison Commandant, Colonel Andrus, had approved their application. She and Mr. Morgan would meet Goering at noon tomorrow.

Based on photographs she had gleaned from various news magazines, she had arranged half of the dining room to resemble Goering's cell: a small table and chair against a white wall with almost no outside illumination.

Flora pointed at a chair against the wall. "Sit there and lean back," she told James.

He sat.

She placed the Six-16 on the back of another chair exactly six feet from James's head. The lighting in Goering's cell would be poor, and the chair would help her keep the camera steady during the long exposure.

"Now look into the lens and don't blink," she said.

Flora shot all six pictures in the roll, experimenting with the shutter speed and the f-stops. She rewound the film into the cartridge and placed it in its canister. "Let's get to the laboratory," she said.

While they waited for the technicians to develop the film, James took Flora on a walk through Nuremberg's downtown. The economy had recovered in this district, mostly because of the trials and the money the press and tourists spent. Flora saw construction crews working on almost every building in the square.

James stood with his hands on his hips in the center of the *platz* and slowly turned a full circle. "You'd hardly know that over ninety percent of this city was destroyed," he said. "This old town district is beginning to look pretty spiffy."

Flora nodded and they walked on. She grabbed James's arm as they paused in front of the Grand Hotel. "Can we go in the club?" she asked. She had read about it in the papers, and could only imagine how glamorous it was inside.

James shook his head. "They only let active duty officers, press, and VIPs in. We don't have a pass."

Tomorrow she'd have a press pass. Maybe she could convince James to take her next weekend.

They walked another half hour until they reached the Palais du Justice. The articles said that the prison cells were deep in the basement, and the Nazis had their own elevator to get to and from the courtroom.

"Are you ready to go in there tomorrow?" James asked.

Playing with the camera and exploring around town with James the past month had been fun, but tomorrow she had to pay for it by confronting the man she considered responsible for her father's death. Worse, she would help him prolong his memory and bury his loot. She stopped and wrapped her arms around her chest to keep from shivering. "I can't believe I have to help that monster win."

James looked at her. "It's the price of freedom, darling," he said. "We may work on the train, but somebody else decides where it stops."

Flora just shook her head.

They were quiet on their walk back to the laboratory, where the technician handed them six mounted 2x2 color transparencies. They remained quiet as James drove back to the Soul Identity house.

In the dining room, Flora pulled the drapes shut and James readied the Kodaslide projector.

While the projector warmed up, she looked over at Baba and the overseer. "It should work this time, Mr. Morgan," she said.

"It had better work—we are out of time," he replied.

James dropped in the first slide and projected the first image of his eyes onto the wall. They looked no better than the ones she had taken through the diffusion filter.

"Can you focus it any clearer?" Flora asked.

James turned the projector lens. "That's as good as it gets."

"Try another one," she said.

James had blinked in the next three slides.

"How many pictures did you take?" Mr. Morgan asked.

"There's two more." Flora held her breath.

This time James's eyes were clear. Baba stepped over to the wall and peered at his projected irises. "Can you make them any bigger?" she asked.

James slid the projector back to the far wall and refocused.

Baba stood looking at James's projected eyes. She ran her fingers around the irises. "Flora, get me a proof sheet," she said.

Flora tacked a blank proof sheet against the wall, aligning the projected eyes with the two top circles. She handed Baba a pencil and stepped out of the way.

While Baba spent the next half hour tracing the lines from James's irises onto the proof sheet, Flora squeezed small amounts of blue, brown, black, white, and yellow oil paint from their collapsible tubes onto a palette. She mixed in some turpentine, and when Baba was done, she handed her the palette and a tiny paint brush.

Flora moved the proof sheet to an easel. Baba stood next to the projected image and mixed the paint on the palette into shades matching James's blue irises. She walked to the easel and filled in the colors on the proof sheet. After an hour, she had completed painting the first eye.

"What the—" James said as he pointed at the wall.

His projected face was crumpling. A growing white circle engulfed first his nose, then his whole head. The room went dark.

Flora opened the drapes.

Mr. Morgan stood holding the end of the projector's electrical cord. "The bulb melted the film," he said. "This is not going to work."

"We have one more slide left," Flora said. "Let's let the bulb cool off, and then keep going."

The overseer nodded. "Let me know how it turns out." He left the room.

Another two hours crept by. Baba finished the second painting, then used her gold reader to calculate the soul identity. Mr. Morgan was pleased when he saw it matched James's identity on file—the camera was going to work after all.

In the morning, to fulfill her duty to Soul Identity and to get Baba to the States, Flora would face the Nazi monster. She just hoped she had the nerve.

ten

FLORA THOUGHT COLONEL BURT Andrus looked like he was trying to be a movie star with his crisp uniform, white shellacked helmet, and wooden baton. She and Mr. Morgan followed Nuremberg Prison's Commandant down the two flights of stairs into the bottom level prison block.

Andrus stopped outside the first prison cell on the right. Flora read "H. Goering" on the metal plate at the top of the door frame.

A pair of soldiers stood outside the white door. One faced out toward the hallway, and the other peered through a small opening into the cell. Andrus tapped the peeping soldier with his baton, and he turned around. Both soldiers saluted.

The Commandant returned the salutes. "At ease," he said. He took out his key ring. "Mr. Goering, the reporters are here."

Flora held her breath. She was about to stand face to face with the man responsible for millions of concentration camp deaths; the man responsible for her father's death. Although she had dreaded its arrival, this moment seemed to have come too quickly for her to prepare. She hoped she could maintain her composure and do her job and get out of there.

Andrus unlocked and opened the door. "You have exactly five minutes," he told Mr. Morgan. He turned and swaggered further down the hallway, tapping his baton against the wall.

The facing-out guard walked into the cell and stood to the right of the doorway. "Enter, but don't touch anything," he said.

Mr. Morgan stepped into the cell, and after a moment's hesitation, Flora followed him.

The cell looked smaller in person than it did in the magazines and in Flora's dining room mock-up. A bed took up the whole left side. On the far wall, a frosted window high above let in scant light—even less than she had feared. Goering sat in a chair in front of a desk on the far right wall. A seat-less toilet bowl lurked in a recess in the corner to the right of the guard.

Reichsmarschall Hermann Goering looked shorter, thinner, and happier than Flora expected. His uniform, mottled with spots where badges and medals once hung, draped loosely on his frame. He stood up from his desk and rubbed his hands together. "Archibald Morgan, finally you have come."

Mr. Morgan shook his hand. "Hello Mr. Goering. The Colonel only gave us a few minutes for our magazine interview, so we must be efficient with our time."

Goering gave him a wink. "Of course, of course, Mr. Morgan," he replied in English. "What questions for your magazine can I answer? Would you like to hear how much I admire the Western political system? Or how about we discuss why you will be fighting the communists in only a few years?"

The overseer's lips twitched upward. "Our magazine is more spiritual in nature. How about you explain to our readers your thoughts on the afterlife?"

Goering smiled. "Very well. Please tell your readers that I am looking forward to my return to this world. I am waiting for the day when I can view the marble monuments that my beloved countrymen will erect for me in a rebuilt Berlin."

Mr. Morgan motioned for Flora to set up her camera. He looked around the cell. "Maybe you can tell us a bit about your current living conditions."

The guard stepped forward. "Colonel Andrus does not allow any questions on prisoner security." He pointed at Flora. "And I must examine your photographic equipment before you take any pictures. You now have four minutes left."

Flora held her camera out to the guard, and he took it and opened the front. "Mind if I take a picture of you, darling?" he asked.

Flora looked at Mr. Morgan, who shook his head. "We only have six pictures, sir," he said. "We cannot afford to waste any."

The guard scowled. "She's the prettiest photographer we've ever had in the cells. If I don't take a picture of the girl, then she don't take a picture of the prisoner." He looked at his watch. "And it seems I was mistaken about the time. Now you only have two minutes left."

Mr. Morgan's eyes narrowed, but then he nodded.

Flora brought over Goering's chair. "Rest the camera here on the chair's back, so it doesn't shake when you take the picture," she told the guard.

He set the camera on the chair and turned it toward Flora. She focused the lens and showed him how to work the exposure lever. "Press here when I smile."

The guard ran his hands on top of hers. "Like this?"

She pulled her hands away. "Like that."

He smiled. "Stand next to the prisoner."

Flora took a deep breath and walked over. She tried not to cringe when Goering put his arm on her shoulder.

The guard took the picture, and Flora walked back to him and retrieved the camera.

Flora advanced the film. She looked through the view finder and frowned. Goering's eyes weren't in the light.

She looked at the guard. "Excuse me, sir. Can we please use the other wall? This side is too dark, and our readers need to see his pale blue," she leaned close to him and dropped her voice to a whisper, "*evil* eyes."

The guard frowned, and Flora summoned up the courage to flash him a smile. "Maybe we could find a way to work a diligent guard into our feature story."

The guard slowly nodded his head. "Mr. Goering," he barked. "Sit on the toilet and put your head in the light."

Goering frowned. "I will not sit on the toilet," he replied. "It is undignified for the highest ranking prisoner in Germany to be sitting on the toilet with guests in his cell."

"Suit yourself." The guard looked at Mr. Morgan. "Are you ready to go?"

The overseer took a deep breath. "Mr. Goering," he said, "we need this picture. You need this picture, sir."

Hermann Goering shook his head and planted his hands on his hips. "This is outrageous," he said to the guard.

The guard shrugged. "Might as well start packing it up," he told Flora.

Goering marched across the tiny prison cell and sat on the bowl. "You guards are despicable," he said as he leaned forward.

Flora looked through the viewfinder and tried not to smile at the thought of how un-monster-like the mighty Hermann Goering looked now. "I need you a little bit lower, Mr. Goering," she said.

The Nazi grimaced as he sank into the bowl. "My trousers are getting wet," he grumbled.

Flora adjusted the camera's f-stop and shutter speed to compensate for the extra light. She took the five remaining pictures.

"We are done," she told the guard.

Goering glared at them. "I am stuck," he said. "Help me stand up."

The guard snickered. "Pull yourself out, prisoner."

The Nazi placed his hands on the rim of the toilet bowl and pushed down. After a minute, he said, "I cannot do it. I need your help."

Flora bit her lip, folded the camera, and tucked it into her handbag.

The guard seemed to be enjoying himself. "Keep trying, prisoner. You'll get there." He turned toward the cell door.

"You cannot leave me," Goering screamed. "I will have your head for this."

The guard stopped. His eyes narrowed, and he reached into his holster and pulled out his night stick. "Did you just threaten me?" he asked.

Goering froze, and with what seemed a huge effort, put a thin smile on his face. "I am sorry, sir." He looked down at the floor. "I will pull myself out once you are gone."

"Damn right you will." The guard slapped the night stick into his palm, then re-holstered it.

Later that afternoon, as she and Mr. Morgan sat in one of Nuremberg's rebuilt cafés and waited for the laboratory to develop the film, Flora decided it was time the overseer shared more information with her. She had done everything he had asked her to do, and now she deserved some answers.

"Was this the first time you met Hermann Goering?" she asked.

He nodded. "Until today I have only communicated through intermediaries."

"Why are you letting him join?" she blurted out.

He cringed and put his finger to his lips. He looked around the café, then back at Flora. "We must use discretion when talking in public places. Please keep your voice down."

"Sorry," she whispered.

He nodded and spoke in a soft voice. "Soul Identity has always allowed anybody membership. And so we must let even unsavory people like Hermann Goering join. We are a business and not a club."

She banged her cup onto its saucer, and some coffee splashed onto the table. "But you know he stole that gold—how can you possibly let him deposit it?"

The overseer shook his head. "We do not know it is stolen." He used his handkerchief to dab at the spill.

"You know that gold is just as dirty as the jewels and paintings." She stuck out her chin. "Tell me I'm wrong."

Morgan sighed and put the handkerchief in his pocket. "We have gone over this many times. The gold will go to the depositary."

"Not if I can help it," she muttered.

He glanced around the café, and then he leaned forward and whispered fiercely, "If you want to stop the gold, you must find proof of its theft. Talk to me about facts, and not feelings." He sat back. "Otherwise my hands are tied."

"We both know those bars can't be traced." She blinked to stop it, but a single tear escaped from her eye and rolled down her cheek.

He handed her his handkerchief. "Look, Flora, I know this is personal for you. But I must honor Goering's wishes and get that gold deposited."

Flora wiped her eyes. "I will keep searching for proof, Mr. Morgan. I'm not giving up."

He nodded. "I understand."

eleven

I SIGHED. "THAT'S YOUR big story about breaking into Nuremberg? You took a picture of Goering's eyes while he sat on the can?"

Madame Flora nodded. "That's it. We rescued the artwork, returned the gems, but allowed that monster to deposit his looted gold. We got pictures of his eyes by pretending we were the press. End of story. You can go home now."

"Not so fast," Archie said. "Did James really refer to my mission as 'Goering's Last Shot'?"

"I thought you knew," she said. Then she faced me. "I think it's good that Goering's money and memories are missing, Scott. I hope you never find them."

"Thanks for the support," I said.

She smiled.

I turned to Archie. "Madame Flora does have a point—why not let these sleeping dogs lie?" I was thinking that I didn't want to help any Nazi, not even a dead one.

Archie glared at me. "Somebody broke into our depositary, and it is our duty to rectify the situation." He pointed at Ann. "Our members trust us to guard their most valuable possessions, and we must honor that trust."

"Archibald, nobody broke in," Ann said. "The records are in order, and your claim of a theft is unfair and unrealistic. If anybody stole anything, they did it before the deposit."

Archie balled his hands into fists. "Ann, I personally deposited twelve barrels of gold and three boxes of Mr. Goering's memories."

"My depositary has no record of that deposit." Ann reached into her briefcase and pulled out a folder. "I went through the books myself last night. No gold, and no papers. Just one journal, deposited on October 14, 1946."

Archie froze, then cocked his head to one side. "Do you happen to have that receipt?"

"As a matter of fact, I do." Ann opened the folder and extracted a yellow carbon copy the size of an index card. "And if you look right here"—she tapped it with her index finger—"you'll find it is signed by none other than Archibald Morgan, overseer."

Archie took the paper and laid it on the coffee table. He leaned forward as he examined it. "It does look like my signature," he said.

I looked at the paper. It was a numbered deposit receipt. I could read Archibald Morgan's signature. The items section read "One journal, handwritten."

Had Archie confused two different events? It had been a long time since the deposit, and he was no spring chicken.

I was thinking of a tactful way to ask him this, but then he stood up, pulled his wallet out of his front pocket, and took out a small zip-top plastic bag. He opened it and withdrew a folded slip of white paper. He carefully pulled on the edges to open it, then laid it next to Ann's paper. "Mr. Goering asked me to destroy this receipt, but I have carried it with me for over six decades," he said. "Here are the items: twelve barrels containing seventy-two pure bars of gold, each bar weighing four hundred ounces, and three boxes of personal papers." He looked up. "Mine does not mention a journal."

Other than a different list of items, the papers shared the same embossed receipt number, and the signatures lined up perfectly.

"Is the journal still in the collection?" I asked Ann.

She shook her head. "Archibald used his overseer ring to remove it yesterday morning."

I thought Madame Flora was about to say something, but she must have thought better of it. After a minute of silence, I asked Archie, "May I see the journal?"

Archie walked over to his desk and pulled a hand-sewn brown leather binding encasing only a handful of small sheets of thick paper out of his drawer. He handed it to me.

Madame Flora couldn't take her eyes off the journal. I looked up, and she turned away, but her eyes darted back to the small book as I opened it.

The writing inside used alien-looking characters. The first page had what looked like three words:

$$\Phi \text{⑪} \Psi \text{Ꮾ} \text{ᚼ} \quad \text{ᛖ} \text{Ꮾ} \text{ᚼ} \text{ᛈ} \text{ᚼ} \text{Ꮾ} \text{ᛈ} \text{Ᏸ}$$
$$\text{Ᏸ} \text{ᐺ} \text{ᚢ} \text{Ɜ}$$

I flipped through the journal and saw that the same writing filled half of the twenty or so bound pages. The other half were blank.

"It looks like a secret code," Ann said. She stood peeking over my shoulder.

"Have you seen this before?" I asked Madame Flora.

She shrugged. "As I said, I wasn't there on the night of the deposit."

Not quite a direct answer, but I nodded and handed the journal back to Archie. I'd have to catch her alone if I wanted to know more.

twelve

"HAVE YOU SOLVED THE great depositary robbery?" Val asked me over our picnic lunch.

I nibbled on our shared "everything" grinder. Val introduced these to me last year, and I had become as hooked as she was to anticipating the flavor of the next bite.

I got a mouthful of grilled eggplant and hummus. Not bad. "I still don't know if there even was a robbery," I said.

We sat on top of a rock on the same hill Val had taken me to the previous summer on our very first date. This time, though, it was in daylight, and the golden autumn sun lit up some amazing fall foliage in the valley below. In front of us we could see a reservoir with an old stone church standing on its shore.

Val pointed. "I've wondered many times why that church is standing all alone, with no houses around."

"Would you like to hear the story?" an Indian-accented voice asked from below us.

Val and I looked down, and we saw an elderly Indian man standing at the base of the rock. He had a small pot belly, and the sun gleamed off his thinning white hair. He smiled up at us.

"Hello," I said. Where did he come from?

The man placed his palms together and made a small head bow. "*Namaste*," he said. "Do you two come here often?"

"Not lately," I said. "Do you live around here?"

"I stay with my son and his wife, just like back in my village when my parents once lived with me," he said. "My son lives nearby, and during the day they work and I go trekking." He climbed up our rock with surprising agility and sat down between us. "This is one of my favorite spots."

"Mine too," Val said. She scooted over to give him a bit more room. She held out a water bottle. "Would you like a drink?"

The man took it and unscrewed the top. He tilted his head back and held the bottle a couple of inches above his lips. He poured the water into his mouth and swallowed without spilling a drop and without stopping the flow.

The man drained the bottle and gave it back to Val. Then he stuck out his hand to me. "Myself Mukesh Rana Malhotra. Please call me Mukesh."

I shook his hand. "I'm Scott, and this is Val."

He gestured below. "You wish to hear more about that stone temple?"

"You know the story?" I asked.

Mukesh nodded. "Last week I met a chap standing outside its door, like he had just finished his *puja*. His family has lived in these villages for almost four hundred years." He swept his arm across the scene below us. "He told me that last century this area was a valley filled with apple orchards and cider mills lining three rivers."

The man frowned. "But the city of Boston needed more water, and the state built this reservoir," he said. "The villagers left the temple standing as a memorial to the one thousand displaced people who lost their homes and jobs."

The three of us sat silently for a moment.

"I am somewhat displaced myself," the old man said. "I chose to spend my life caring for my parents instead of pursuing my career. Now that they both are gone, I have come to live with my son."

"That is very honorable," Val said.

"It was *dharma*, my duty," he said. "We all must do our duties." Mukesh stood up. "I must finish my trek before my grandson comes home from school." He turned to Val. "Thank you for the water. Please carry on with your meal."

"It was nice meeting you," Val said.

"The pleasure was mine," he said. The old man climbed down the rock and headed off. We listened to the fading sounds of his humming as we finished our grinders.

I put our bottles and wrappers back into the bag. "I've been learning about displaced people all morning," I said. I told Val about Madame Flora's Croatian origins, her father's fate, and what drove her and her grandmother to Nuremberg.

"Flora's grandmother had to read Hermann Goering's soul identity?" she asked. "I wouldn't wish that on anybody."

"It was the price of their tickets to America," I said. "Besides, she did it from a photograph. It was Archie and young Flora who had to face the Reichsmarschall and take his picture."

"Are Flora and Mr. Morgan getting along now?" she asked.

I explained how the bickering had continued all morning. "But I've got her telling the story now, and it seems she knows a lot more than Archie."

"Can you trust what she says?"

I shrugged. "I don't really think I can trust either of them."

She nodded. "So what was lost from Goering's collection?"

I did some calculations in my head. "Archie claims there was over twenty-five million dollars' worth of gold and three boxes of the Nazi's memoirs. And in its place, a handwritten journal."

"Where did that come from?"

I shrugged. "It was written in some weird alphabet." I told her how Madame Flora acted when she saw it. "I wonder if she remembered it from Goering's cell."

"I feel for her." Val shuddered. "Imagine standing face to face with the monster responsible for the concentration camps that killed your family, knowing your grandmother will die if you don't help him."

And as we climbed down the hill and drove back to headquarters, I couldn't shake that image.

thirteen

Present Day
Sterling, Massachusetts

VAL AND I MET everybody back in the executive overseer's office after lunch, and I spent an hour asking Archie and Madame Flora more questions about the stories they had told me. I re-examined the conflicting depositary receipts, and finally I grilled Ann on depositary procedures.

Other than the different items listed on the two receipts, nothing else looked suspicious.

It was now three o'clock. I turned to Archie. "Do you really think I can catch your thief with only this information?" I asked.

He leaned forward. "You must, Scott," he said. "We need to know how they robbed our depositary."

Ann sighed. "They didn't—"

I raised my hand to cut her off. "Let's not go there," I said.

What I needed was something fresh. "Let me see that journal," I said to Archie. "Maybe it'll have a clue."

"No," Madame Flora said.

We all looked at her.

She sat with her arms crossed. "It belongs back in its soul line collection," she said. "It is private property." She shook her finger at Archie. "You know better than to have removed it."

"Flora, Scott needs it to track down the perpetrator," Archie said.

"You used your ring to pry open an account in which you have no right to stick your nose." Madame Flora turned to Ann. "We don't even know if a crime was committed."

Ann looked at her for a moment, and then nodded. "She's got a point, Archibald. The journal belongs in the depositary. Your ring lets you look at it, but not Scott."

Archie turned to Berry.

Berry's eyes went from Archie to Madame Flora to me. "I'm siding with the ladies on this one," he finally said. "Theft or not, the journal belongs in its collection, and not in Scott's hands." He paused. "As distasteful as it sounds, we must safeguard that book, along with whatever secrets it contains, for Goering's future carriers."

Archie banged his fists on the arms of his chair. But after a minute he nodded and said, "I will return it this evening."

"We can do it now," Ann said. "It'll only take a minute."

Archie shook his head. "I wish to examine it again," he said.

Ann looked at Madame Flora, who nodded. "Take as long as you need, Archibald," the old Gypsy said. "Just don't share it with Scott."

"You have my word that I will return it directly this evening." He stood up. "You will have to excuse Mr. Berringer, Ann, and me. We must attend a staff meeting."

After the three headed out the door, I looked at Archie's desk and wondered if I could take a peek at the journal.

"Don't even think about it, Scott," Madame Flora said.

I stared at her for a minute. Then I turned to Val. "So where does that leave my investigation?" I asked her.

"On a wild goose chase." Madame Flora's voice was sharp. "Go home, Scott. Archibald is wasting your time." She stood up and walked to the window, then whirled around and faced Val and me. "If you don't, then mark my words—we'll all be sorry that Goering's soul line collection was opened."

fourteen

Present Day
Sterling, Massachusetts

AFTER MADAME FLORA MADE her unhappy prediction, the three of us walked out of the overseer's office and rode the elevator down. Madame Flora didn't say a word, but she did give us a tight smile as she exited on the first floor.

Val and I continued down to the dungeon, but when the doors opened, I held up my hand. "I'm going back up to get that journal," I said.

Val just looked at me.

"We can copy it before Archie gets back from his staff meeting."

She scrunched up her forehead. "Flora was pretty adamant about you not getting it."

"All the more reason," I said. I pressed the button for the third floor. "We've got no other clues, and I can't solve a sixty-four year old robbery based on those two receipts."

She closed her eyes and didn't open them until the doors opened back at the third floor. "Okay," she said as we stepped into the foyer. "Though I still don't think it's right."

When we reached Archie's office, I took a quick peek down the hallway. Nobody was around, so we hustled inside, then shut and locked the door.

We walked over to the overseer's large desk. "Did you see which drawer?" Val asked.

I opened the middle one on the left side and lifted out the journal.

"It's so small," she said.

I pointed to the first sheet. "Here's that crazy writing I told you about."

$$\Phi\,\text{Ⅲ}\,\Psi\,\text{Ⅼ}\,\text{ⅰ}\quad\text{Ⅲ}\,\text{Ⅼ}\,\text{ⅰ}\,\Psi\,\text{ⅰ}\,\text{Ⅼ}\,P\,B$$
$$\text{Ꚕ}\,\text{Ѵ}\,\text{Ⴕ}\,\Im$$

Val took the sheet. "Are they runes?"

I shrugged. "We'll have to figure it out."

"The first letter looks like a Russian, or maybe a Greek, F." She handed it back to me.

"It all looks Greek to me," I said. Then I heard the door handle rattle.

I slid the journal back into the drawer and closed it softly.

Somebody knocked on the door.

Val whispered in my ear, "What do we do?"

I pointed to the chairs around the coffee table on the other side of the room, and we tiptoed over and hid behind two of them just as we heard a key turn in the lock.

The door opened and closed softly. I heard footsteps heading toward the desk, and after a second or two I risked a quick look.

Madame Flora stood behind Archie's desk, angling away from us. She opened the top drawer and rifled through the papers, then closed it with a whispered curse.

I looked at Val and mouthed "Flora."

The fortune teller opened the middle drawer and let out a cackle as she lifted out the journal. She sat down at Archie's desk, and since she was now facing more or less toward us, I pulled my head back behind the chair.

I heard pagers turn, punctuated by the old lady's sighs, gasps, and after a minute, weeping. When I heard the chair roll back, I risked another look.

Madame Flora stood behind Archie's desk. The journal was open to the first page. Her left hand gripped its cover, and she tugged on its pages with her right.

Should I stop her before she destroyed the journal, or should we stay hidden? Exposing ourselves didn't make much sense to me, as the old lady had already blocked us once, but I looked over to Val and pointed at the desk to get her opinion.

She shook her head emphatically and put her finger to her lips.

I turned back. Madame Flora let out a quiet moan and started ripping out one page at a time. The sound of each tear slid down my back and made me shiver, and I cursed myself for not stopping her.

After she ripped out ten pages, she closed the journal and slipped it back in the drawer. She took the removed pages and tore them each in half, then did it again.

She gathered the tiny paper quarters into a loose pile. Then she brought Archie's metal trash can up to the lip of the desk and swept the pile into it.

I mentally urged her to leave the room, but instead she carried the trash can over to the window. This caused Val and me to spin around and hide on the other sides of our chairs.

We both watched Madame Flora struggle to open the window, her scrawny body silhouetted by the fading sun. After a minute she stopped and banged her fist against the frame.

Then she snorted, pulled a lighter out of her pocket, flicked it on, and held its flame up to one of the quarter papers. After it was half consumed, she dropped it in the can, took a deep breath, and blew a puff of air after it.

The old lady sat hunched over the can, the flames casting a dancing orange glow over her wrinkled face. She tilted the can back and forth, then fell into a coughing spasm when a cloud of smoke rose up around her.

After a minute the flames and her coughing subsided. She remained still for a minute, then stood up, her knees cracking loudly. She carried the trash can over to the desk while Val and I crept back to the other sides of our chairs.

Madame Flora opened the middle drawer and poured the ashes inside. "Share that all you want," she whispered fiercely. She set the trash can down and closed the drawer. She walked to the door, paused for a minute, then stepped into the hallway, pulling the door shut behind her.

Leaving me with my only clue up in smoke.

fifteen

"SHE BLOCKED US," I said to Val as the two of us sat in her dungeon office. "I needed that journal."

We left what remained of the journal in Archie's drawer. Not that it mattered: except for the initial cover page, Madame Flora had left only blanks inside.

Val was typing on her keyboard. "You can mourn the loss of the journal," she said, "but I've got to finish this—we're going live next week."

When Val's team launched mysoulidentity.com, not only would members be able to access their accounts, but anybody with a browser and an Internet connection would be able to set up a just-for-fun soul line collection. They'd be able to record their memories, save pictures, and post their learned lessons for others to see, all from a social-networking-style immersive interface.

The overseers felt mysoulidentity.com could fill a need for people who were searching for a purpose in life, but who didn't want to deal with the trappings of an organized religion. They also felt it would be a good way to attract new members.

"Are you linked to the real depositary?" I asked.

She nodded. "That code passed testing today. Take a look."

I pulled her mouse and keyboard over and clicked on the login page. "Will my membership id work?" I asked.

She pointed at the "member registration" link.

I created an account for myself and logged in. The depositary tab remained grayed out. "Why can't I view my real soul line collection?" I asked.

"Because your soul identity needs verification by a trusted source." She smiled. "Which is, as I recall, something you forced me to add."

"Good girl," I said. "So how does one get verified?"

"One either goes to their local depositary, or one asks a delivery person to come to them."

"So let's go to the depositary," I said.

Her mouth fell open. "You're actually going to open your soul line collection?"

Just last week, when Bob dropped off my membership package and I learned that a soul line collection was waiting for me, I told Val I wasn't ready to open it. So I couldn't fault her for being surprised. But with no other clues to help Archie figure out who broke in, I had to get myself into the depositary.

"I'm actually going to do it," I said. It was time, anyway.

"You want me to come?"

"Of course."

We headed upstairs together.

sixteen

I SMILED AT THE lady behind the acrylic window. "You were here last year."

"I remember you, Mr. Waverly," she said. "You came in with Mr. Morgan. Now what can I do for you?"

I leaned on the countertop. "I'd like to see my own soul line collection."

She pulled her yellow keyboard in front of her. "Account number?"

I passed her my membership card, and she started typing. After a minute, she looked up at me. "I'm ready to verify your identity," she said.

I put on the goggles and looked at the blinking red light. "Can I blink?" I asked.

"Of course you can…okay, Mr. Waverly, take them off. You're verified."

I pointed at Val. "I'm bringing her with me."

The lady slid me an index card. "After you complete this waiver."

I filled it out, and she slid a smart card under the window. "Room six, through the door and on your left."

"Thanks," I said. "How long will it take to dig up my collection?"

She smiled. "We've been expecting your visit, so only a minute or two." She pressed a buzzer, and the door to her right swung open.

Val and I headed down the hall to room six. I inserted the card in the door. We entered, and the door hissed as it closed behind us.

I put the card into the slot on the wall and closed my eyes. After we were disinfected, we sat down at the small table.

Val sat across from me. "What did she mean, they were expecting your visit?"

I shrugged. "Ann probably told them I was in town."

"Lots of people are in town."

Good point. "Maybe I have a really special soul line collection, and it's stuffed full of riches."

"That would be nice." She smiled. "Are you nervous?"

"Of course."

After a few minutes, the interior door opened, and a middle-aged lady in a green lab coat wheeled a metal cart into the room. "Your soul line collection, sir," she said. She held out a clipboard.

I signed "John Doe" in the box.

She looked at my signature and frowned. "You may think this is a big joke, buster, but I'm not amused. Sign it correctly, or I throw you and your friend out of here."

I narrowed my eyes. "How do you know that's not my real signature?"

She glared right back at me. Then she flipped the papers on her clipboard. "I've got your real signature right here, Mr. Waverly." She held it up so I could see it. "And if you would scribble something that comes close to resembling it, you can get on with your business, and I can get on with mine. It's a busy day today."

I signed, this time with my real signature.

She glanced at the clipboard and nodded. "Much better. Just remove your card when you're ready to go, and I'll be back to put everything away." She closed the door behind her as she left.

Val laughed. "She's got your number."

"Yeah. Nice to see they're taking it seriously." I looked at the cart and took a deep breath.

It was pretty exciting to think that somebody years before had left articles for me to find. Maybe I'd learn something that would change my life.

Or maybe I'd discover my previous soul line carrier was a creep or a criminal, like the poor person who one day would open the collection left behind by Hermann Goering. I shivered, and hoped that wasn't me.

Time to do it. "Let's start with the proof sheets," I said. I lifted the slim wooden case off the top of the box and laid it on the table. I opened it and took out two sheets of paper encased in stiff plastic holders.

"Two sheets—you're a level two member," Val said. She tapped the top sheet. "These brown eyes are yours. I'd know them anywhere."

I nodded. "And what about these bright blue eyes?" I slid it over and read, "Edward 'Ned' Callaghan. New South Wales, Australia."

Val ran her finger down the proof sheet. "He joined way back in 1912," she said.

I laid one proof sheet on top of the other, like Archie showed me last year, and I flipped on the tabletop light. The soul identities at the bottom of each sheet aligned perfectly.

I looked up at Val, and saw her staring at me with shining eyes. I reached over and squeezed her hand.

It was time to find out what Ned Callaghan had sent to the future. I put the proof sheets back in the wooden box and opened the cart's side door. A piece of paper and a small hammer sat on the shelves.

I passed the hammer to Val, then pulled out the paper and laid it flat on the table. On it were just a handful of sentences, which I read out loud:

If you are reading this, you are luckyer then me.

My wife and baby boy are both dead from tyfuss. Doc sed it was the water, so don't drink it if you come here.

I am quittin White Cliffs and depositing me hammer, becos its all I have left. The opal mine bought me 2 caskets and 4 bottles of rum. Sorrie I cant leave more.

Ned

I set the paper down. "I hope this wasn't the high point in Ned's life," I said.

"I'm sure it wasn't," Val said. She examined the hammer. "He carved his name in the handle."

I took it from her, ran my fingers over the "Ned C," and sighed. "So Ned's opal hammer is my inheritance?"

"And his letter."

"I was hoping for more of a life lesson than 'don't drink the water in White Cliffs.'"

She tilted her head. "Are you disappointed?"

That was a question I couldn't really answer without sounding shallow.

"I guess I was hoping for something a little more meaningful." Maybe I dodged that bullet.

"At least you have somebody in your soul line. Ned was right—you are luckier than him."

Good point. I tried to picture Ned Callaghan, opal miner, his wife and child recently dead, reaching out to Soul Identity in the hopes of leaving a trace of his life for the future. How dare I be disappointed?

I'd have to find out more about Ned, so I could honor his memory. I turned the paper over and saw more writing on the back. "Hold on," I said, "there's more."

Surviveing a mine cavein

Last year at full moon I et me tucker and headed back to me claim, as the opal bug was biting me hard. I clumb down the hole with pick and shovel, and found a ratter named Raddy scratchin my walls trying to pinch my opals. Fair dinkum.

I was sore, so I swung me pick at him. He swung back, then one of us fell into the main prop and caused a cavein. Next thing I know, all but me boots were berried in potch and stone.

That ratter pulled me out of the rubbell, but the tunnel was blocked and we were diggin for eight days in the dark with nothin but our own piss to drink and memories to eat.

The tunnel kept collapseing, so me and Raddy dug out to Old Man Cleats hole fifteen chain away. We were knackered and almost dead, but still manged to scare the piss out of him when we showd up in his claim.

We staid alive by not quittin. One dug wile the other slept until we got out. The lads say thats how we kept from going batty.

Now Raddy the ratter and me are mates. He spun a good tale about Soul Identity, and sed this story would do for a memory. Hope it helps.

I looked up and grinned. "Now that's a story." I laid the paper and the hammer in the cart and closed the door.

Val smiled.

As I was returning the wooden proof box to the top of the cart, I noticed that it had been sitting on top of a small stack of papers with a Post-it note attached. I pulled off the note and read it out loud.

"Scott—a copy of the journal I showed you this morning, in case I am prevented from giving you the original—Archie."

Son of a gun. I let out a laugh. "We must have been born lucky."

"That was pretty clever of Mr. Morgan," Val said.

"And it explains why the receptionist said she was expecting me." I flipped through the stack. Each sheet held a copy of two pages of the now-destroyed journal.

I put the wooden box away, but I rolled up the copied journal and stuffed it in my pocket. "Score this round for Archie," I said.

seventeen

Present Day
Sterling, Massachusetts

WE CHECKED INTO THE guesthouse that evening. George and Sue led Val and me to a large, palatial suite on the top floor of the brand-new three story building.

This guesthouse had been built on the same site as the one Feret's henchmen had blown up last year.

"We reopened last month, and we've saved this room for you two to break in." George smiled. "Before you ask, I want you to know I personally verified that the hot water functions properly."

"Did you include a gadget room?" I asked.

He winked. "With an even better couch than before."

"Georgie, let's leave these two alone," Sue said. She handed us each a key. "We'll see you at breakfast."

We parked ourselves at the dining table. I handed Val the copied journal and fired up my laptop. "Let's see if we can figure this out," I said.

She flipped through the sheets. "Do you think it's a cipher?"

"It depends on the audience."

She frowned. "Explain."

"If it's a targeted message to somebody else, then it's encrypted, and it will be a bear for us to break. But if it's a diary the author wants to re-read someday, it's either just an alphabet and language we don't recognize, or it's encoded with a simple substitution scheme."

"Which do you think it is?"

I took the journal and flipped through the pages. "It's Madame Flora's diary. See this word on the first page?"

She nodded.

"It's also one of the first words on every few pages. It's probably a date. Any decent encryption algorithm would have randomized it."

"Do you think you can figure it out?"

I smiled. "Of course I can."

Famous last words. I glanced up at Val an hour later. "I've gotten nowhere," I said.

She closed her laptop. "What did you find?"

"Nothing. I can't find any system that uses numbers like this."

She frowned. "What if they're letters? Roman numerals use letters."

That was interesting. I took a look at the journal again; the word I thought was a date contained characters that were also used in the text.

I searched the Web for information on letters representing numbers. While Latin used I, V, and X to represent one, five, and ten, the more ancient Hebrew and Greek languages used their first nine letters to represent one through nine, the next nine letters to represent ten through ninety, and the next set to represent one hundred through nine hundred.

"But these letters aren't Roman, Greek, or Hebrew," I said.

There was a knock at the door, and as Val got up, I tucked the copy of the journal into my laptop bag.

"Flora, what a surprise," Val said. "Come on in."

Madame Flora frowned. "I need to talk to Scott." She entered the room and stood in front of me, hands on her hips.

"Hello, Madame Flora," I said. I wondered if she felt more in control now that she had destroyed the journal.

"Stop your investigation," she said.

I pointed to the chair next to me. "Let's talk about it."

After she sat, I asked, "Why's it bothering you?"

She stared at me. "You have to ask after what you heard today?"

"I heard that Hermann Goering joined Soul Identity and opened a soul line collection before they hung him at Nuremberg."

"Actually, he committed suicide," Madame Flora said. "Just a few hours ahead of the hangman."

I hadn't known that. But it didn't really matter. "I also heard that his money and memories have gone missing, and a cryptic journal has appeared," I said.

"That journal doesn't matter," she said quickly.

Of course it didn't, now that she thought she had destroyed it.

"I think the journal holds the key," I said. "I'm going to ask Archie for it tomorrow."

I watched her try to hide the smile lifting the corners of her lips. "You can ask, but I can guarantee you that he won't let you read it."

I couldn't wait to wave my copy into her smug face. But only after I figured it out.

She stared at me. "You two are in grave danger."

"Danger?" Val asked.

Madame Flora faced her and spoke with an ominous voice. "Even over sixty years later, the Nazis are waiting to pounce once Hermann Goering's belongings surface."

"How would they know that Soul Identity has them?" I asked.

"They just do," she said.

I waited for her to elaborate.

"If you had any sense, you'd steer clear of these dangerous people," she said.

"Do you think they broke in and raided Goering's collection?" I asked.

"I suppose it's possible."

Again she had avoided a straight answer. I crossed my arms. "Then they wouldn't be waiting to pounce, would they?"

That seemed to catch her. "I...I don't know." She stared at the table for a minute. "You need to know about the mess you're stepping into. Let me tell you how evil these Nazis are."

eighteen

THEY SAT IN THE back of the darkened room, watching Flora's grandmother trace Goering's irises onto a proof sheet. Three of the five images had come out clear, so even if the projector overheated and melted a slide, there were two backups available.

James leaned close. "I've heard that the Nazi underground is poking into Goering's affairs," he whispered to Flora.

She shrugged. "I don't care any more." She had compromised her principles to save Baba, and now the Reichsmarschall had won. She felt sick to her stomach, and she didn't want to talk about it.

But James apparently still cared. "They claim Goering promised to give the gold back," he said, "but he changed his mind after he was indicted."

It was somewhat interesting after all. She threw a glance at Baba, then turned back to James. "How do you know they're Nazis?" she whispered.

"The Schutzstaffel tattoo."

This elite SS military group was responsible, Flora learned during the trials, for the party's race-centric activities, including the enslavement and killing of the Jews, Gypsies, priests, and homosexuals. Unfortunately for most SS members, they had their blood type tattooed on the underside of their left arms. Flora thought it ironic the Allies were using these symbols of German practicality to identify and imprison the most vicious Nazis.

Baba turned around. "Is the paint ready?" she asked.

"Sorry, Baba." Flora glanced up at Hermann Goering's pale blue projected eyes, then squeezed the tubes of paint onto the palette and mixed in the turpentine. She handed Baba the palette, then transferred the proof sheet to the easel.

"Let's let the projector cool down a tad," James said. He pulled the plug and the room went dark.

An hour later, Flora and James sat in the back and watched Baba paint Goering's eyes.

Flora couldn't stop thinking about the Nazi underground. If they could demonstrate that Goering had stolen their gold, Mr. Morgan would have to stop the deposit.

Was it too much to hope for? She looked at James. "Do the Nazis know we have the gold?"

"They suspect we do, but I didn't confirm it."

"I want to talk to them," she whispered.

He shook his head. "These guys are too dangerous."

She grabbed his arm. "We have to try. We can't let that monster win."

James stared at her.

She silently willed him to say yes.

He nodded his head. "I'll set up a meeting."

Flora darted a glance at Baba, then leaned over and kissed him on the cheek.

nineteen

JAMES SET UP THE meeting with the Nazis for today, the last Saturday of September. The defense had rested in the war crimes trial, and the world awaited the verdict. Mr. Morgan was busy working out transfer details with Soul Identity's Swiss depositary representatives. Flora and James had the day off.

James drove the Jeep onto the main street. "It should take us thirty minutes to get there," he said.

Flora sat next to him and thought about what she would ask the Nazis.

"I still don't see why we need to talk to them," James said.

Why was this so hard for him to understand? "Once they admit Goering stole the gold from them, Mr. Morgan won't deposit it."

James shook his head. "They'd never admit that."

"They want the gold, don't they?"

"Of course."

Flora smiled. "So we tell them they can't have it unless we get the truth about its origins."

James glanced at her, then back at the road. He looked at her again. "How old are you, hon?"

"Seventeen."

"Seventeen." He shook his head. "Well, I guess I was pretty naïve, too, ten years ago."

She crossed her arms. "Are you mocking me, James Little?"

He looked in the mirror, then maneuvered the Jeep over to the side of the road. He flipped the ignition lever down and the engine stopped.

She stared out the windshield, arms still crossed.

"Flora, look at me," he said.

She twisted in her seat, then looked up to meet his gaze.

"Do you want these Nazis to get that gold?" he asked.

"Are you crazy? Of course not!"

"Then smarten up. Most of the Nazis we missed have escaped to Spain and South America. Some joined the French Foreign Legion. Now only the wily ones are left—ones smart enough to be able to hide in

Occupied Germany for over a year. If you go waltzing in and tell them that you have their gold, what do you think they're going to do?"

"They'll tell us the truth." She stared at him. "Why won't you understand this?"

"Because you're not thinking!" He pulled his pistol out of his holster and held it in the air. "If I were them, I'd just force us to tell them where the gold is." He pointed the pistol at Flora. "And then I'd kill us both."

She opened her mouth to retort, but then turned back and slumped in her seat. James was right: there was no reason for the Nazis to help them. Her naïve plan would get them both killed. Baba would be left alone, and Mr. Morgan would still deposit Goering's gold.

"Do you have a better idea?" she asked.

"I do," he said. "When we meet with the Nazis, you keep quiet." He holstered the pistol. "I mean it, Flora. Not a peep out of you. I have some experience dealing with these kinds of guys, and it's a man's job."

"What do I get to do?" She aimed these words at the windshield.

"Take your photographs like you planned. But don't say anything." He stretched his hand to her cheek and gently turned her face toward him. "Trust me on this one. Stow away that feisty temper until we're back home."

She glared at him, but she knew he was right. She nodded.

He patted her cheek and smiled. "Then let's go and save the world." He flipped the ignition lever and the Jeep rumbled to life.

After a few minutes, James turned off the road and drove into the woods. He parked behind a large bush.

Flora looked around. "Where are the Nazis?"

He pointed. "Five minutes through the woods." He undid his belt, pulled off the holster, and stuck the pistol in his side pocket. Then he bent down and grasped a small pine tree he had run over, jerking it out of the ground with a grunt. He turned it over and swept its branches over their tire tracks. He threw the tree in front of the Jeep. "Let's go," he said.

Flora reached behind the seat and pulled out her camera case. She hopped out and caught up to him as he strode into the forest.

As they drew near the edge of a clearing, James stopped and put his finger to his lips. He pointed to the remnants of a dilapidated barn a hundred yards away. "That's where we're meeting them," he whispered.

Flora shifted to get a better view through the trees. The barn stood surrounded by mown fields in the clearing. She could see one person: a shirtless, barefoot man standing at attention next to an ancient door. "That's a Nazi?" she asked.

"Not just any Nazi. He's ex-SS. Remember, they're in hiding, so don't let their appearance fool you. They're mean and dangerous." James pulled out his pistol. "Can you squeeze this into the bottom of your camera case?" He held it by the barrel and extended it to her.

It was the first time Flora had touched a gun. She closed her eyes and wrapped her fingers around the grip. The textured handle felt cold and murderous.

She opened her eyes. "How does it work?" she asked.

"*It?* This is my standard issue M1911A1 pistol, the most dependable sidearm in the world." He moved Flora's index finger to the guard. "Feel the curve? That's the trigger. You can squeeze that seven times before you're out."

She hefted it. "It's heavy."

"Almost three pounds with a full clip. Use both hands, and just point and shoot. But not at me." He showed her where to put her left hand, and how to squeeze the grip safety.

She removed the camera and the lens cloth from the case. She laid the pistol in the bottom, covered it with the lens cloth, and put the camera on top. The case barely closed, but Flora was able to buckle it shut.

James whispered instructions as they walked out of the woods and across the field. "Ask no questions. Show no emotion. And don't take out the pistol unless you're ready to kill somebody."

When they were halfway across the field, the shirtless man slipped into the barn.

Flora glanced at the empty fields and shivered. "This is scary," she whispered.

James stopped. "You want to go home?"

She glared at him. "Of course not." And that gave her the determination to march the rest of the way to the barn.

James rapped on the door, and it swung open.

"Come inside," a voice commanded in German.

"Outside is better," James called. He turned and marched back into the field. Flora followed him. They stopped after twenty feet, faced the barn, and waited.

The shirtless man stood in the doorway and scowled. Flora could see his ribcage poking at his taut skin. "The *Untersturmführer* commands you to come in," he said.

"Please tell your storm leader that we will meet with him outside," James said. "Until we get to know each other better."

The man vanished into the barn's darkness, then reappeared carrying a wooden dining chair. He placed it just outside the door and went back inside.

Flora heard murmuring, then a suppressed moan. A tall blond man in a dirty, pale-gray SS uniform appeared in the doorway. His right hand gripped a cane, and his left rested on the shirtless man's shoulder. A soiled brown bandage encircled his right thigh.

The shirtless man stepped over the threshold. The officer squinted in the light and carefully limped out. He fell into the chair and grimaced, using his hands to retract his right leg.

"Do you have our gold?" he asked in a raspy voice.

"Herr Goering insists the gold belongs to him," James said.

"The gold belongs to the Party—not to that traitor."

James threw a look at Flora, then back at the SS officer. "That may be true," he said. "But my employer requires evidence of your ownership before releasing it."

The officer beckoned his helper, then murmured in his ear. The shirtless man stepped into the barn. The officer glanced back, then focused on James. "My *Sturmmann* will bring our documents."

The storm trooper returned grasping a leather portfolio. He handed it to the officer, who undid the clasps and pulled out four pages of carbon copies.

James stepped forward, and the officer handed him the papers. "You may examine them, but they must remain here," he said.

James nodded. He motioned to Flora, and together they tried to make sense of them.

The officer leaned forward and gave a few hacking coughs. "The top sheet is from Degussa," he said. "It shows their purchase of five hundred and nine bags of gold teeth, pocket watches, fountain pens, and eyeglass frames from the Dachau camp."

Flora went light-headed, and she gripped James's arm. She had heard in the war crimes trials how the German company had set up gold smelting foundries next to each concentration camp.

James looked at the blond officer. "Herr Goering's gold bars are not marked from Degussa," he said. "They are stamped with the Reichsbank's insignia."

The officer smiled. "You are correct. The second paper shows the sale from Degussa in Dachau to the Reichsbank in Frankfurt, nineteen days later, of nine hundred kilograms of pure gold."

James looked at the second page, then handed it to Flora.

Flora verified the dates, and did some mental math. At twelve and a half kilograms per bar, this made seventy-two gold bars—exactly what was in Soul Identity's Nuremberg basement.

The officer pointed. "The third paper shows the resulting Reichsbank gold bars. The serial numbers and dates on the bars are listed." He smiled. "The bank was quite thorough in its deception."

Flora looked at the sheet. The dates on the gold bars were all prior to 1939, just like the bars in the basement.

"And the last page?" James asked.

"A copy of the orders last April to the Reichsbank to have the gold delivered to me in Berlin." The SS officer scowled. "The Reichsmarschall's goons hijacked the gold and shot the deliverymen."

James re-scanned each page. "These seem to be in order." He looked down at the seated officer. "Of course, I will need to have them verified by my employer."

"*Nein!*" The officer slapped his legs, then winced. "The papers shall remain with me," he said. "Bring your men here."

James shook his head. "The men won't come here."

"*Sturmann!*" the officer barked.

The shirtless storm trooper reached inside the door. He withdrew a rifle, worked the bolt action, and aimed it at Flora.

Flora couldn't move. She could feel her heart racing in her chest. James had been right; these men were too dangerous for them to handle. They were going to die for nothing more than her foolish idea.

"Your *fraulein* will stay with us until you return with the gold," the officer said in his raspy voice.

James stood still for a full minute. Then he shook his head. "I cannot leave her here."

The officer shrugged. "Then you both shall die."

Flora knew Mr. Morgan would be too cautious to mount a rescue. If James left, she would perish in this barn for sure.

But why should James sacrifice his life? It was her silly idea to come here. Not his. She would have to help him leave. "Go," she whispered in English. "Get out of here, and get Baba to America."

He shook his head. "I will not leave you here to die."

"You must." She tightened her grip on the camera case. She still had James's pistol; she still had a chance to save herself. She swallowed and looked up at him. "Don't let Goering get that gold."

James addressed the SS officer. "My employer will want a photograph of you and the *fraulein*, and of the papers, too. Otherwise he may not believe me." He pointed at Flora's case.

What was he doing? Flora shook her head, but she saw the officer nod, and then James reached out and pried from her fingers her last hope of escape.

The officer held out his hand. "Let me inspect the case."

James nodded as he unbuckled it. "Of course. Here, let me get that camera out for you." He handed the papers to Flora and reached inside.

"Halt!" the officer shouted.

The storm trooper spun his rifle and swung the butt at James's arms.

James pulled back, but the rifle struck the edge of the case and ripped it out of his hands.

Flora held her breath as the case fell. It bounced, flipped over, and dumped the camera, cloth, and pistol onto the ground.

James lunged for the pistol, but the storm trooper swung again, and this time connected with James's forehead with a loud thud.

James fell face down on the ground.

The shirtless man stepped forward and pounded his rifle butt into the back of James's head.

James's arms and legs jerked once, and then his body went limp.

The SS officer extended his cane and used it to drag the pistol to his feet. He bent down and picked it up.

"You will give me my papers." The officer pointed the pistol at Flora. She stood frozen.

He shifted his aim and fired over her head. The shot echoed in the clearing. "Now, *fraulein*."

Flora felt her knees buckling, and she fought to keep them rigid. She opened her hand and let the papers drop to the ground.

The officer pointed, and the shirtless man stepped forward and swung the rifle toward her head.

Her last conscious thought was of Baba.

She woke with a gasp, her head pounding. She was unable to see far in the dim light, but she could hear the sounds of a muted conversation.

Where was she?

Flora turned her head and stifled a scream as her nose brushed against somebody's cheek. It was James. The memories of the Nazis and the clearing and the papers rushed back at her.

She and James must be inside the barn. The officer and the storm trooper were talking outside. They held her and James captive.

Was James even alive?

Flora quietly pulled herself to her knees, fighting nausea from the overwhelming pain in her head. She leaned close to his chest.

He was breathing.

She looked around. They lay with their feet against the barn wall, directly across from the entrance. A small table and a few wooden boxes stood on her right, and two tiny cots occupied the space on her left. She couldn't see the officer and storm trooper, but it sounded like they were just outside the doorway. The officer probably still sat in the dining chair.

Flora turned back to James. His shirt and shoes were missing. She checked and was relieved to find her own clothes intact.

They had to get out of here.

Flora shook James's shoulder, but he didn't move. She decided they needed a weapon. She crawled over to the boxes next to the table.

The first box held a half loaf of bread, a plate, two chipped teacups, and a bent spoon.

The second box held the leather portfolio. Flora opened it up and withdrew the four sheets of paper she had dropped earlier. Somebody had smoothed out the crumpled parts.

Flora had just put the papers on the table when she saw the storm trooper enter the barn. He was clad in James's shirt and boots. He carried an oil lamp in one hand and the rifle in the other. The light from the lamp almost reached her.

Flora dropped to the floor behind the boxes. She peeked out between them, and saw the man set the lamp on the table.

She cursed as he spotted the papers. Before he did anything, she leaped up, grabbed the second box, and ran at the man. She thrust the box as hard as she could into his stomach.

The man fell to the ground, and the rifle clattered to the floor. Flora picked it up and rammed the butt into the storm trooper's crotch.

He gave a strangled moan and curled into a fetal ball. Flora swung the rifle by its barrel and clipped the soldier on his ear.

The storm trooper's body lay still.

"*Sturmann?*" a voice called.

Flora flipped the rifle around. She worked the bolt action like the storm trooper had done. She placed the butt firmly against her right shoulder, then walked toward the door. Her finger rested on the trigger guard.

The officer appeared in the doorway. He held a cane in one hand, and the door frame in the other.

Flora closed her eyes as she pulled the trigger.

Click.

She opened her eyes.

The officer bared his teeth. "No bullets, *fraulein.*"

The storm trooper had tricked James with an empty rifle.

There was no time to lose. Flora flipped the rifle around and swung the stock at the officer's head.

The Nazi dropped his cane, let go of the door frame, and grabbed the stock in both of his hands.

Flora held onto the barrel and tried to yank it out of his grasp.

The officer lost his balance and fell into Flora.

She stumbled backward into the table. The oil lamp crashed to the floor, smashing its reservoir.

Flora twisted, and she and the officer hit the ground. With a desperate push, Flora shoved him into the puddle of oil.

Blue flames spread across the slick. They cast shadows onto the barn walls. The flames licked at the officer's blond hair.

He tried to leverage himself up, but his palms slipped in the oil, and he fell back into the flames.

The papers—Flora struggled to get up and grab them before they burned.

The officer grabbed the rifle and used it to pull himself to his feet. A cry escaped his lips, and Flora could see the pain twist his face. He hobbled over to the papers.

Flora scrambled back and grabbed the cane. She swung it at the officer, and it connected directly with the wound on this thigh.

The officer screamed and fell down, right on top of the papers.

The fire was spreading. An expanding orange ring had ignited the straw on the floor. Flora had to get out of the barn. She threw a look at James.

She made one last try for the papers, but the officer was able to deflect her attack with his good leg. The kick tumbled her onto the storm trooper, and she felt something crack in his chest.

She forced herself to her knees and crawled to James. She grabbed his legs and pulled with all her might. Somehow she dragged him out the door, wincing as his head bumped over the threshold.

By the time she got James out of the barn, the fire had spread across the floor and was working its way up the walls.

The SS officer burst out of the doorway and collapsed on the ground. He clutched the papers in his burnt hands.

Flora bent down and pulled them out of his grasp. Only slivers remained—the rest was charred and illegible. The officer let out a low groan.

Flora took the charred bits and stuffed them down her blouse. She stood up and kicked the officer in the head, as hard as she could. She kicked him again. Then she wrapped her arms around James's legs and pulled him toward the woods.

twenty

"IT TOOK ME OVER four hours to drag James through the woods and get him home," Madame Flora told us.

"So that's why James always acted a bit odd." Val said.

Madame Flora nodded. "He never recovered from his head injuries. It was a year before he came back to work, and then all Archibald could do for him was put him in the elevator. He didn't remember Nuremberg, and he never did recognize me."

Maybe that was for the best. "What happened when you showed Archie the scraps of paper?" I asked.

She scowled. "He refused to accept my word of what we had read, and James wasn't able to corroborate. All that sacrifice—for nothing."

It looked to me like it was all James's sacrifice.

I was still trying to wrap my head around the complexities in Archie and Madame Flora's relationship. I was sure the journal held the answers.

But first things first: I needed to track the gold. Young Flora's scheme must have failed, or Archie would have returned the gold, and it wouldn't be missing now. "So I'm guessing the Nazis never got to assert their ownership," I said.

"Archibald could have declared the gold stolen, with or without their admission," she said. "He was just too scared."

"What could he have been scared of?" I asked. "He was an overseer—a master of Soul Identity."

"You've been here a year, and you've got a lot to learn," she said. "Archibald was brand new, living under the thumb of executive overseer Isabella Vida." She frowned at me. "And let me tell you this—Vida's thumb was heavy. She ran this place like it was her own empire. Sterling after the war was a beehive of political intrigue—always buzzing with plots and counterplots, back-stabbings, and vendettas."

I had a hard time picturing Soul Identity steered by anything other than the gentle hands of Archibald Morgan. "You're claiming that Archie had no choice but to accept Goering as a member and deposit his loot," I said.

"He had a choice, and he chose to let the gold in." She shook her head. "Increasing Vida's collection of famous and infamous members was the primary objective those days. Archibald viewed Goering's deposit as his price of admission to Vida's inner circle."

Isabella Vida must have been a real piece of work. "She was more manipulative than Feret?" I asked.

"Feret was an amateur." Her face hardened. "Isabella Vida, friend of presidents and board member of museums, was a snake. She was the coldest, most calculating person I've ever met."

And here I thought, ever since she shot Feret, old Madame Flora held that honor. "When did Archie take the reins?" I asked.

"Around twenty years ago," she said. "His success with Goering gave him enough power to be elected as the new executive overseer after Vida died."

"He certainly doesn't seem to be that political," I said.

"No, they got lucky with him," Madame Flora said. "When Archibald became executive overseer, the world was changing and democracy was blooming, and he capitalized on it." She was quiet for a moment. "I get frustrated at Archibald, especially at how he always puts business first, but I'll give him his due—once he worked his way to executive overseer, he did transform Soul Identity into a kinder, gentler, happier organization."

I noticed how Madame Flora's features softened as she talked about Archie. Were the hard looks and sharp tongue she used on him earlier today just her public defense? Or was she trying to scam me, like she did last year when she had me convinced that she didn't know how to work a fax machine?

The old Gypsy lady knew a lot more than she was admitting. "Why do you say we're in danger now?" I asked.

"The Nazis have been chasing that gold ever since James and I confirmed Soul Identity had it. They're strong, and they're motivated by revenge." She stood up and poked her finger into my chest. "I'm going back to my room. Heed my warning, Scott. Stop your investigation before you get somebody hurt."

Val showed Madame Flora out, then came back and sat down next to me. "That was a little spooky," she said. "Are you going to stop?"

"Are you crazy?" I pulled the copy of the journal out of my laptop bag. "She just got me more interested."

twenty-one

Present Day
Sterling, Massachusetts

IT WAS ALMOST MIDNIGHT when I threw the copied journal pages onto the table. They slid toward the edge, and Val saved them from falling to the floor.

"Any luck?" she asked me.

"None." I slumped in my chair. "Maybe the alphabet is from outer space. Does Soul Identity believe in extra-terrestrials?"

She smiled. "Don't be silly."

"Just in case, I'll search for alien alphabets." I opened my laptop and ran a search. The results spanned from Klingon to cartoon alphabets to characters drawn by those claiming to have been abducted by aliens. None of the characters matched ones in the journal.

Then I clicked on a link for *Alien Adventure*, a 1999 Belgian movie. The plot summary told how a space gypsy tribe called the Glagoliths stumbled onto a not-yet-opened amusement park on Earth.

"Hold on—Glagoliths?" Val asked. "I've heard that word before." She typed on her laptop, then smiled at me. "You found it."

I leaned over and looked at the same style characters from the journal on her screen. "Found what?"

"Glagolitic writing."

"Is it alien?"

She threw a pencil at me. "It's an ancient Slavic writing language—the precursor to Cyrillic. We learned about it in Soviet History class." She clicked her mouse. "Here's the full alphabet."

I grabbed the pencil and the first page of the journal. "Let's see what it says."

After a couple minutes, I smiled and held up the sheet.

ⰗⰎⰑⰓⰀ ⰄⰓⰀⰁⰀⰓⰐⰉ
FLORA DRABARNI
ⰝⰜⰍⰅ
Ch Ts K E

Val pointed at the last four characters. "That's not a word."

"It's got to be a date," I said. "Look up Glagolitic numbers."

Val typed at her keyboard, then turned the laptop so I could read it.

The old Slavs used letters to represent each number, similar to the ancient Greeks and Hebrews. I added them to the journal.

Ⱇ Ⱌ Ⰽ Ⰵ

Ch Ts K E

1,000 900 40 6

"Where was Glagolitic writing used?" I asked.

She looked at her screen. "The Yugoslav coastal area."

"Like Istria?" Madame Flora's homeland, according to the twins.

"Especially Istria."

I flipped through the pages and saw the journal contained four entries, all from 1946.

Thirty minutes later, I read the first sentence out loud: "*Bengeski niamsi, te bisterdon tumare anava.*"

"That's not English. And it's not Slavic-sounding, either," Val said.

"Or Italian or German," I added.

She smiled. "Is it alien?"

I thought about that movie again…the plot mentioned a space gypsy tribe.

Flora was a Gypsy. "It must be Romany," I said.

Val typed on her keyboard. Then she frowned. "Did you know that Romany's an ever-shrinking language? They only have three thousand words left."

"You found an online dictionary?"

"I did." She took the sheet from me.

After a bit, Val grinned. "You're such a smarty. Here's your translation—*Cursed Germans, may your names be forgotten.*"

"If I close my eyes and concentrate, I can hear that bit of melodrama coming out of the mouth of a seventeen-year-old Flora," I said. I rubbed my hands together. "This may take us a while."

By sunrise we had completed the first two entries. Flora had extended the limited Romany vocabulary with a mix of Italian, Croatian, German, and English, and we were able to translate almost every sentence.

I looked at Val and rubbed my eyes. "It sure starts with a bang."

Flora's Journal

Cursed Germans, may your names be forgotten. May malignant diseases waste your bodies. And may your grasp at immortality fall short.

ONCE UPON A TIME a young princess lived with her father the king and her fairy godmother in a beautiful castle by the sea. The fairy used her magic to bring people joy and comfort.

Then disaster struck. Evil wolves killed the king and captured the castle. The princess and her godmother escaped and hid, alone and starving, deep in the woods.

The wolves destroyed many more castles, and they killed many more good people. A vast army joined together to fight against them. After many years, they defeated the wolves, and they rounded up the surviving leaders and put them in a cage so they could kill them.

The strongest wolf in the cage had fierce magical teeth, made out of the bones of his victims.

The princess and her godmother still starved in the woods, for although the people had won and they had rescued the beautiful castle, they kept it for themselves.

One day a knight in shining armor sent a message to the fairy godmother and the princess. He offered them a new castle in a land far away. But to get there, he wanted the fairy godmother to use her magic and make the strongest wolf immortal.

The princess didn't want to help the wolf who killed her father. She didn't want to help the wolf use his magical teeth forever and ever.

But her fairy godmother said they would perish if they remained in the woods, so they agreed to help, and they traveled to the wolf cage. While the fairy prepared a special talisman for the wolf, the princess decided to destroy the magical teeth before they too became immortal.

The captain refused to help her, even though she pleaded with him many times. One brave knight did volunteer, and he and the princess set off together on a quest to destroy the teeth. But although they tried valiantly, cunning wolves tricked them and almost killed the brave knight.

Now the princess doesn't know what to do. The wolf still needs to be defanged. The captain doesn't care. And time is running out.

But the princess will never give up. Never.

1 October 1946

When you are given, eat. When you are beaten, run away.

THE CAPTAIN CAME TO the princess, who had been hiding in her room for the three days since the brave knight was wounded. The talisman was ready, and the wolf's magical teeth would soon be deposited in a safe place, there to await his return from death.

The captain asked the princess to befriend a guard and pass messages to the wolf. She didn't want to help, but the captain forced her to by swearing that he'd harm her fairy godmother if she didn't.

So the princess searched for other ways to destroy the wolf's magical teeth. Her fairy godmother made a special truth-telling potion to use against the captain.

When the princess gave the captain the potion, he told her where the magical teeth would be hidden. He told her he had to save them so he could become a general and help kill future wolves. And then he confessed his love for her.

When the captain left, the princess was horribly confused. She wanted to help the captain, but she was still determined to destroy the wolf's magical teeth.

twenty-two

VAL LET OUT A whistle. "The first entry matches what she told us, but the next one—Flora and Mr. Morgan—wow."

I couldn't wait to hear how the fairy tale ended. I held up the translation. "Time to show Madame Flora our copy. Maybe that'll shock her into filling in the gaps."

We walked downstairs and knocked on Madame Flora's door. When she opened it, I pushed past her and sat down on her couch without saying a word. Val sat next to me.

The old lady stood in her bathrobe, her arms crossed. After a long moment of silence, she cleared her throat and asked, "Are we playing charades?"

"Good idea," I said. I held up three fingers.

"Three words," Val said.

I nodded and held up a single finger.

"First word," Madame Flora said.

I nodded and pointed at her.

"Flora," Val said.

I nodded and held up two fingers.

"Second word," Madame Flora said.

I pointed at her again.

"Drabarni," Val said.

I nodded and held up three fingers.

"Let's cut this short," Val said. "Third word is 1946. As in your journal from 1946, found in Hermann Goering's soul line collection."

Madame Flora sucked in a big gulp of air. She dropped her hands to her sides. "Archibald snuck you a copy, didn't he?"

I touched my nose. "Bingo. And it's a good thing, too, since you burned the original."

"How do you know that?"

I smiled. "We also thought we should get to the journal before Archie returned it. We watched you destroy it."

She closed her eyes. "And now you've figured out my code?" She opened them and stared at me.

I nodded. "Mostly Romany in a Glagolitic script."

She seemed to collapse into a chair across from the couch. "How much of it did you understand?" She bit her lip.

"We've decoded half of it," I said. "Right now we have a wounded brave knight and a captain in love with a confused princess."

Madame Flora sighed. "Scott, you mustn't tell Archibald you can read it."

"Why not?" I asked.

"You will cause irreparable damage for all of us." Madame Flora sat forward on her seat, her hands gripping the ends of her bathrobe. "You mustn't tell him."

I looked at Val. "What do you think?"

"I think she owes us the rest of the story before we can agree to that," Val said.

"Me too." I pointed at Madame Flora. "Translate your fairy tale into fact, and we'll reserve judgment until you're done."

Madame Flora's gaze swung from Val to me. She nodded, and said, "Once you hear me out, I'm sure you'll understand."

twenty-three

October 1946
Nuremberg, Occupied Germany

BABA HAD GIVEN IT to Flora last week, the night she completed calculating Goering's soul identity. "Write it down," she said, pressing the leather-bound journal into her hands.

"Write what, Baba?" she asked.

"Everything that happens to you from this day forward." Baba handed her a fountain pen. "Today marks the first day of our new life. You must record all that happens." She grabbed Flora's shoulders and stared fiercely into her eyes. "You must form new dreams."

So Flora took the journal, and she wrote about the disastrous negotiations with the Nazi underground.

The overseer knocked on the door just as she finished, and Flora glared at him. "Get out of my room," she said. She moved to her bed and hugged her pillow to her chest.

Archibald Morgan shook his finger at her. "You put my mission in jeopardy, yet you dare talk to me like this?"

"It was your fault—not mine. It didn't have to happen that way, and you know it."

"I know it?" His hands clenched into fists. "What do you think I could have done?"

"Turned the gold over to the authorities," she yelled. "We both know it's stolen."

His chin dropped toward his chest. "Knowing is not enough," he said softly. "I told you I needed proof."

"And James and I got you that proof." She spat that out. "We almost died on Saturday—but that's not good enough for you, is it?"

He shook his head. "I have only your word and four scraps of burnt paper. James is barely coherent—he remembers nothing. And the only thing I saw in that clearing was a burnt-down barn."

She turned away from him. They had been so close.

Flora had been mentally punishing herself ever since that hellish trip back from the barn. Baba had tried talking to her about it, but she gave up as Flora maintained her stony silence. Not even the historic news that afternoon of Goering's conviction and death sentence could cheer her up.

Why was the overseer bothering her, anyway?

"I need your help, Flora," he said after a minute. "Just one more time."

She turned back to him. "Haven't I done enough, Mr. Morgan?"

"I thought you had," he said. "But the depositary team has reviewed my paperwork, and they now require a new form. Mr. Goering needs to sign a release and attestation for us."

"So have him sign it."

He sighed. "Mr. Goering's lawyer, Dr. Stahmer, only trusted James. Now that he is hurt…" His shoulders slumped.

Maybe she had succeeded after all. "What happens if he doesn't sign the release? Will he be able to deposit the gold?"

"He will not." The overseer cleared his throat. "But before you get any ideas, let me make something crystal clear—if Mr. Goering does not deposit that gold, I will rescind the offer we made to your grandmother."

"Go ahead. I dare you."

Archibald Morgan nodded. "Very well. The two of you are to leave the residence tonight. I do not wish to do this, but you leave me no choice. You may take one week's worth of medicine for her." He turned around and stepped over the threshold and into the hallway.

"You're a cold-hearted bastard," she said under her breath.

He stopped, but he didn't turn around. "Excuse me?"

She clenched her fists. "All right."

Silence for a moment. Then he asked, "All right what?"

"I'll help you, Mr. Morgan. You can count on me."

He turned around and gave her a thin smile. "I hoped I could." He reached into his jacket pocket and pulled out a small black and white photograph and a folded sheaf of papers.

Flora got up and walked over to him. She looked at the picture. "Who's the soldier?" she asked.

"Private Steven Lee. He is one of Colonel Andrus's guards. James identified him as a weak link. I need your help getting to him."

"My help?"

"Three weeks ago, I asked James to come up with a backup plan in case Mr. Goering's lawyer blocked our access." He held up the papers and frowned. "I will not lie to you, Flora. This is a delicate and, shall I say, a very personal assignment. And now that Mr. Goering has been sentenced to death, I need you to work quickly."

It wasn't like she had a choice, was it? "Yes sir," was all she could say. She closed her eyes for a moment and steeled herself for what she was about to do. She walked back to her bed and picked up a small cloth bag hanging from the post. Then she returned to the overseer. "Mr. Morgan, there is something you could do for me."

He smiled. "Certainly."

Funny how nice he acted, once he'd gotten his way. Flora reached into the bag and withdrew a hypodermic syringe. Then she quickly jabbed the needle into the overseer's arm and depressed the plunger.

He clapped his hand to his arm. "What did you do, Flora? That hurt."

"I need the whole story, Mr. Morgan." She grabbed his arm and pulled him into the room, next to her chair. "You'd better sit down before you fall." Baba said the drug took only took a few seconds to take effect.

The overseer lurched forward and collapsed onto the chair. His body slumped to the left.

Flora grabbed Mr. Morgan's shoulders and pulled him upright. She straightened his neck like Baba showed her. Then she dropped the syringe into the cloth bag and hung it back over the bedpost.

The Soul Identity team wasn't the only one with a backup plan. Two weeks ago, Baba and Flora had taken the sodium thiopental from the Army medical kits, just in case the overseer tried to cheat them out of their trip to America.

Baba said the drug made a person feel drunk, and it took away their inhibitions. She said that Flora could ask the overseer about the trip, and with a little cajoling, he'd cough up the details.

But Flora chose to learn more about the gold instead.

He opened his eyes. "This feels pretty good," he said.

"How good, Mr. Morgan?" she asked.

"Like I have no cares in the world." He closed his eyes. "Like I am sailing on a calm sea into a red sunset."

Flora thought he sounded like a totally different person. "You grew up on the water?"

"I did. Prince Edward Island, in Canada." He opened his eyes and smiled. "You would love it there, Flora. It is beautiful and clean and quiet. The sea would remind you of your own Istria."

"You know where I'm from?" she asked.

"Of course I do."

She had no time for this small talk; Baba said a dose of the drug only lasted nine minutes. "Mr. Morgan, when are you sending Mr. Goering's gold to the depositary?"

"As soon as he signs his release. The depositary team is waiting on that last form."

"Do they know what they're depositing?"

"Not yet."

"They don't know about the gold?"

He shook his head. "Because of the possibility of you finding proof of its theft, I have not disclosed the contents of the deposit."

There was still hope. "Is the team in Nuremberg?"

Morgan nodded. "They have been waiting at the Grand Hotel for the past five days." He sighed. "James getting hurt has caused me many problems."

"Because you don't have the release?"

"Precisely." He closed his eyes for a minute.

She reached out and shook his shoulder.

Morgan opened his eyes and stared at Flora. "You would not believe how difficult this assignment has been, Flora. Ms. Vida has threatened to have me killed if I fail to establish Mr. Goering's soul line collection."

"Who is Ms. Vida?"

"Isabella Vida is the executive overseer and the absolute dictator of Soul Identity. Every move I make here in Nuremberg gets broadcasted back to her." He shivered. "And if I mess this up, she will have me neutralized."

Mr. Morgan wasn't as big a boss as she thought him to be. That could explain why he was so pig-headed. Or not. "Mr. Morgan, do you believe Goering's gold was stolen?"

"Yes, Mr. Goering stole that gold." He said that flatly, with no more emotion than he'd say yes, my hair is light brown.

The drug was letting her peer into this new dimension of the overseer's character. "If you know it's stolen," she said, "then why are you letting him deposit it?"

"Because I cannot afford to fail." Morgan leaned forward. "Soul Identity's politicians would like nothing more than to watch me mess this up.

Those vultures pick apart the fallen for their own sustenance. I dare not make a mistake."

"But I had proof!" she cried.

He shook his head. "Your proof went up in smoke, and with James hurt, nobody can corroborate your story," he said. "On the other hand, if I can get Mr. Goering signed up before his execution, I will score a win against the vultures and cement my position as Miss Vida's successor."

Flora forgot for a minute he was drugged. "You're going to use Goering and the gold as a stepping stone for your career?"

He nodded. "I am."

So she was wrong in her assessment. He was less of a bastard and more of an opportunist. "But that gold is bloodstained!"

"Nazi gold shines as bright as any other. And if I can use it to build a better Soul Identity for the future, I will." He closed his eyes again.

Flora shook his shoulder. "Mr. Morgan, wake up."

The overseer opened his eyes and looked around her bedroom. Then he turned to Flora. "I have something I need to tell you."

She doubted she could absorb anything else.

"We have worked together for three months now," he said.

"Three months exactly."

He nodded. "We have worked very close together, have we not?"

"Yes, we have, Mr. Morgan." Where was he going with this?

"Please call me Archibald."

She nodded.

"Go ahead, Flora. Call me Archibald."

"Archibald."

He closed his eyes and smiled. "It sounds nice when you say it."

Maybe she had used too big a dose of the truth serum.

His eyes remained closed. "When you first arrived, I thought you were intolerable," he said. "You burned with anger." He opened his eyes wide and stared into hers. "But then I learned it was not anger, but passion. You really did want to right the world's wrongs."

"I still do."

He nodded. "I know. I see how much the wrongs matter to you, and how you invest everything you have to solve them. I am overwhelmed in my admiration."

Flora was also overwhelmed. Was this the real Archibald Morgan peeking out?

"Your passion to right these wrongs is what makes you so determined," he said. "My own determination is driven by my vision for a better future. We are not so different, Flora."

That was a new perspective. Two people, driven by different goals, each determined to make the world a better place.

The overseer continued. "Your passion invigorates me in ways I have never felt. I spend half the night thinking about you, and the other half dreaming about us. I have fallen in love with you, Flora Drabarni. I want to unite your passion with my vision, for I believe that together we could form an unbeatable pair. We belong together, Flora," he said.

She stared at him, speechless.

"These last few days without you around have been worse than torture," he said. "I need you."

For a brief moment, Flora's heart soared, and she lost herself to the idea of running into the safety of this man's arms. Flora and Archibald, fulfilling their dreams together, changing the world together.

But the un-drugged Archibald Morgan had layers of armor that prevented him from ever expressing these thoughts. In another minute he'd be back to reality, back focused on his opportunities. And she'd be back to hating what he represented.

She needed to wake him properly. Baba had shown her how to make enough pointed suggestions so he wouldn't recall anything they had discussed.

And while she worked to help him forget, her soul cried out for him to remember.

twenty-four

LAST YEAR MADAME FLORA injected Archie and Anne with sodium thiopental to fake their deaths. She also injected Bob to learn what Feret was up to. At the time, she casually mentioned that she had used it on some clients. Who would have thought she had been relying on truth serum for over sixty years?

Who would have thought she and Archie may have had something going on for over sixty years?

"Archie doesn't know, does he?" I asked her.

She shook her head. "And there's no way he ever should."

We'd see about that.

It was almost noon, and we had been up all night. Val and I headed back to our room and collapsed on the bed. We woke three hours later and got dressed.

"What are you going to tell Mr. Morgan?" Val asked.

"Until we get the rest of the story out of Madame Flora, I'm keeping quiet."

She pursed her lips.

"If we tell him now, Madame Flora won't help us sort out the rest of the story," I said.

"So we have to act just like her?"

I thought about that. "You mean we're doing the wrong things for the right reasons."

She nodded.

That did seem to be the theme of the story so far: Flora helped Archie to get her grandmother medicine. Her grandmother read Goering's eyes so Archie would bring her and Flora to America. Archie helped Goering so he could climb Soul Identity's hierarchy.

And here I was suggesting that we hide what we know so we could hear the rest of the story. Val was right to call me on it.

"You think we should go to Archie now?" I asked.

She shook her head. "Flora is right—it will cause irreparable damage."

"But we'll have to tell him what we learned, sooner or later."

She made a face. "That's going to be tough."

I wasn't looking forward to that, either. "Maybe after we find out what happened to the gold."

The translating was getting easier. I took the next few pages and marked the words we already had solved. That saved us half the work. While I forged through the new words, Val manned the online dictionaries. It took us three hours to complete the remaining pages and head back to Madame Flora.

Flora's Journal

With one behind you can't sit on two horses.

THE PRINCESS SOUGHT OUT the wolf's guard. Besotted with her beauty, he helped her pass messages between the captain and the evil wolf.

She spent many hours pondering all that had happened. She began to look favorably upon the captain, and to admire the strength he showed as he performed his quest.

But she still sought to destroy the wolf's magic teeth. The captain brought her to the dungeon to see them. She gasped at the power the wolf would hold when he returned to life. Yet when she begged the captain to crush them, still he refused.

So she used more truth-telling potion on the captain, down there in the dungeon, right next to the wolf's magic teeth.

The captain told her how and when the teeth would be transferred to the knights' cave. Then he again professed his love for her. And this time, the princess felt her own heart jump. She realized she was in love with this captain of the knights.

She told the captain she loved him, and then she showed him, and then she helped him forget.

Later that night, finally, a plan, forged out of her love for her captain, and out of her hatred for everything the wolf represented, took shape.

14 October 1946

There are lies more believable than truth

HER PLAN WAS SO simple it was brilliant: trick the captain into giving the magical teeth to the princess's friends, and find something else to place in the cave.

What could she put in place of the magical teeth? After thinking long and hard, she chose to deposit her story. Then, when the wolf returned to life, he would learn how the brave princess had thwarted him.

And how would she trick the captain? A friend of her godmother had offered to help; he and his men would fool the captain and take the magical teeth someplace safe.

The princess is very excited: tomorrow the wolf's teeth will be out of the knights' hands. Tomorrow they start their journey back to the families of the wolf's victims.

Soon she and her fairy godmother will be safe in a new castle. Soon her knight captain will become a general, and soon he and the princess will live happily ever after.

twenty-five

THE YOUNG LADY OPENED the basement apartment door and rubbed her eyes. "*Bitte?*"

Flora thought the girl was quite pretty, even with her tousled hair, bleary eyes, and patched nightgown at five in the morning. She smiled at her. "You are Helga Brunne?"

The girl nodded and yawned.

"You are an acquaintance of Private Steven Lee?"

That seemed to wake her up. "I am his friend," she said with a subtle emphasis on the last word.

Flora already knew this from the impressive research James had done before he got hurt. Now for the tricky part. "I have a message and a package for you from Private Lee," she said. "He would have delivered them himself, but he had to leave the city an hour ago on a secret mission."

"He left Nuremberg?" Helga's face filled with worry.

"*Ja.* An emergency prisoner escort."

"But he was meeting me here for lunch."

"That is correct," Flora said briskly. "And Private Lee sent me here to tell you he will not be able to come."

"Sent you?" Helga's eyes narrowed. "Why should I trust you?"

It was a good question. James's papers told Flora that eighteen-year-old Helga Brunne was Lee's girlfriend. Apparently Lee passed on cigarettes, candy, and other Army "extras" to Helga, who sold them on the black market to feed herself and her grandmother. Flora knew that if she were Helga, she'd also be suspicious of anybody threatening her welfare.

And this was why Flora had brought the envelope. She held it out. "Do not trust me, *fraulein.* Trust the package he left for you."

Helga took the envelope and pulled out a wad of bills. She whisked the money into her bathrobe pocket, and then pulled some papers out of the envelope. She unfolded and read them. "These are train tickets?"

"*Ja.* The US Military transport. Private Lee wishes you and your grandmother to await his arrival in Paris. You will also find a voucher for two nights at the Hotel du Nord. The two hundred American dollars is your extra spending money while you wait for him."

Helga stuffed the tickets back in the envelope. "He wants us in Paris?"

Flora smiled. "Paris. Now hurry and get you and your grandmother ready. The train leaves at seven this morning."

Helga's face fell. "My grandmother has sprained her ankle, and she cannot travel."

If Flora didn't get rid of both Helga and her grandmother for the next few days, the plan to reach Goering would fail. "Can I help you bring her to the *hauptbahnhof*?"

Helga shook her head. "She cannot walk at all. Not even to the toilet—I have to bring her a bucket." She looked at Flora. "I am sorry, but please tell Steven I cannot come to Paris."

Cannot come to Paris! For a moment Flora fought to breathe as despair squeezed her chest.

But then images of James tumbled through her head: James driving the Jeep, turning his head to smile at her. James patting her cheek. James blushing after she kissed him. And finally, James in the clearing, declaring "I will not leave you here to die."

If she could just fulfill James's plan, her bouts of guilt might subside. James had identified what it would take to turn Private Steven Lee into Soul Identity's new conduit with Hermann Goering. How dare this silly little German girl stand in the way?

Flora snatched the envelope out of Helga's hands. "Very well. I will convey your reply to him."

"I'm sorry," Helga called as Flora headed to the stairway.

Flora turned back and smiled and said in a breathy voice, "It's no problem at all. I am happy to go in your place. I've always wanted to go to Paris, and seeing it on the arm of your handsome GI will be *wunderbar*."

"You'll go in my place?" Helga's voice was barely audible.

Flora smiled. "Naturally. My own American went home to his wife last month, and I've been looking for another. Private Lee seems almost perfect." She turned to go.

"Wait!"

Flora turned back.

"Why did Steven send you?"

"I work the ticket counter at the *hauptbahnhof*. Your soldier was quite distraught a few hours ago. He was thrilled when I offered to deliver his package to you."

Flora could see that Helga was almost there, and she pressed on. "It's a shame you can't come, but one girl's loss is another girl's gain, *nein?*"

She stood on the platform and waved. Two soldiers had just carried Helga's protesting grandmother into the car. The train whistled, the wheels began to turn, and in another minute, Helga and her grandmother were on their way to Paris.

Giving Flora three whole days to seduce Private Steven Lee and open an alternative conduit to Goering.

twenty-six

JAMES TURNED HIS HEAD as Flora opened the door. He lay on the bed, feet raised in a tangle of stirrups, weights, and pulleys. A white bandage wrapped his head.

Flora winced as she looked at him. The doctors said that she had broken both of James's ankles and one of his hips as she dragged him through the forest and back to the Jeep. That was on top of the head wounds he received from the Nazis.

James smiled at her.

"Did I wake you up?" she asked, still in the doorway.

He shook his head. "Just waiting for the end of the line, ma'am. Soon we'll be off."

She slumped against the door frame. So James was still busy playing conductor on the locomotive in his head. Archibald said he might never recover.

Archibald—she'd been mentally referring to him that way since she drugged him and he told her how he felt.

But Flora wasn't here to examine her feelings for the overseer. She walked over to the bed. "James, do you know who I am?" she asked.

He smiled. "Of course. You're one of my special passengers. Where's a nice girl like you going, anyway?"

"I'm not your passenger, James."

He closed his eyes for a minute.

Flora waited.

Finally he asked, "Do you work here too?"

"I do."

He nodded and opened his eyes. "Then what can I do for you, pretty lady?"

She pulled out his research and plans which Archibald had given her. "Do you remember writing these?" she asked him.

He took the papers, glanced at each of them, and shook his head. "It looks like my writing," he said, "but it can't be. I've never been to Germany in my life." He handed the pages back. "Sorry, hon."

"James, you have to remember. I need your help!" Flora's voice was sharp. The plans he had assembled shocked her, and she wanted a confirmation for what he had planned for her to do.

He shrank back into his bed. "There's no need to get mad at me, ma'am. You could file a complaint with the office—maybe they could help you."

She sighed and sat down in the chair next to him. "No, I'm sorry for getting upset. I'm just very lonely—I lost my friend last week, and I can't seem to find him anywhere."

He looked at her. "In these dark days of depression, many people have suffered big losses, and we all seem to get upset easily. But don't worry, little lady—soon we'll reach the end of the line. Mark my word—better days are coming!"

She nodded. "I really hope you're right."

She sat next to him for the next half hour and watched James as he alternated between examining his fingernails and looking out the window. Her fears dissipated, but the overwhelming sense of guilt for the pain she had caused him remained.

She stood up and wiped her eyes. Enough time spent mourning what could have been. No matter how shocking, no matter how unsavory, she would do what James had planned and finish this mission. Hopefully it would begin to make up for the damage she had caused him.

He glanced at her. "We're almost at the station, hon. You only need to hold on for a little longer."

She smiled through a fresh set of tears. "Thank you, James. I'll try."

twenty-seven

October 1946
Nuremberg, Occupied Germany

FLORA WATCHED THE SOLDIER'S white helmet descend toward the Brunnes's basement apartment. A minute later she watched it come back up.

The helmet crowned a frowning American face. Private Steven Lee must be wondering where his girlfriend had gone. Maybe he was even a little worried—how could Helga's crippled grandmother have left?

Time to strike. Flora set her path to intersect with his in the middle of the street. As she got close, she looked directly in the soldier's eyes and flashed him a big smile.

James had noted that Private Steven Lee had a special thing for pretty brunettes. It seemed he was right; the soldier stopped in front of her, looked her up and down, and grinned.

"Do you speak English?" he asked.

"Of course I do," she said in her most cultured voice. "Did you steal that white helmet?"

His grin was replaced by a frown. "Of course not."

She gazed right into his eyes, then looked down at the ground. "They told us monsters guarded the Nazis, but you look like a movie star to me."

She heard him chuckle. "Twenty-sixth regiment honor guard, ma'am. I'm with the prisoners every day."

She looked up and caught him admiring her figure. When his gaze made it back up to her eyes, she asked, "And you stayed so handsome and happy? How did you do it?" She took a tiny step closer.

He blushed. "It is a tough job, but I had some help from my girl, Helga." He glanced back at the basement apartment.

Flora nodded. "Of course." She stuck out her hand. "It was nice to meet you, Private…"

"Lee. Steven Lee." He took her hand in his.

"I'm Mona." She let her fingertips flutter against his wrist ever so slightly.

He held onto her hand and cleared his throat. "I have a couple hours before my shift starts—would you like to have lunch with me, Mona?"

She tossed her head in the direction of the apartment. "What would Helga say?"

He shrugged. "She's not home, and I'm hungry."

Flora pretended to think for a moment, and then grabbed his arm. "I suppose I could have lunch with you."

It was the first time either of them had been inside the Grand Hotel—Flora's press pass had gotten them past the suspicious American guards. She was careful to hide her real name on the pass from Lee.

The club echoed with laughter—something Flora hadn't experienced in a public place since she was a little girl. Before the war.

"You are a reporter?" Lee asked in what she thought was a faintly accusing tone.

She shook her head. "I am a photographer."

"Have you been inside the prison?"

She nodded. "Once. Your Colonel Andrus let me in to take a picture of Hermann Goering." She leaned forward in her chair. "But enough about me. Now the trial is over, do you still have guard duty?"

He smiled. "I do. Two four-hour shifts every day."

"Tell me what it's like, guarding them."

"They've gone quiet, I guess, now they've been convicted." He shrugged. "But just a week ago, it was a whole different story. Goering was strutting around, trying to rally the military men. Speer was sitting with the apologists, moaning about how evil they were, and how they needed to be punished. Now all of them sit in their cells, meet with their priests, and write letters. Lots of letters."

For the rest of the meal, Flora sat and listened to Lee's descriptions of families visiting the condemned, and her mind wandered to her own visit with Goering. She hoped the Nazi's every day had turned into a hellish nightmare—death was too good for him.

The bill came, and after Lee paid, he stared at her. "Did you hear anything I said?"

She smiled. "Private Lee, you have treated me to a wonderful meal at the grandest hotel in town, and you regaled me with amazing stories. I feel like the luckiest girl in the world, escorted by a handsome American soldier."

"Are you crazy?" He pointed around the room. "All these newspaper reporters and radiomen—the swaggering French, the debonair English, the brooding Russians—you could have your pick of anybody in this room."

She took a look around and pretended to consider what he said. Then she smiled at him. "But you're a special guard who is part of history. Why would I choose to be with somebody who only reports on the things you see and do every single day?"

He smiled, and Flora knew she had him.

They walked out of the Grand Hotel, Flora holding onto Lee's arm. "So how do I know you're really a guard?" she asked him.

He pulled a picture from his pocket. "Take a look at this. Autographed by von Schirach, just today."

She looked at the picture of the former Hitler Youth leader. "They autograph their photographs for you?"

"They do. Then I usually give them to..." his voice trailed off.

"Helga," she finished for him. "So she can sell them and help feed her family."

He nodded. "How did you know?" he asked.

She leaned over and kissed his cheek. "You are a very noble man, Private Steven Lee."

"You think so?" He looked worried.

"I do." She squeezed his arm. "But even noble men need some excitement in their lives. What time does your next four-hour shift end?"

That evening, as Flora waited for Lee to meet her, she finally confronted her feelings on whether it was right to use the soldier to get her way.

She knew precisely what Baba would say: it was wrong, under any circumstance.

But Baba also read Goering's identity, knowing it would legitimize his theft and allow his memories to survive. She had compromised on her own principles to get herself and Flora to America.

Archibald had blamed Flora for hurting James and destroying the communications link with Goering. He had threatened to renege on his deal with Baba. Going along with James's plan was the price he was charging Flora for redemption.

And the price was high: to reach Goering, she would sacrifice a precious piece of herself. Sex was new territory for Flora, and she was afraid.

At least she had no fear of falling in love with him. Private Steven Lee was cheating on his girlfriend, after all. He was using Flora as much as she was using him.

She saw Lee striding her way, whistling. "Hello, Mona," he said when he reached her.

She smiled. "I was hoping you weren't too scared to see me again."

"Should I be scared?"

"Terrified." She only hoped her own fear wasn't noticeable. She slipped her arm through his as they walked down the street. "What do you have planned for us tonight?"

He stopped and looked at her. "You said something about excitement."

She gave his arm a little squeeze. "I did. But first I have something to show you."

They reached the Gooseherder's Fountain and sat at its base. Flora pulled a gold fountain pen out of her bag. "I was given this pen by Hermann Goering," she said. "He told me it was a Pelikan 100 with special Toledo engraving."

His eyes widened. "Goering gave this to you?"

She nodded. "After I took his picture. He said I was the prettiest, most efficient photographer he ever met." She sighed. "But now his lawyer, Dr. Stahmer, says I stole it, and I need to give it back."

"And if you don't?" He held the pen in the air.

"He'll report me, and I'll get thrown out of my apartment." She put her hand on his shoulder. "But you could help me, Private Lee."

"You want me to talk to his lawyer?"

She shook her head. "I think if I could get Herr Goering to say it belonged to me, all would be good."

"How would he do that?" Lee was staring at her.

She shrugged. "He could write something to prove it was a gift. Here, I'll show you." Flora took the fountain pen and pulled off the black rubber bottom cover. She removed two sheets of paper wrapped around the piston.

The soldier read from the first paper, "I hereby grant the bearer of this note ownership in all my property they have in their possession. I certify nobody else has any claims on this property."

Flora pointed at a line on the bottom. "He needs to sign right there, and put the date after it."

Private Lee nodded. "What about this paper?" Again he read it out loud. "The overseer has been most efficient and useful, and is to be commended."

"That's me," she said. "Something I can show my boss and maybe even get promoted."

"Overseer?" Lee asked.

Flora pretended to study the writing. "I may have garbled the words," she said. "Directly translated from German, it means professional photographer." She held her breath and hoped the soldier would buy it.

He nodded and handed the pages back.

She wrapped them around the piston, pushed it into the bottom, and gave him the pen. "So you can help me?"

He looked at her with solemn eyes. "You're asking me to do something illegal."

Uh oh. She tried a smile. "But it is exciting, isn't it?"

"Maybe," he said. "But still, it's a big risk, and I could get into deep trouble." He looked down at the ground and cleared his throat. "What kind of excitement will you give me in return?"

Late that night, Flora made her way back to the Soul Identity house. She went to the washroom and scrubbed her hands and lips and breasts and genitals until her skin was raw. She crept to her room before anybody could see her, limping slightly from a newly-felt pain between her legs.

As she lay in bed and thought about what she had done with Private Lee, she worked to summon up outrage at the overseer for forcing her into this humiliating situation. But try as she might, she found she couldn't be angry with Archibald. In fact, she closed her eyes and imagined it had been him kissing and stroking and entering her body.

twenty-eight

SHE SAW THE OVERSEER at breakfast.

"How is your mission?" he asked.

"Under way," was all Flora could manage. She didn't look at him, and after a minute of apparently finding nothing to say, he finished his coffee and left the room.

She met Private Lee back at the same fountain later that morning, and she did her best to smile after he kissed her on the lips.

"Last night was incredible, Mona," he said. He put his arms behind him on the fountain ledge and leaned with his face up toward the morning sun. "I haven't been able to think of anything else."

At least they agreed on that, though his thoughts probably weren't filled with as much despair as hers. "Me too, Steven," she managed to say.

Lee reached into his pocket. "Here's your pen, my lady."

As she reached out to grab it, he smiled and jerked it out of her grasp. "It's going cost you."

She steadied her voice. "How much?"

"Another evening of your time." He smiled. "Just like last night, but longer."

She held out her hand. "Let me see."

Flora pulled off the cover and unwrapped the papers. They were unsigned! She looked up at Lee.

He held a note in his hand. "Goering asked me to give this to you."

She took the note. It was written in German, and she read it to herself.

Fraulein—our mutual soldier friend told me how sweet you taste. I encouraged him to sample you again, as it seemed fair payment for the embarrassment you caused me. I refuse to sign the papers until you help me get from Dr. Stahmer the special medicine I need to hasten my depature.

"What does it say?" the soldier asked.

Flora's mind raced to find a credible explanation. "Herr Goering says he won't sign until I spend another night with you." She forced another smile. "He must really like you."

Lee grinned. "He sure does." He laughed out loud. "That dirty old fox!"

After making plans to meet the soldier in the evening, Flora returned to Soul Identity to speak with Archibald.

"He must be referring to cyanide," the overseer said after she relayed Goering's request. "That seems to be the choice of most of the Nazi leadership."

"He deserves to be hung," Flora said. "If you let him escape the noose by helping him commit suicide, you'll turn him back into a hero."

He shrugged. "I do not care how he dies, so long as he signs the release first."

She saw his point. The clock was ticking, and if Goering hung before he signed, Archibald lost, James suffered for nothing, and Baba was as good as dead. They had no choice but to do what the Nazi wanted. "If you get me the cyanide today," she said, "I'll have his signature tomorrow."

He nodded. "Let me see what I can do."

While waiting for Archibald to return with the poison, Flora stopped by Baba's room. The old lady was sitting by the window, looking at a tiny silver locket. When she saw Flora, she smiled. "Come here and look at my pictures," she said.

Flora knelt on the floor and glanced at the photographs inside the locket. One was of a young couple, and the other of a small boy. "Is that you and Zedza?" she asked.

Baba nodded. "I don't know how he did it, but one of your grandfather's old friends found me here in Nuremberg and returned my locket."

"Why did this friend have your locket?"

"Your grandfather took it with him when he went to war. Old Ned must have held onto it for the past thirty years."

"Old Ned?"

Baba smiled. "A dear friend from Australia. Major Edward Callaghan, but your grandfather called him Ned. He's here for the execution."

That was a subject Flora didn't want to discuss. She tapped the photographs. "Your parents must have had to beat the boys away with a stick."

"I wasn't nearly as pretty as my granddaughter." Baba pointed at the man. "You've got your grandfather's cheekbones."

"Tell me about him."

Baba closed her eyes and smiled. "A wild man, my parents said. But Radik was ambitious, and full of high ideals, and always finding ways to get into trouble." She looked at Flora. "You're an awful lot like him."

"I'll bet he never got his friends almost killed."

"You still blame yourself over James Little, don't you?"

Flora nodded and bit her lip.

"You must stop that," Baba commanded. "And just so you know, your grandfather made his share of mistakes too."

This was new territory. Baba practically worshipped the memory of her long-deceased husband. His name had been invoked many times over the years to convince Flora to study harder, or to act more ladylike. If the great Radovan Drabarni had any flaws, Baba had them well covered with a layer of historical perfection.

"Mistakes?" Flora asked.

Baba nodded. "Two big ones that I know about. One of them cost him his job as foreman of the Hungarian opal mines."

Flora knew her grandfather had been a miner, but she thought it had been in Australia. "Hungary?"

"At the time it was Hungary. The mines have since closed. But back in the nineties, your grandfather was in charge of mining the Dubnik opal mines. Until his first mistake."

"What did he do?"

Baba looked out the window for a minute before saying anything. "Radik came home one evening and told me he had just sent a crew down an un-shored tunnel. The mine needed to complete a shipment to Budapest, and they were behind schedule. Your grandfather worried all night about a cave-in." She stopped and sighed.

"Did they make it?"

She shook her head. "We sold everything we had and sent most of our money to the boys' families. Then we headed to Australia to start afresh."

Flora knew the story from there. Among other jobs, her grandfather had been mildly successful in the Australian opal mines. Baba had told her about Flora's father being born in the underground town of White Cliffs, and how Radovan had volunteered to serve in the Great War, where he was killed by the Turks at Gallipoli. After the war, Baba had returned to her hometown in Istria with her twelve-year-old son.

"Did he ever forgive himself?" Flora asked.

"Never," Baba said. "And for the first two years, he was a nuisance to everybody in White Cliffs. That's when he made his second big mistake—he tried to steal some opals."

"Zedza was a thief?" This was just getting worse.

"I said he tried to steal, but fortunately Old Ned caught him in his mine before he took anything." Baba frowned. "The mine collapsed, they both nearly died, and that finally shocked some sense into him. Your grandfather became a great man, Flora, but only after making great mistakes."

So her sainted grandfather had his own alternative history. "Why haven't you told me this before?"

"Because you weren't ready to hear it."

Both of them were silent for a minute.

"And now you think I'm ready?" Flora asked. "Now that I'm a failure too?"

Baba stroked Flora's hair. "You've proven your strength, my child. You've shown your convictions are stronger than your desires. Now you must learn from your mistakes and become a great woman."

The overseer returned that afternoon. "Dr. Stahmer anticipated my request," he said. He held out a small brass cylinder a half-inch wide and two inches long. "He retrieved this just last week from one of Mr. Goering's hiding places." He unscrewed the top and flipped it over. A green glass capsule fell into his hand.

"Is that the cyanide?" Flora asked.

Archibald nodded. "When Mr. Goering bites down on this, he will experience a very painful, but self-inflicted, death." He slid the capsule back into the cylinder and screwed on the top.

Flora pulled out the fountain pen and pulled off the rubber cap. "We'll have to hide it in here," she said, pointing to the piston.

The overseer grasped the piston in his hands and wiggled it loose. He unscrewed the cap and handed it to Flora.

Flora slid the brass cylinder into the cap and reassembled the pen.

"It is as if it were meant to be there." Archibald looked at Flora. "You will deliver this tonight?"

Flora nodded. "I'll bring you the signed release tomorrow."

After another long evening with Private Steven Lee and another harsh scrub in the bathroom, Flora crept to her bedroom and dreamt of her overseer.

twenty-nine

October 1946
Nuremberg, Occupied Germany

FLORA HELD THE SIGNED release at exactly the height of the over-seer's eyes. She released it, and the paper drifted down and landed on his desktop.

Archibald picked it up and read it. A smile crossed his face. "You did it, Flora."

She had, but at what cost? She shook this thought from her head and forced out a smile. "It was James's plan."

But he didn't seem to hear. He let out a whoop and jumped out of his chair. He rushed around the desk and hugged Flora, then gave her a big kiss.

Without even thinking about it, Flora twisted free, lifted her arm, and slapped Archibald Morgan as hard as she could.

His hand flew up to his cheek.

Flora took a step back. "Damn you for what you made me do!" she cried. She turned and ran from the room.

An hour later the overseer knocked on Flora's open door.

"Go away," she said. She lay on her bed facing him.

"Flora, we must talk."

She turned and faced the wall.

After a minute, she heard him close the door. Relieved, she turned over, and bit back a scream when she saw him standing over her.

"Flora, I must speak with you."

She sighed. "If you must."

He sat down on the chair and put his hands on his knees. "I owe you an apology."

"You owe me your career." Maybe even his life.

At that he was silent. Then he nodded. "You are correct. I do. Your actions have saved me my job, and I am in your debt, Flora."

At last he acknowledged this. Too bad it came too late.

They sat quiet for a long moment. Then he cleared his throat. "Soon everything will go to the depositary, and soon we will go to America."

"Can you show me the gold?" she asked.

He smiled. "You asked just in time. I have not yet sealed the final barrel."

She got up, and she grabbed her purse. Maybe she'd get a chance to drug him again.

Downstairs, Archibald pulled out his chain necklace and selected the larger of the keys. He bent toward the basement door and unlocked it. He pulled on the door handle. It screeched as it opened.

Flora followed the overseer down the stairs and closed the door behind her.

When they reached the bottom, he flipped on a light switch and extinguished his flashlight.

Twelve wooden barrels the size of beer kegs and three long and narrow wooden boxes stood against the far wall. A desk and chair sat in front. The overseer walked over to the last keg and slid off its wooden cover.

The keg was full of sawdust. He brushed some aside and pulled out a canvas-wrapped, rectangle-shaped object. He grunted as he extended it toward her. "Careful, it is heavy."

Flora grabbed it with both hands, and was surprised at the weight when the overseer let go. She hefted it up over the desk and set it down. It made a dull clink.

Archibald unwrapped the canvas, and the yellow metal gleamed in the light. The bar was about eight inches long, three inches wide, and two inches deep.

It was hard to believe something so small weighed almost twenty-eight pounds. Flora rubbed the cool metal with just her fingertips. She traced the serial number and date with her fingers, but she avoided the German eagle and swastika. She closed her eyes and thought that part of her father could be inside the bar.

Not just her father, but parts of each of the millions of slaughtered Jews, Gypsies, homosexuals, priests, and prisoners of war were entombed in that bar of gold. She felt a buzzing in her head, and she swayed with dizziness.

She opened her eyes. The buzzing stopped. Archibald Morgan stood before her with a solemn expression on his face.

"You can still do the right thing," she said.

He raised his eyebrows. "The right thing is to deposit Mr. Goering's belongings."

She pointed at the wooden boxes. "Those papers are his belongings. But you and I both know he stole the gold."

He shook his head. "I am sorry, Flora. The gold must go to the depositary."

She grabbed his arm. "You have the power to do something great. Please don't let that monster steal the gold." But even as she said the words, she realized she had lost. Archibald Morgan was a man of facts and reason, and she knew he would not be swayed by her emotional arguments.

He gave her a sad smile as he wrapped the bar in its canvas. "I have the power to do my job, Flora."

She watched him bury the bar back in the sawdust. He placed the lid on the keg and nailed it down. He ran a length of red tape through holes drilled above the lid in each of the keg's staves. When he finished, the tape's crisscrosses resembled a spider web suspended an inch above the center of the lid.

The overseer picked up a large metal sealing tool and two small tablets of wax. He held the wax over both sides of the center of the tape, where it all came together, then squeezed it with the tool.

When he opened the tool's jaws, the wax remained, attached to the middle of the red tape. "Now we are ready for the depositary team," he said.

As he turned around, Flora was ready for him with her hypodermic syringe. She jabbed it into his arm and depressed the plunger.

He looked at her and at the syringe.

"Sit down before you fall down," she said. She guided him to the chair, and he collapsed into it. The sealing tool hit the floor with a clang.

After a minute he opened his eyes, smiled at her, and then closed them again.

Had she overdosed him? "Mr. Morgan, are you all right?"

"Call me Archibald," he said softly.

The dose was fine. "Archibald, when is the depositary team coming?"

"Six days from now, at five in the afternoon," he said. "I wanted them here sooner, but they said it would take them that long to verify Mr. Goering's signature on the release."

"They're depositing everything?"

He nodded. "Then I get to go home."

"To much acclaim, I would imagine." She tried to keep the bitterness out of her voice.

He smiled. "Yes, this will cement my position as next in line for executive overseer." He leaned forward. "And then I will do some real good."

"What will you do?" Despite her disgust at his self-serving decisions, she was interested in his plans.

"Transform Soul Identity out of politics and into a smooth-running business," he said. "There will be no more currying favor, no more plots, and no more subterfuge. I will bring peace to the organization."

If she was honest with herself, it did sound good. She could picture Archibald at the helm of Soul Identity, ruling with a firm but fair hand.

And she'd be right there with him, helping him, guiding him. With her passion and his vision they'd fight together against the evils of the world, and they'd live together happily ever after.

He reached out and grabbed her hands. "I owe my success of this mission to you, Flora. You are my heroine, and I love you."

And then, thinking she could replace her nightmares of the past few months with his dreams of a better tomorrow, she pulled her hands free and wrapped her arms around his neck. Their lips crushed together, seeking each other hungrily.

She invested herself in that kiss, and as he returned it, she felt her frustration and pain and anger melt away, replaced by a raw hunger. Her body, shamed by Private Steven Lee, responded in new and urgent ways.

Archibald pulled his head back and stared in her eyes. "Flora…"

And then she was on the desk but under him, and then they were fumbling with each others' clothes. A minute later she cried out with joy as he filled her. She wrapped her legs around him and pulled him in even closer. He was the man she wanted; this was the love she needed.

They held each other when it was over, Archibald stroking her face, Flora kissing his hands. She wished the moment would last forever.

She sat up with a start. How many minutes had it been? Too long, she was sure. The thiopental might have worn off. She threw off his arm and searched for her purse.

"What are you doing?" he asked.

"Getting something," she said. "Relax for a minute."

She refilled the syringe with the remainder of the serum and injected it into his arm. Archibald's eyes rolled up and he collapsed back on the desk.

She stood over him and cupped his face in her hands and covered it with kisses. "My sweet, sweet overseer," she said.

But only sweet while drugged. Flora knew by now that Archibald Morgan was more interested in his career at Soul Identity than he was in her.

And to be fair, Flora was more interested in fixing the wrongs of the world than she was in Archibald Morgan. So she took her undergarments and wiped him clean, got them both dressed, and as he slowly woke up, she used everything Baba had taught her about the power of suggestion to help the overseer forget what had happened.

thirty

MADAME FLORA GAVE US a rueful smile. "Did you see that coming?"

She and Archie doing the wild thing: yes. She and Archie creating one of the world's great unsolved mysteries: no. "I can't believe you guys helped Goering kill himself," I said.

"He only swallowed the cyanide a few hours before he'd have hung," she said.

"And I can't believe Mr. Morgan had you sleep with Private Lee," Val said.

"It wasn't so bad," she said. "Besides, if I hadn't done it with him, I never would have had the nerve to do it with Archibald."

I scratched my head. "Are you sure he has no residual memories from that night?"

"I'm sure." She smiled. "If he did, he would've told me by now, and I would've made him pay his share of child support."

Whoa—I didn't see that coming either. "He got you pregnant?"

"With my only child. Jamie." She sighed. "Archibald's only child, too, I would imagine."

"Only Mr. Morgan doesn't know he's a father," Val said.

Madame Flora shook her head. "And you can't tell him, either."

"Are you sure Archie's the father?" I asked. "What about Private Lee?"

"Lee used his US Army-supplied condoms," she said. "My Jamie was definitely Archibald's son."

"Does he know who his father is?" I asked.

"Jamie died as a journalist in Vietnam forty years ago. I never told him."

"Something's not adding up," Val said. "How can Rose and Marie be your grandchildren?"

"They're really my great-granddaughters," Madame Flora said. "When Jamie died in Vietnam, his wife ran away and left me their little girl. I raised her as my own daughter."

"And she's the twins' mother?" I asked.

Madame Flora nodded. "They don't know about Archibald either."

"When do you plan to tell them?" Val asked.

"When the time is right."

"What are you waiting for?" I asked.

She smiled. "For us to recover the gold."

Somehow I knew she was going to say that. "So you did find a way to hide it," I said.

Madame Flora laughed. "Poor Archibald really thought he deposited it, but I fooled him after all."

thirty-one

FLORA WAITED IN THE lobby of the Grand Hotel for Major Ned Callaghan to come down from his room.

Baba had been sure that Callaghan, her grandfather's best friend and fellow soldier from the Great War, would be happy to help Flora. "Old Ned will enjoy taking the mickey out of Soul Identity," she said.

Flora could only hope Baba was right. Without a fake depositary team to receive the gold, her plan would fail.

She looked up as a middle-aged man with a cane approached her. "Stone the bloody crows, you're the spitting image of your grandfather," he said. "Only much prettier." He passed the cane to his left hand and stuck out his right. "Ned Callaghan."

Flora shook his hand. "Flora Drabarni, and thank you for meeting me."

"No worries." He looked around the lobby. "You up for a waltz around town? There's too many ears here."

She nodded, and they headed out into the afternoon sun. The day was bright and the air crisp. They walked to the Gooseherder's fountain and sat down. Flora tried not to think about last week's meetings here with Private Lee.

"Something nagging at you?" Callaghan asked.

Flora sighed. "Just some bad thoughts."

He nodded. "The whole continent is buggered with them." He laid the cane across his lap. "Your grandmother said you needed my help."

"I do." Now how to start? "Major Callaghan, Baba said you were friends with my grandfather."

"Aye, his best mate," he said. "Your grandfather was a top class fella. I knew him since we mined opals together in White Cliffs."

"Were you there when he died?"

He nodded and looked into the distance. "We were digger mates in the first war."

"Digger mates?"

"Soldiers. They started calling us diggers during Gallipoli."

Baba had told her about the senseless slaughter that the Australian and New Zealand soldiers suffered on the Turkish peninsula. "But you survived," she said. Unlike her grandfather.

He poked his thumb at his chest. "You're looking at one of the few who made it all the way from Alexandria to Gallipoli to home. We fought Johnny Turk from April to November," he said, "and then we tucked our tails between our legs and ran away."

"So it was all pointless."

Callaghan's grip on this cane was tight. "Aye." After a minute of silence, he asked, "Would you like to hear about your grandfather in Gallipoli?"

She nodded. Baba had not known the details.

He sat, head bowed, for another moment before starting. "By August most of our men were either blown to bits or dead from dysentery. Your grandfather and I dug a tunnel to the Turks' front lines and hid there. When the rest of the army attacked, we blew out its roof and rose right out of the ground. We scared the piss out of those buggers.

"We tricked Johnny Turk every way we could," he said. He smiled at Flora. "Raddy was one of the best we had. He rigged up automatic firing rifles, hoisted silhouettes of the Kaiser, and even posted scarecrow troops."

Major Callaghan sighed. "Then in early November a fierce storm blew in. The water in our canteens froze solid, with us still in summer uniforms. Raddy was one of the few diggers with any snow experience, and he taught the rest of us how to survive."

"What happened to him?"

Callaghan went silent and stared over the rooftops. He swallowed a couple times and pawed at his eyes.

Flora waited for him to continue.

"A week before we finally evacuated, a Turk hand grenade bounced into the corner of our trench. One man jumped on it and saved the rest of our lives." Callaghan looked at her intently. "Your grandfather was a true hero."

Flora felt a chill run down her spine.

Major Callaghan planted the tip of his cane on the ground and stared at it. "I held him in my arms as he died."

They sat quietly for a few minutes.

He turned to look at her. "Did you see your grandmother's locket?"

She nodded.

"Raddy pulled it off his neck and made me promise to return it to your grandmother." Major Callaghan cleared his throat. "But when I got back to Australia, she had already left for Istria. It wasn't until this war that I was deployed again in Europe."

"You fought in this war?"

"Commissioned a Major, I was. We sat in Greece until the evacuation, and in 1941 me and me lads were captured at the Battle of Crete. I spent most of the war in different camps—Crete, Greece, Belgrade, and Dresden. At the end we were set loose somewhere behind the Russian Front." He shook his head. "After VE day, I headed to Istria to find your grandmother. Then I followed your trail to Nuremberg."

"And you fulfilled your promise."

"Aye. Now Raddy can rest in peace." He stood up slowly. "My knee needs stretching. Let's walk while we chin wag."

As they headed toward the prison, Flora took his arm. "Major Callaghan, did you know my father?"

He smiled. "When he was barely walking. A right cute lad, he was."

She pointed at the Palais du Justice. "He was killed by those monsters," she blurted out.

He glanced at her. "I know, darling. Your grandmother told me."

"But it's worse than that," she said. "What do you know about Soul Identity?"

"Not much, I'm afraid. I joined years ago when your grandfather suggested it would help me, but I haven't stayed with it."

"That fat bastard Hermann Goering is now a member."

He grunted.

"We're supposed to deposit his gold this week," she said. She gripped his arm. "But it's not his—that gold was stolen from my father and others, and I need you to help me get it back."

He stopped walking and turned to face Flora. "Do you have a plan?"

She nodded. "But I can't do it alone." She explained it to him.

Major Callaghan scratched his chin. "It sounds doable. But where are you going to stash all that gold? The Art Looting Investigation Unit has found every hidey hole in this country."

She grinned. "I know a place you're going to love."

thirty-two

October 1946
Nuremberg, Occupied Germany

IT WAS THE AFTERNOON of the fourteenth. The real depositary team was coming in an hour, and Flora was panicking.

If she didn't get Archibald out of the house, he'd turn over the gold to the depositary team. She cursed at her own stupidity of using up the remaining thiopental.

She paced the hallway between the overseer's office and the front door. What could she do?

The only solution was to use James. And although it sickened her stomach, she steeled herself with the thought that if he was in his right mind, he'd approve.

Or maybe he wouldn't, but after all it was his idea that she sleep with Private Lee. If James Little could exploit her to get his mission accomplished, she could return the favor.

She climbed the stairs and peeked through a crack in James's door. He dozed in the bed, his legs still held upright in stirrups. His face and chest were dappled by the late afternoon sunlight.

Flora tiptoed into the room and closed the door. James stirred, and for a minute she thought he had awoken, but soon his breathing returned to normal.

She squeezed into the space between the bed's headboard and the wall. She slipped the pillow out from underneath James's head, moving slowly and carefully so he didn't wake up.

When she had the pillow in her hands, she crept around from the head of the bed and stood along its side, next to the window.

She threw a glance at the door. Still closed. Now was her chance. She quickly climbed onto the bed rail and flung herself onto his chest. She kneeled on his shoulders and brought the pillow down over his face, pushing hard with both hands to make sure she smothered him properly.

James's arms flailed at her, but she twisted back and forth and avoided getting hit. He clawed at the pillow and tried to wrench it away from his face. Flora put all her strength into holding the pillow firm. She spread her legs out and pinned his upper arms with her knees.

After a minute James's body stopped writhing. In another half a minute his fingers stopped twitching. Flora lifted the pillow, set it on his chest, and slapped James twice across the face.

He still wasn't breathing, so she slapped him again, this time much harder. James gasped for air and convulsed, and she snatched up the pillow and smothered him again.

This time it only took a few seconds for his body to stop moving. She removed the pillow and slapped him hard on both cheeks. James started breathing again, but he lay still.

Flora slid the pillow back under his head. She rolled off of him and stood on the floor on the side closest to the door, her chest pounding. She looked at James lying helpless, and she reached out and caressed his forehead. Could she really go through with this?

She could. She had to. She took a deep breath, grabbed his right wrist, and pulled. But she was unable to shift him. She'd have to roll him. She reached across his chest and grabbed his left arm, planted her foot against the bed, and pulled with all her might.

James rolled toward her. She went around to the other side of the bed and pushed against his shoulders.

His body teetered on the edge of the mattress before it fell. The side of his head hit the floor with a sickening thud. His legs remained twisted, tied to their stirrups and weights.

Flora rushed around the bed and back to the door. She slipped out and closed the door behind her. She stood still and willed the hammering in her chest to subside. What had she just done?

She opened the door a crack and let out a scream that echoed through the house. "Mr. Morgan, come quickly!"

The overseer ran up the stairs and into James's room. "What happened?"

Flora threw up her arms. "I just opened the door, and there he was!"

He knelt beside James and put his hand on his chest. "At least he is breathing." He stood up and untied James's legs. "Help me pull him forward."

She grabbed James's arms and pulled him enough so Archibald could get his feet onto the floor.

"We must get him to a doctor," the overseer said. Together they got James down the stairs, out the door, and sprawled across the back seat of the Jeep.

Then he climbed behind the wheel. He turned to Flora. "Hurry and get in."

That wouldn't work—she needed to stay at the house. "The depositary team is coming," she said. "Let me take James to the infirmary, and you can meet with them."

He shook his head. "James is more important than the deposit."

Exactly what she was hoping he'd say.

He pointed at the door. "Stay here, and when they come, tell them to return tomorrow afternoon." He flipped on the ignition, shifted into gear, and sped away.

Flora spent the next ten minutes practicing the overseer's signature in his office. She heard the sounds of a truck engine, and she peeked out the front room's window. A green flatbed truck had parked against the curb, and three men in green uniforms walked toward her.

It was a shame she no longer had the camera to capture the details of their uniforms. She committed them to memory instead. At the very least, Major Callaghan would need to know where to sew the Soul Identity logo and the nametags.

She opened the front door. One steel-haired man wearing square glasses and carrying a briefcase stood between two young men.

"May I help you?" she asked.

The man in glasses stepped forward. "Overseer Morgan, *bitte*." He spoke in German with a light Swiss accent.

"You are the Soul Identity depositary team?"

He nodded. "I am Herr Burri."

"Overseer Morgan sends his regrets, but one of his employees needed emergency medical care." The truth was the easy part—now for the lie. "He asked me to represent him in the transaction."

The men looked at each other. Then the older man nodded his head. He looked at her expectantly.

What was he waiting for?

Burri cleared his throat. "You are to ask me for the password, *fraulein*."

She shook her head. "I'm sorry, but Mr. Morgan left in such a rush, he may not have given me the full details."

He nodded. "I understand." He stood still, his mouth taught.

After another moment of silence, she realized it was her turn to speak. "Very well, what is the password, please?"

"Passion." He said this in English.

She nodded. "That is correct. Please come inside."

Burri shook his head. "*Nein, fraulein.* We must follow procedure. Please provide me your password first."

"My password?" Flora felt a rise of panic.

He sighed. "Without verifying your password, we cannot accept any proxy deposits. Surely you know this."

She nodded. "I do. I'm sorry—I'm overwhelmed with concern for our employee. Let me get my thoughts organized."

He nodded and shifted his briefcase from one hand to the other.

She had to calm down and think. Passion—why would Archibald use a word like that?

The overseer would have chosen passwords that others couldn't guess, based on information only he knew. So if she was going to figure it out, she had to think like him.

Maybe the password was 'Flora'. The drugged Archibald did say that he was in love with her passion.

She looked at Burri. "How many tries do I get?"

"One." He wore a stern expression on his face. "Maybe we should come back tomorrow?"

"No! Just give me a minute to remember."

She realized it couldn't be 'Flora'. She would be standing next to the overseer if he was here, and she couldn't imagine an un-drugged Archibald putting himself in a situation where he would say her name. He was too careful to expose himself like that.

What could it be? If Archibald was in love with her passion, what did he love about himself?

Then she smiled. "Vision," she said.

Burri smiled back. "*Sehr gute, fraulein.* Let us go inside to complete the paperwork. My men will wait here."

Flora led Burri down the hallway and into the overseer's office. "Please have a seat," she said. She sat behind Archibald's desk and folded her hands. "Are there any other formalities?"

Burri opened his briefcase. "Overseer Morgan told me to be prepared for as many as three boxes and twelve barrels. I have brought the requisite custom forms for you to complete." He laid the forms on the desktop.

"I'm afraid our client has had a change of heart," she said. "Only a single item, our client's journal, will be deposited." She pulled an open envelope containing her journal out of the drawer and slid it toward Burri.

He removed the journal from the envelope and examined it. "Then there is no need for customs forms. I will write you a receipt." He removed a paper-bound book from his briefcase and opened it on the desk. He placed a sheet of carbon paper under the first page and a sheet of cardboard under the second.

Burri held his pen above the page and looked up at her. "One journal, handwritten. Yes?"

Flora nodded.

He wrote onto the form, then looked up again. "What is the soul identity of your client?"

She steadied her voice. "Soul identity?"

The older man sighed. "*Fraulein*, in order for the journal to reach your client's collection, you must provide us with your client's soul identity. It is a number."

"Where do I find this number?" she asked.

He stared at her. "Does your client have a membership card?"

She opened the middle drawer and rummaged under the papers. There—a small card with the Soul Identity logo embossed on it lay on the bottom. She handed it to Burri.

He looked at the card and then at her. "Your client is Hermann Goering?"

She nodded.

He took a deep breath, and copied the numbers off the card and onto the receipt. He handed the card back to Flora and wiped his fingers on his pants.

Flora stared at him. "You don't like the idea of depositing something from a Nazi?"

"No, *fraulein*, I do not."

She felt her voice go hard as she repeated the overseer's words. "Soul Identity does not discriminate against anybody. We are a business, and not a club."

Burri stiffened in his seat. "Precisely, *fraulein*." He turned the receipt book to her. "You must sign Mr. Morgan's name here."

She picked up a fountain pen. "Here?"

He nodded.

She wrote the overseer's signature, and it looked just like his real one. She gave Burri the book.

He tore out the top copy of the receipt and handed it to her. He put the journal and the receipt book into his briefcase. "That is all?"

"Yes." She stood up and held out her hand. "Thank you, Herr Burri. I realize this work is distasteful, and I appreciate your professionalism."

He looked at her hand, then turned away. "I will show myself out."

After the door banged shut, Flora buried her head in her hands. Did Archibald feel this dirty when he had to defend his actions?

The overseer returned later that night. "The doctors say James will be fine," he said. "He had quite a bump on his head, but they think no additional damage was done."

That was a relief. She didn't want James to suffer any more than what was necessary.

"The depositary team came this afternoon," she said. "I asked them to return tomorrow."

He smiled. "Thank you, Flora. I knew I could count on you."

thirty-three

October 1946
Nuremberg, Occupied Germany

FLORA SPENT ALL THE next morning and half the afternoon rehearsing with Major Callaghan and two German men he had hired.

"Let's go through this once more," she said for maybe the twentieth time.

"Crikey, Flora. If we haven't nailed it yet, we never will," Callaghan said. "Besides, this green uniform needs to be pressed before its debut. Give the lads a couple hours' break."

He was right. Everything was in order: the uniforms pressed, the logos and nametags attached, the receipt scraped clean, and the flatbed truck ready to roll.

"I'll see you at five then," she said. She had just enough time to stop at the infirmary and visit James before heading back to the Soul Identity house.

Flora could see Archibald pacing in his office when she came in the front door. She walked down the hallway toward him.

He whirled around when she knocked on his door frame. "Where have you been?" he snapped. "The depositary team will be here any minute."

"I visited with James," she said. "Should I have stayed here instead?"

He was silent for a moment. "I am glad you checked on him, Flora," he said. "And I apologize for my short temper. I just want everything to go smoothly with this most important deposit."

"I understand, Mr. Morgan," she said. "Can I get you anything?"

"Just some coffee once they arrive, if you please."

When Major Callaghan rapped his knuckles on the front door, Flora opened it and saw him and his two helpers standing in their green uniforms. They had parked their green flatbed truck out front, just like the real team did yesterday. "May I help you?" she asked.

"Mr. Callaghan to see Overseer Morgan."

The overseer stepped into the doorway. "I am Archibald Morgan."

"Please come inside," Flora said.

The overseer held up his hand. "We first need to verify them, Flora." He looked at Callaghan. "Where is Mr. Burri?"

"Puking his guts out, the poor bugger. He sent me instead."

Archibald narrowed his eyes. "May I see your Soul Identity membership card?"

Flora winced. She should have thought of this.

Callaghan's eyes flitted to Flora, then back to the overseer. "What use is seeing me bloody card?"

"I need to be sure who you are, Mr. Callaghan." Archibald held out his hand.

The Major again threw a glance at Flora.

She had to try to help. "Mr. Morgan, this man came with Mr. Burri yesterday. I can vouch for him."

The overseer didn't take his eyes off the Major's. "And did you check his card yesterday, Flora?"

"No," she finally said.

"Then you may have been fooled. Mr. Callaghan needs to prove that he is part of Soul Identity."

Callaghan reached into his pocket and pulled out his wallet. He fumbled through the papers and withdrew an etched, gold-plated card. "Me card," he said, "all the way from White Cliffs, Australia." He handed it to Archibald.

The overseer examined both sides, then handed it back. "Thank you," he said. "What is the password, please?"

Callaghan scratched his head. "I believe Herr Burri said it was 'passion'."

The overseer nodded. "That is correct." He remained in the doorway and stared at the Major.

Callaghan cleared his throat. "Overseer Morgan, what is your password?"

"Vision." Archibald smiled. "Please come inside, Mr. Callaghan." He turned and walked toward his office.

Flora glared at the Major as he left his helpers and stepped inside. He wiped his forehead, then followed the overseer.

Flora closed the front door and waited. After a minute, she heard Archibald call for her.

She stuck her head into the office. "Yes, Mr. Morgan?"

He sat behind his desk, with Callaghan across from him. "Please bring me a coffee." He looked at the Major. "Mr. Callaghan, can I offer you anything?"

"I'll have a cuppa tea, if you please," he said. He smiled at her. "Half milk, half sugar, and half tea."

Flora nodded and closed the door behind her. She tried to hear what they were saying, but she couldn't make out the words.

When she returned with the drinks, she heard peals of laughter coming from the office. She opened the door and saw the two of them sitting back in their chairs, still chuckling.

The overseer looked up. "Mr. Callaghan has just done a grand and a rather accurate impression of Hermann Goering."

What was the Major doing? She set the cups and saucers on the desk. "Which Hermann Goering did you mimic, Mr. Callaghan?" she asked. "The charming, dashing one that the reporters seem to love? Or the evil, insidious one that ordered the deaths of my father and millions of others?"

Silence in the room. Then Archibald cleared his throat. "Thank you, Flora," he said flatly. "That will be all."

She bit her lip. Why couldn't she control her temper? She cursed at her stupidity as she left the office.

The door opened two minutes later, and the men stepped out. Flora watched the overseer fold the receipt and put it in his pocket. The two walked over to the basement stairs, and Archibald used the key around his neck to unlock the door. They descended, and Flora heard Callaghan's cane tap on each step. A minute later she followed.

She saw Archibald pointing at the wooden boxes. "And these are his papers. Three boxes of them," he said to the Major.

Callaghan pulled out his copy of the receipt. "So that's it then. Twelve barrels, each containing six gold bars, each bar weighing four hundred ounces. And three boxes," he said. He looked up at the overseer. "I'll go call the lads, and if you don't mind, I'll stay up top this time. Me leg is killing me."

The overseer nodded, then froze when he saw Flora on the stairs.

"Can I help with anything?" she asked him.

He pursed his lips, then shook his head. "I am afraid not. But stay down here until the men are finished—I don't need any more trouble from you."

"Yes, Mr. Morgan." She pressed herself against the wall to allow Major Callaghan to pass, then came down the remaining steps. "I apologize for my outburst."

The overseer looked at her for a moment before nodding. "I suppose we both have been jumpy," he said. "But soon this assignment will be over, and the four of us will be on our way to America." He cocked his head. "Are you looking forward to that?"

"Baba needs it, but I'm not so sure," she said. She also wasn't sure if it was the right time to talk about her change of plans, but she decided to plow on. "Mr. Morgan, while James recovers enough to leave, I'd like to visit my home town."

His eyebrows went up. "All the way in Istria?"

She nodded. "I want to say goodbye to my remaining friends and family."

He shook his head. "That is impossible, Flora. We leave here on the twenty-second—just seven days from now. There is no time to reach Istria and back."

She tilted her head back just a little. "I can make it. And it's important."

"Is it important enough to risk your move to America?"

That caused her to pause. Baba would be left fending for herself in a strange land.

She was saved from answering by the arrival of Callaghan's men.

Archibald pointed them to the boxes of papers first. When they left, he turned to Flora. "I would much rather you stayed with me," he said.

"Why do you want me with you?" She held her breath. Could he say what he did when he was drugged?

He stared at her. He seemed to struggle with something inside his head.

Finally he said, "I want my mission to be a success, and leaving you behind could spoil that."

She exhaled. How foolish she was to even hope for his candid answer. "When will you leave Paris for America?" she asked.

"At noon on the twenty-eighth."

"I can meet you in Paris that morning."

He shook his head. "I cannot take the risk, Flora. You will stay here with me."

She was down to her final weapon. She reached into her purse. "Before I forget, I have a gift for you," she said. She pulled out a slip of paper. "Hermann Goering sent you a note. 'The overseer has been most efficient and useful, and is to be commended'," she read. "It's signed and dated the sixth of October, 1946."

He took the paper and read it to himself. He seemed to be fighting back a smile. Then he looked at her. "How did you get this?"

"I put it with the release, and he signed them both." She looked down at the floor. "I thought it was the least I could do for you, after all you've done for me and Baba."

He put the paper in his pocket. "Thank you, Flora."

Still looking down, she said, "I really would like to meet you in Paris on the twenty-eighth." She looked up at him.

He shook his head. "That is unacceptable."

Before she could protest, the men returned for their next load, and as Archibald directed them, she gritted her teeth. She needed time to bury the gold, and she wasn't going to let Ned Callaghan and his men do it without her. Why couldn't the overseer let her go?

Callaghan's men headed up the stairs with their next loads. She crossed her arms. "What do you mean, 'unacceptable'?" she asked.

He smiled. "We must do paperwork on the afternoon of the twenty-seventh. If you promise me you will reach Paris by then, you may go to Istria."

She laughed and ran over and gave him a hug. "Thank you, Mr. Morgan!"

He put his arms around her. "Just be careful, Flora," he said gruffly. He let go when they heard the men start down the stairs.

When the fake depositary team left, the overseer's mood lightened. He called Flora and her grandmother to his office.

Flora and Baba watched him pour champagne into three glass tumblers. "I brought this bottle with me from America," he said. "I could not find flutes, and the champagne is not properly chilled, but I suppose it will do." He handed them each a glass. "Let us toast the end of a most successful mission."

"And for a safe journey to America," Baba said. She turned to Flora and raised her glass. "And Istria."

"Let's not forget James," Flora said. "He paid a very big price to ensure your mission's success."

Archibald nodded. "We will never forget James," he declared.

After they finished the champagne, Archibald opened his office wardrobe and pulled out a dark brown robe. "Tonight I will attempt one final visit," he said. "Dr. Stahmer has agreed to help me pose as Mr. Goering's priest."

"Why tonight?" Baba asked.

He slipped into the robe. "The gallows were completed today, and the Nazis will be executed as soon as tomorrow morning. Mr. Goering wants confirmation before he—"

"—cheats the hangman," Flora said.

"Correct." He looked at Flora and Baba and gave a half-smile. "Now if you will excuse me, duty calls."

thirty-four

"YOU AND THE MAJOR really pulled it off," I said to Madame Flora.

"We did," she said. "And Archibald never knew." Her smile faded. "Until he used that damned ring."

"Ann will be pleased to hear there was no depositary theft," Val said.

"So where'd you hide it?" I asked.

She crossed her arms. "I'm not telling."

"Why not?"

"You'll just return it to the depositary, and my sacrifice will have been in vain."

"Your sacrifice?" Val asked. "What about James? You practically ruined his life!"

"Archibald gave James a good job," Madame Flora said. "He was honored as a centuriat, and only last year he retired."

Val stood up and marched over to Madame Flora, hands on her hips. "He was brain damaged, Flora," she said firmly. "Because of your insistence to meet with the Nazis. And if that wasn't enough, you beat him up even more."

Madame Flora nodded. "I did whatever it took to stop that gold from reaching the depositary."

Val pointed her finger an inch from the old lady's nose. "You alone decided your cause was greater. You gave yourself an excuse to do bad things." She dropped her arm and stood staring at her.

"How dare you stand here and judge my actions sixty-four years later?" Madame Flora cried. "No matter how wrong you think it looks today, I could not let the killer of my father win."

"He might as well have won," I said. "Nobody benefits from stashed gold."

"That's true," she said. "I still must return the gold to the hands of those it was taken from."

"Why haven't you done that already?" Val asked. "Wasn't it important enough?"

Madame Flora frowned. "I wanted to. But first I took care of Baba until she died. Then the iron curtain descended, and I couldn't return to its hiding place," she said. "Besides, the Nazis are always watching."

"You said that last night," I said. "But then you told us you killed the Nazis at the barn."

She shook her head. "I only killed one of them. Somehow the *Untersturmführer* survived the barn fire, and he followed me and Major Callaghan all the way to…" Her voice trailed off.

"Where?" I asked.

She smiled. "Where we hid the gold. Where it is today."

I'd have to squeeze the location out of her, but we could do that in front of Archie.

"What happened to Major Callaghan, anyway?" I asked, trying to make it sound casual.

Madame Flora shrugged. "It's not important."

"It is to me."

She looked at me. "Why?"

Val came and sat next to me. She took my hand. "Oddly enough, Ned Callaghan and Scott share a soul line. Your grandfather's Australian friend is Scott's previous carrier."

Madame Flora nodded slowly. "That is most interesting."

Spooky seemed a more apt description.

I squeezed Val's hand and turned to Madame Flora. "Ned mentioned your grandfather in the notes he put in his collection."

"What did he say?" she asked.

"Not much," I said. "It was Ned's version of the big mistake your grandmother told you about."

"Tell me," she commanded.

"All right." I took a minute to recall the story Val and I had read in the depositary. "Ned said he caught Raddy trying to steal opals from his dig. They got into a fight, and somehow the mine caved in. It took a few days to dig out, and by the time they reached the surface, they were best friends."

We all sat silently for a few minutes.

Then Madame Flora pointed at me and spoke slowly. "Scott, not only is it your duty, but it is also your moral obligation to help me retrieve that gold and get it to its deserving parties. You need to finish the job your soul line ancestor and I started."

I noticed Val was biting her lip. She didn't seem thrilled with this idea.

And neither was I. From what we had learned, Madame Flora didn't leave many happy people in her wake. This wasn't my kind of assignment. "With all due respect," I said, "my answer is no. Tell us where the gold is, and Soul Identity can send out a retrieval team."

Val smiled at me. "Thank you," she whispered.

Madame Flora shrugged. "It's your choice, Scott. I'm almost eighty, and this is probably my last chance to recover that gold."

"What would you do with it?" Val asked.

The old lady's answer was prompt. "I'd set up a foundation to improve the lives of victims across Eastern Europe."

"How much did you say the gold was worth?" Val asked me.

"Around twenty-five million bucks." I looked at Madame Flora. "Why not give it to the Romany people?"

"Because they'd waste it, and it would all end up in some loan shark's hands," she said. "I've thought about this for a long time—just handing over the money isn't restitution. They didn't lose it, and they shouldn't benefit from it."

"What kinds of victims would you help?" Val asked.

"People who are discriminated against. I want to give them hope and help them become valuable members of society," Madame Flora said. "Many cities in Eastern Europe are throwing the Roma out of their downtowns. They're building them new ghettos on their outskirts, where crime and unemployment run rampant."

"So how could you give them hope?" Val asked.

"They need community anchors," she said. "I'd set up a grocery store and use it to fund some jobs. Then I'd make micro-loans at decent rates and put the loan sharks out of business. And I'd start a small craft school so the young people can learn to make a living. These three things would help each Roma community."

"Don't charities already help them?" I asked. I thought about the quarter million dollars we had just committed to a Roma charity.

She nodded. "But it's never enough. There are millions of Roma spread across the continent, and the charities are fighting uphill battles in each neighborhood. I've given them every dime from every Soul Identity commission I've ever received, but it's still not enough," she said. "The gold is important to me emotionally, that's true. But the gold will also help the Roma. And you two ought to help me retrieve it."

I shot a glance at Val, and I saw that Madame Flora's story was working—Val stared at her, unblinking, nodding her head.

Had the old lady hypnotized her?

"Why make this our fight?" I asked Madame Flora.

They both shot me dirty looks.

"It's everyone's fight," Val said.

Oops—I had used the wrong words. But I needed to shut this down before we got ourselves sucked in over our heads. "How many people went with you to hide the gold?" I asked Madame Flora.

"Two others—Major Callaghan and one helper."

"And how many of them survived the task?" I asked.

She was silent for a moment. "Why does that matter?"

"Yesterday you told us that the Nazis made it way too dangerous to look for the gold," I said. "Then last night you told us how James was almost killed."

"But—"

"I'm not done," I said. "This morning we learned how you and Archie helped Goering commit suicide. And last year we saw you in action in Venice," I said. "I want you to help me calculate our chances for survival."

"I won't lie to you," she said.

Of course she would.

"The chances are not that good."

That meant the odds were way against us.

She sighed. "Only I made it back."

Oh boy.

Val looked at me with a solemn expression. "Regardless of our chances, we need to help Flora."

Was she serious? "You'd risk our lives for some Nazi gold?" I asked.

Her chin went up. "I'd risk my life to make a difference."

I pondered this turn of events. "Surely there are other opportunities to make a difference," I finally said.

"This one's ours," she said. "Somehow we're being called to it."

Game over—if Val was in, there was no way I'd be out. And if I was honest with myself, I did want to soak up everything I could about Ned Callaghan. Not that I felt any physical connection to him, but his memories and his attempt at relevancy had become my responsibility since I opened our soul line collection.

I looked at Madame Flora and waited until she wiped off the little smile that had started to lift the corners of her wrinkled face. "I have two conditions," I said.

She raised her eyebrows.

"First, Soul Identity needs to back this treasure hunt."

"Why?" she asked.

"You need their resources, and I want to get paid," I said. "That means we need Archie. This afternoon, you're going to explain how you tricked him out of the deposit, and you're going to invite him to join us."

She grimaced. "I'm not sure I can do that."

And I was sure she could. "I've learned how resourceful you are," I said. "You'll find a way."

She sighed and looked at Val, but when Val didn't respond, she turned back to me and nodded.

"Good," I said. "Second, you will tell me everything you know about Ned Callaghan. What he told you, and what happened to him on your little trip to hide the gold." I figured I could augment Ned's rather bleak memories in our soul line collection. It was the least I could do for our future carriers.

"What if I tell you about him as we go?"

She wanted to use her knowledge of Ned as leverage over me. So be it. "That's fine," I said.

Val raised her hand. "I also have a condition." She faced the old lady. "You must tell Mr. Morgan the whole story. How you used him, how you loved him, and how he was the father of your son."

Madame Flora crossed her arms.

"He has every right to know the truth," Val said.

"Would you have me break his heart?"

Val glared at her. "After you lectured Scott on his moral obligation to help finish what you and Ned Callaghan started, how can you even ask that question?"

Madame Flora sighed. "You're right," she said. "But can I open that can of worms once we're in Europe?"

Val nodded. "As long as Mr. Morgan has the full story by the time we recover the gold and get back."

If we got back.

thirty-five

MADAME FLORA AND I parked ourselves at Archie's coffee table and waited for him to get off the phone.

He wrapped up his call and came over to stand behind an empty chair. He looked at us each in turn. "You both seem uneasy," he said at last.

Madame Flora rolled her eyes at me.

"Your dear friend Madame Flora has something important to share with you," I said.

Archie raised his eyebrows. "That sounds ominous."

"Sit down, Archibald," Madame Flora said. "This may take a while."

He sat.

"May I see that depositary receipt you showed us yesterday?" she asked him.

Archie pulled the plastic bag out of his wallet and removed the small slip of paper. He handed it to her.

Madame Flora glanced at it and chuckled. "It's amazing you never noticed." She gave it back to him.

Archie peered at it, but then he shook his head and held it out to me. "What am I missing?" he asked.

I took it. It looked fine to me—what was she laughing at?

Then I saw it. I passed it back to Archie. "What day did you make the deposit?" I asked him.

He extended his arm and squinted through his glasses at the receipt. "Just like it says—the fourteenth of October." He looked at Madame Flora. "What are you getting at?"

"You were planning to make the deposit on the fourteenth," Madame Flora said. "But you didn't."

Archie bowed his head for a moment. "I had forgotten that," he said. "I could not make the deposit, because James had fallen out of bed. I asked you…" his eyes narrowed.

"You asked me to reschedule the team for the next day," she said. "But I didn't. I deposited that journal you found instead of the gold. They gave me the receipt, and I used a razor blade to scrape off the item list and your signature. I couldn't remove the date because of that line underneath it."

Archie stared at her. "And the next day?"

"And the next day," she said, "I sent a fake team, who filled out that receipt for what you thought was the real deposit."

Archie dropped the receipt onto the coffee table. "You re-used a depositary receipt?" His voice rose in volume. "You forged my name onto the original? You assembled a fake depositary team?"

"I did." Madame Flora frowned. "And even with your ring, you never would have known it was me without your little security consultant to figure it out."

Archie swung around to face me, awfully quick for an eighty-four year old. "Are you in on this?"

Did my soul line ancestor count? "Archie, it was sixty-four years ago. I wasn't even born then," I said. "You asked me to catch the thief and find out how Goering's gold was stolen." I pointed at Madame Flora. "I found your thief. Now listen to her, and she'll tell you how she did it."

She glared at me. "Stop calling me a thief. The Nazis stole the gold, and then Goering stole it from them. All I did was keep it out of his soul line collection."

Archie walked over to his desk. He turned around and came back to his seat. He looked at me for a minute, then at Madame Flora. He got up again and went to the window.

Madame Flora cleared her throat, but I shushed her.

After a few minutes he came back and sat down. He stared at Madame Flora. "Your story is preposterous," he said. Then he turned to me. "Scott, you have fingered the wrong person. There is no way Flora could have stolen the gold."

Madame Flora sighed. "I knew this wasn't going to be easy," she said to me.

"You don't think she did it?" I asked Archie.

He shook his head. "We had too much security, Scott. We used double passwords. And I personally checked the identity of the depositary team leader before I turned over the gold." He turned to Madame Flora. "Are you protecting the real thief with your false confession?"

"I most certainly am not!" she said. Her arms were crossed and her eyes were smoldering. "I tricked you, plain and simple. I smothered James, then I pulled him onto the floor so you'd have to leave. I guessed your secret password, and I signed your name. Then I watched you hand Goering's gold to my men."

Archie's shoulders sagged. "Why would you do this?" he asked.

"To stop you," she said. "You knew it was wrong!"

They both went silent. I bit my tongue and waited.

Finally Archie spoke. He was looking at the floor. "What you did was just as wrong, Flora." His eyes flicked up at hers, then back down. "You deliberately sabotaged a Soul Identity mission. You violated its integrity."

"I did what I had to do," she said. She pursed her lips. "And the sooner you agree with me, the sooner we can go get that gold."

He raised his eyes and met hers. "To return it to the depositary?"

"No, you silly old goat. To return it to the families of the victims."

Another few minutes of silence. Then Archie turned to me. "How did you figure it all out?"

Madame Flora threw me a sharp glance.

Val had asked her to tell the whole story, including that he was a daddy, but only once we recovered the gold. I wasn't going to spoil it for her. Besides, watching them handle this old dispute was painful enough without throwing lost love opportunities into the mix.

"A few lucky guesses," I said to Archie. "Plus, she was acting pretty weird in the meetings yesterday when she saw the journal."

He seemed to buy my lame explanation. He turned back to Madame Flora. "I want the full story."

She shook her head. "Only after we get the gold," she said. "Are you going to help?"

More silence. They glared at each other.

Time to help break this log jam. "Archie," I said, "you admitted yesterday that you were wrong, and that you hated yourself for doing business with Goering." I pointed at Madame Flora. "She's right—it's time to finish the job. It's time for Soul Identity to step up to the plate."

He kept his eyes on her as he nodded. "Where did you hide it?" he asked her.

"Not until you commit," she said.

"I am committed," he said. "And so are Soul Identity's resources." He held up his hand. "But I am coming with you."

Madame Flora smiled. "You're more than welcome to come, Archibald. You are part of this." She clapped her hands twice. "We'll start our journey in Nuremberg."

"You hid the gold in the city?" I asked.

She shook her head. "It's a long way from there," she said. "I'll work with George and Sue to handle the logistics. Rose and Marie will come too. They need to learn more about their heritage." She pointed at me. "You and Val need to spend a week in training."

"Training?" I asked.

"Diving," she said. "The gold is buried underwater."

Great.

"When do you want to leave, Flora?" Archie asked.

"Soon," she said. "It's already October—if we don't hurry, the mountains will be snowed in till spring."

thirty-six

I TRIED TO KICK my way up to the surface. I couldn't get enough air in my lungs, no matter how hard I sucked on the regulator. Frantic shouts came over the intercom, but I ignored them. I had only one thing on my mind—I had to get out of the water.

I broke through the surface into the moonlight and ripped the mask off my face and the regulator out of my mouth. I gulped the air and tried to think of happy thoughts.

Christian Nielsen, our dive master, popped up a moment later and tore off his own mask. He slapped his palm hard against the water and sent up a great splash. Then he swam to the boat and clambered onto the dive platform.

Christian's eight-year-old son Julian walked back to the stern. "Dad, give the man a break," he said.

"He could get us all killed by acting like that," Christian said. He pointed at me. "Do that next week, and you'll both end up in a compression chamber."

At that moment, I didn't really care. "There's not going to be a next week," I gasped.

Val surfaced next to me. She turned to the instructor. "I think Scott was better this time."

"Bullshit," Christian said. "He panicked again. We're done here—this isn't gonna work."

"I think he can do it," Julian said. He gave me a smile. "I know he can."

Christian faced his son. "What makes you so sure, Julian?"

"Sometimes I just know," he said. "You know I'm right, Dad."

Our dive instructor frowned. "My son is usually a better judge of talent than I am," he said to Val and me. Then he turned back to Julian. "But this time I think you're wrong."

The boy shook his head. "No, I'm not. Mr. Waverly can do it." He looked at Val. "When I was little, my mom sang me lullabies after I had nightmares. Do you know any lullabies?"

Val smiled. "I do, Julian. That's a good idea."

"It's a stupid idea," Christian said. "Start the engines, son. We're heading back."

"Wait," I said. I gritted my teeth. "Let's try it again."

The dive master shrugged. Then he twisted his wrist to read his dive computer. "You've got time for only one more shot," he said. "It's now or never."

I threw a grimace at Val and then put on my mask. I bit down on the mouthpiece and dove under the waves.

I never would have thought I'd get a panic attack. But there it was: a big gnarly monster living inside of me. And it would mess up our trip if I couldn't figure out how to dive in dark places without becoming a danger to everybody else.

I'd been in plenty of tight spaces before. Last year, when Val and I hid in the trunk of Bob's limo, I didn't panic. And I stayed calm when Andre Feret tossed us into an airless closet in Venice—along with the body of the assistant he had shot.

But diving in the dark was different. Maybe it was the cold water squeezing my wetsuit. Maybe it was how my wrist-attached flashlight only pierced a few feet of the murk in front of me. Whatever it was, the panic overwhelmed me, and I wanted nothing but to push myself off the bottom of the Chesapeake Bay, leap out of the water, rip off my wetsuit, and gulp fresh air—not the recycled stuff the rebreather pumped into my lungs.

Fortunately, we were diving in only twenty feet, and we didn't have to worry about decompression. An old culvert lay on the bottom, and our instructor was having us retrieve a stainless steel toolbox he had buried at the deep end. Val had done it the first time without a hitch, but this was my third and final attempt.

"Ready?" Val asked. The rebreather's regulators garbled our voices, but we could understand each other.

"As much as I'll ever be." I kicked forward and glided up to the culvert. The entrance was lit by my and Val's lights. One last glance back at Val and the dive master, and I swam into the opening.

And my panic monster came hurtling back to join me in that tiny space in the middle of all the murk. My body screamed for me to return to land. My heart raced, and I let loose a strangled cry. My flippers thrashed in the water.

I heard somebody on the intercom, barely audible over the din of my own heartbeats. What were they saying? I scrunched my eyes shut and balled my fists and tried to hear.

It was Val, singing softly in Russian. It was a tune I had never heard before, and I couldn't understand the garbled words, but listening to her voice calmed me down just enough to stop my thrashing.

I pictured the waves of Val's singing carrying me gently up the culvert. I kept my eyes closed, and I gave gentle kicks to propel myself along. And after a few minutes, my head bumped into something. I opened my eyes, and the toolbox gleamed in the beam of my flashlight. I had made it, with Julian's idea and Val's help. We'd be able to do this in Europe next week.

That night, as we lay in our bed before the morning's trip to Germany, I closed my eyes and could still feel the gentle rocking of the waves. I opened them to the moonlight and rolled onto my side. "What was that lullaby you sang in the water?" I asked Val.

She smiled. "It's not quite a lullaby. It's a love song that tells of a beautiful girl dreaming for her prince."

I made a face. "You stopped my panic attack with a love song?"

"It worked." She kissed the tip of my nose. "You were in such bad shape."

I rolled onto my back, bringing her on top of me. "Can you sing it again?"

She snuggled into my arms, her lips close to my ear. "I'll sing you the first few verses."

I closed my eyes and listened to her beautiful, calming voice. "Tell me the lyrics," I said when she stopped.

She propped herself up on her elbows and smiled. "The golden rays of the sun are caressing the shore. The waves are washing up, and somewhere far away, a beautiful ship is floating, its scarlet sail blooming."

I raised my head up off the pillow and gave her a long kiss. "You saved me, my beautiful girl," I murmured. "What shall be your reward?"

"I'll get it myself," she said, her hand sliding down my side and across my hip.

thirty-seven

GEORGE AND SUE MET Val and me as we came through the Nuremberg customs early in the afternoon. Val and I had arrived three days after everybody else, giving the others time to explore the city while we spent extra time diving. The others had come on Soul Identity's jet. We had flown commercial.

George wore lederhosen, a white shirt, and thick gray socks. He hooked his thumbs under the suspender straps and smiled. "Welcome to Bavaria," he said.

"Where's the hat and hiking stick?" I asked.

"Back in the hotel where they belong," Sue said. "Next to the new dirndl you won't ever see me wear."

George smiled. "She looks fabulous in it," he said. "It's one of the made-for-tourists dirndls, so it shows lots of cleavage."

Sue shook her head, but she was smiling. "Let's get you out of the airport and checked into the hotel."

Once we closed the door of our hotel room, Val burst out laughing. "George gets so excited when he travels. Remember how he was in Venice?"

I put my arms around her. "I've been imagining how you'd look in one of those dirndls."

She gave me a kiss. "Just keep imagining," she said. "Sue said we're having dinner at the Bratwurstglocklein, and I hear their waitresses wear some revealing ones."

"Cool." I sat down on the bed and patted the space next to me. It was time to have the conversation that we both had been avoiding the last few days. "Val, I can't shake the bad feeling I have about this little adventure."

She sat down and grabbed my hand. "I have it too. But then I tell myself that we're doing the right thing, and it sort of fades away."

"How do you know it's the right thing?"

She sat quietly for a minute before speaking. "By the time I was a teenager, the Soviet Union was in its perestroika days, so things weren't that bad. But my parents told me how it was in their generation. Success in those days wasn't driven by hard work and determination, but by who you snitched on and how you played the game." She squeezed my hand. "My mom said our next door neighbors, the nicest, gentlest family you could imagine, got hauled off to Siberia because their other neighbor's cousins slandered them to get their flat. My parents were too afraid to speak out, and they lived in constant fear of losing their own place to another one of the cousins."

We sat quietly for a moment.

"When my parents told me that story," she continued, "I swore that I'd never do what they did—I'd never shy away from doing what is right, and I'd always help people with their struggles—no matter the consequences." She looked at me with shining eyes. "And this is my chance. I can help the victims, and I can help Flora conquer her life struggle."

I could understand where Val was coming from. But should we put our lives in danger to satisfy Madame Flora's warped sense of what was right?

I stood up and grabbed both her hands. "It's not just the diving and my stupid panic attacks that are bothering me. If we can believe her, the Nazis are still out hunting for that gold, and they'll want revenge. Are you willing to risk dying for your convictions?"

She stared right into my eyes. "We've been put in this situation for a reason, Scott. Flora is right—your connection to Ned Callaghan is more than just a random coincidence. We are here to make a difference."

"But it's only twenty-five million dollars," I said. "Soul Identity's annual budget is what, several billion? Couldn't Archie divert some of that toward a fund for Madame Flora's victims?"

"He's too straight an arrow to do that. And besides, Flora still needs to complete her life struggle. She needs our help."

Val was committed. And so was I—partly because I agreed with her, and partly because I couldn't imagine letting her go without me.

We met the rest of our party at Bratwurstglocklein that evening. George wore his lederhosen, but he still hadn't cajoled Sue into her dirndl.

The restaurant was on the lower level of an old building. Waitresses carried plates of bratwurst and glasses of beer to the busy tables. The wooden floors gleamed from what must have been constant polishing.

The eight of us sat on two long wooden benches placed on either side of a narrow table.

The twins were reading the history of the restaurant from the back of the menu. "Listen to this," Rose said. "The oldest bratwurst place in Nuremberg, established in 1313." She looked up. "Did you eat here during the trial, Grandma?"

Madame Flora nodded. "Only once—on a date with a soldier named Private Lee." She glanced across the table at Archie.

"I also dined here," Archie said. "With James, the first weekend after I arrived." He looked around. "It is almost the same as it was, though the waitresses' dirndls are much more revealing than they were in 1946."

"I'll drink to progress," George said, hoisting his empty glass in the air. "Another hefeweizen, *bitte schoen*," he said to the shapely waitress.

We ate sausages with spicy mustard and a white asparagus salad, and we washed it all down with beer. When we were done, George cleared his throat. "This is a good time to review our itinerary," he said. "We meet tomorrow morning at seven, where we will follow Flora's route as she headed to..." he looked at Madame Flora.

"East," she said.

"Grandma, don't you think it's time to tell us where we're going?" Marie asked.

Madame Flora lowered her voice to a harsh whisper. "I told you already—they might be listening."

"Who's listening?" I asked.

"The Nazis!" she whispered.

"Why would the Nazis be listening?" I said this a little too loudly, and the other patrons in the restaurant went silent.

"Keep your voice down," Madame Flora hissed. She looked around at the other tables and let out a nervous laugh.

The other diners went back to their own conversations.

"After all we saw today, Grandma must think she's back at the trial," Rose said to Marie.

"Where did you guys go?" Val asked Rose.

"Today was the Palace of Justice. We saw Courtroom 600, and then we rode the elevator down to Hermann Goering's cell." Rose shivered. "Grandma told us how she and Mr. Morgan took his photograph in there."

Marie laughed. "And how she got him to sit in the toilet." Her smile faded. "After that, George drove us to a forest where Grandma said James got hurt." She dropped her voice to a whisper. "She and Mr. Morgan got into a huge fight about whose fault it was."

"Who won the fight?" I asked.

She shrugged. "Nobody. It sounded like a discussion they've had many times before—like they were an old married couple."

"Speaking of which…" Rose turned to Archie. "Mr. Morgan, how come you never got married?"

Archie put down his stein and smiled at her. "I seem to have always put my duties ahead of my personal life."

"Didn't you ever want children?" Marie asked. "Or grandchildren?"

He sighed. "I have been so deeply involved in Soul Identity that I never thought too much about it," he said. Then he leaned toward Marie with a twinkle in his eye. "When I was young, my grandfather used to say, 'If I had known grandchildren would be so much fun, I would have had them first.'" He turned to Madame Flora. "Was he right?"

She shook her head. "My son, granddaughter, and now these two have been my life's joy. I'm sorry to say this, Archibald, but you've missed out on the best part of life by not having children."

Wasn't she the one who never told Archie about their child? I was about to say something, but then Val kicked my shin, and I realized I had better be quiet.

Archie sighed. "We all make our choices, Flora."

Before Madame Flora could reply, I jumped in. "George, can you at least share tomorrow's mode of transportation?"

George grinned. "We're flying. We'll go slow, but we'll cover in a few hours what took Flora four and a half days to do back in forty-six."

"Is everything arranged on site?" Madame Flora asked him.

He nodded. "We'll arrive simultaneously with the rest of the diving equipment."

The eight of us met in the lobby of the Grand Hotel after breakfast. George and Sue ushered us outside to a waiting van. We piled our luggage in the back, rode to the Nuremberg airport, and got onto the green Soul Identity jet.

Val and I sat around a table with Archie and Madame Flora. Once we were airborne, the twins came by. "Now can you tell us where we're going, Grandma?" Marie asked.

Rose chimed in. "And how you got there?"

Madame Flora nodded and beckoned to George and Sue. "It's time I tell you about our mad dash from Nuremberg to Dubnik."

"Dubnik?" Archie asked.

I smiled. "Of course—the opal mines your grandfather once worked at."

thirty-eight

THE TRUCK LURCHED THROUGH another large pothole. Were the barrels strong enough to survive the rough trip?

"We should have taken the autobahn," Flora said to Major Callaghan.

"Too many patrols and too many questions, lass," he replied. "One sniff of that gold and I reckon our bodies would never be found."

It was almost midnight on the fifteenth of October. When Archibald left in his robes for his second and final visit with Hermann Goering, Flora packed her bags, kissed Baba goodbye, and waited for the Major and his men to pick her up.

They had come at eight o'clock, in the same green truck they had loaded the gold on earlier that evening. The flatbed and its contents, along with the major's two helpers, sat under a canvas-covered frame.

Not really sat; more like rattled around. "If those barrels break open, we'll never get the gold hidden," she said.

"Only a few more miles, lass, and we'll be in Regensburg."

Why worry about the barrels splitting, when she should be thinking about how they'd make it back to Paris by the twenty-seventh? It would be close: three days to float down the Danube to Bratislava, another day to take a train to Presov, and two days to hide the gold in Dubnik's opal mines. That would leave them only five days to reach Paris.

Baba would be on her own in America if anything went wrong. But Flora couldn't turn back now; she would stop at nothing to keep the gold hidden.

They'd almost blown it that afternoon with Archibald, when he asked for the Major's identification. "How has your Soul Identity card survived all these years?" Flora asked him.

He gave a laugh. "Luckily the War Department recovered my wallet and mess kit from Cyprus. I got them back only last month in Berlin."

She shook her head. "I was sure Mr. Morgan had found us out."

"You were looking like a 'roo caught in the headlights," he said. "At that moment you truly reminded me of old Raddy."

"My scared look?"

He nodded. "Your old Pap had it when I caught him ratting opals from me mine in White Cliffs." He navigated the truck around a gaping hole. "That was before we became mates, Flora. Raddy was going through a dry spell, I reckon."

"My grandfather stole your opals?"

"Aye. I caught him in my hole one night, and we got into a terrible fight. We slammed into the main prop, and the bloody roof caved in. We dug for a week, and when we finally climbed out, we had become best mates." He put his hand on his chest. "Your grandfather saved me, Flora, when he could've let me die. I was buried head-down in potch, but he grabbed me boots and pulled me out."

She thought about the grenade in Gallipoli. "He twice saved your life."

He nodded. "And the poor bastard died that second time. That's why I told your grand-mum I'd help you on your fools' errand. What little bit of life I do have left I owe to Raddy."

They reached a river's bank in Regensburg in the gray early morning hours, and the Major and his men transferred the barrels and boxes to a squat, rusted barge.

"We'll float down the Danube," the Major said, "right under the noses of the patrols. I told the captain we're smuggling cognac to the Carlton-Savoy Hotel in Bratislava—I promised him a barrel if he gets us there in three days."

Flora's mouth tightened. "Don't you dare give him my gold."

"Count the barrels, girlie. I added one full of cognac. Fair dinkum." He chuckled. "He needed a reason to evade the patrols and rush us to the back of beyond."

She pointed to his men, who were assisting as the captain prepared the boat for launch. The three of them spoke in German. "Your two men are his crew?"

"Aye. I told the buggers to keep their traps shut in Nuremberg. They also think we're carrying cognac."

She smiled. Baba was right about Major Ned Cunningham—he was a treasure.

Flora sat on the prow of the barge, her legs dangling over the edge. She pulled the inner wax carton out of another "K" ration breakfast package.

She was glad she had thought to pack these—the crew was grateful to have more than just their dry brown bread and ersatz coffee.

The edge of the sun had just popped up over the Danube in front of her. It streaked the sky in shades of pink and orange. The water ahead was calm.

Major Callaghan limped up. "The billy's piping hot—are you ready for your cuppa?"

She nodded. This was their third dawn on the barge, and they had settled into a comfortable routine of greeting the sun with her coffee, his tea, and their rations. "I'm going to miss this," she said.

The Major grunted as he filled her cup with hot water. "It's pretty, but it's not home."

"Where is home, Major Callaghan?"

He sighed. "Until six years ago, I'd still have called myself an Aussie. But I've been gone so bloody long I'm not so sure anymore."

"Do you have a family?"

"Aye, I did. A regular May-December romance, it was. A tram picked a fight with me back in early 'thirty-nine, and I fell for me eighteen-year-old nurse. Betty and I married a month before I shipped out." His face clouded over. "I knew it was too good to be true."

"What happened?"

"The bloody government told her I was dead five years ago, and she up and married last year. Another digger, but this one her age and not forty years older."

She was shocked. "What are you going to do?"

The Major shrugged. "Let her be, I reckon. Betty doesn't need an old bugger like me rattling around the house. She needs somebody young and strong to help her raise our daughter Kate."

He coughed and turned away, but not before Flora saw the tears in his eyes reflecting the rising sun. She reached out and patted his arm.

He gripped her hand in his, and the two of them watched the sun rise. Then he sighed. "I'm unlucky in love, I reckon. This is the second family I've lost."

She had heard from Baba how Ned Callaghan's first wife and infant son had died during a typhus outbreak in White Cliffs. Ned had turned his claim over to her grandfather and had gone on a walkabout, fully intending to die in the outback.

She wondered what had kept him alive. "How did you and my grand-father find each other after you left White Cliffs?" she asked.

The Major straightened up. "I spent the next year and a half with me dilly bag, drifting around the country. Sometimes I would ride the rails, and one day I stopped in Ballarat, an almost-dried-up gold town. I heard somebody hollering 'Old Ned!', and I spotted your grandfather waving his bloody hat at me."

He smiled. "That was back in 1913. He took me home, and I boarded with him and your grand-mum," he said. "I worked for Raddy in his new blacksmith shop until we both were volunteered for the war."

"The one he didn't make it home from."

"Aye." They sat in silence for a few more minutes. "He was a right chap, Flora. When I returned to Ballarat and found your grand-mum and father gone, I ran his blacksmith shop for twenty years. Until I got bug-gered by that bloody tram."

They finished their hot drinks and stood up. Flora handed Callaghan his cane. "The captain says we'll be at the Carlton-Savoy by noon," she said.

He nodded. "We have seats on the three o'clock train to Presov."

"Will the captain let you take Dieter?" She and Ned would need his help in the mines.

"Aye, Dieter rides with us." The other two would sail on to Budapest, load up, and pick them up from Bratislava four days later. He turned to-ward her. "If the three of us are late, you won't make it to Paris in time."

"We won't be late," she said. She hoped she was right.

thirty-nine

"WHILE FLORA FLOATED DOWN the Danube," Archie said, "I visited Mr. Goering." A faint smile crossed his lips. "I spent a long and painful following afternoon answering Colonel Andrus's questions regarding Hermann Goering's suicide."

Shamelessly facilitated by Soul Identity. "Did they ever suspect you?" I asked.

He shrugged. "The media wakes up every few years with another theory," he said. "And every now and then another old soldier issues a confession about how he inadvertently slipped Hermann Goering the cyanide. I certainly am not going to reveal to them our role in the matter."

Marie pointed out the window at the river below us. Small fields encased it, and young evergreen forests rimmed the edges. "Is that the Danube down there?" she asked.

George glanced out. "Yes, and that city you see up ahead is Bratislava. We're over halfway to Kosice."

I had pulled out a map. "Why not Presov?" I asked. "It looks like it's the closest city."

"The airport is now army-only," he said. "Kosice is twenty miles away."

"Flora, I thought you mentioned the opal mines were in Hungary," Val said, looking over my shoulder. "Dubnik's in Slovakia."

"Now it is," Madame Flora said. "When my grandfather was there, that land was part of Hungary."

"As part of our prep work, I researched the history," George said. "After World War One, this area joined up with the brand-new Czecho-Slovakia. Then during World War Two, it became part of the Slovak Republic. The Soviets re-united Czechoslovakia until 1993, when the two split into the Czech Republic and Slovakia."

"Was it the turmoil that kept you away?" I asked Madame Flora.

She nodded. "Baba died in 1948, but the communists got here before I could organize a trip."

"They've been gone twenty years, Grandma. Since we were born," Rose said. "Are you sure your gold is still there?"

"How can I be sure?" she asked. "Nobody's mined there since 1918, though recently I heard a visitor's center will open, and a diving group is organizing tours."

"Who wants to dive in a mine?" Marie asked.

"Lots of people," George said. "Thrill seekers. The lower half of the Viliam gallery has been flooded for sixty-something years, and supposedly it's fabulous. I found some diving sites that rave about the crystal-clear waters and opals shining in the walls."

Rose looked at her grandmother. "Is this why you had me and Marie spend two summers taking diving lessons?"

The old lady smiled.

I sat down with Madame Flora, Archie, and George when we were an hour away. "You buried the gold in an abandoned opal mine," I said to Madame Flora.

She nodded.

"And since the mine is now flooded, we'll have to dive to recover it."

George held up his hand. "I ordered four suits and rebreathers for you young people to use."

I looked at him. "Do you have a map of the mine?"

"Of course." He reached into an overhead compartment and pulled out a tube. He withdrew a map, unrolled it, and spread it on the table. "After some detective work, we got our hands on these plans," he said. "They were made in 1918, right before operations shut down."

I looked at the map. "This place is huge," I said.

"More than thirteen miles of tunnels." George tapped one particularly complex section. "This gallery is the part that's underwater. It's a quarter-mile in. Multiple levels are connected to each other by shafts and rail ramps. Most of them connect back to this other gallery here, but not all of them. Some dead-end into the cave walls, and others look like blind alleys."

I couldn't think of a worse place to dive. Val would be in jeopardy of wearing out her singing voice as she kept me calm.

I turned to Madame Flora. "Where's it hidden?"

"I'm not telling you. Not yet."

"Are you sure you remember?"

She turned on that wide-eyed stare of hers. "I'm sure."

The pilot dropped under some clouds, and Val and I got a great view of the High Tatras to the north, the part of the Carpathians marking the border between Slovakia and Poland.

"Good thing the gold's not up there," Val said. "Those mountains are covered with snow."

"And look at those cliffs." I reached out and took her hand. "I'm really not looking forward to the diving. Are you still feeling committed?"

"Absolutely." She squeezed my hand. "You'll be okay."

"Just stay close to me and be ready to sing if I panic."

"You don't have to dive, you know."

"And let you girls have all the fun?"

We sat quietly for a minute. Then I said, "There's another reason I want to dive. Old Ned has drawn me in—now I need to be there."

It seemed to me that the stories I'd heard from the World War Two era were filled with larger-than-life heroes and villains, and packed with high-definition drama, romance, and tragedy. Was this part of history a golden age, or did it just stand out as the New World's bridge between the Great Depression and its rise to prosperity?

Ned Callaghan was an old man by the time he made his trip with Flora. Though his personal life was in shambles, he fought in both world wars, and it seemed he died helping the granddaughter of a man who twice saved his life. In just a week, he'd become a hero to me, one I was bound to by our shared soul identity. I wanted to ensure his relevancy, and the best way I could do that would be to learn all I could about him, and then put his story into our soul line collection. I couldn't wait to hear the rest of his final adventure.

I wanted to help him finish his mission. And that's why I had to dive.

We landed at Kosice airport and got into a large green van. George climbed into the driver's seat. "We'll head directly to the mines," he said. "It should take less than an hour."

I turned to Madame Flora. "What happened when you brought the gold to Dubnik?"

forty

October 1946
Dubnik Mine, Czechoslovakia

FLORA GRIPPED THEIR GUIDE Vlado's outstretched hand and hopped down from the back of the horse-drawn wagon. "I felt every bump of that trip," she told him, even though she figured he didn't understand.

She stretched and looked around the clearing. Two rusting ore cars sat on railroad tracks, which ran into what must have been the mine's entrance in the side of a hill. A wooden shack stood beside the tracks.

They had arrived five hours earlier at Presov Station, and while the Major arranged transportation to the mine, Flora searched for a guide who spoke German and English. They both were partially successful: they were now the proud owners of two wagons, and they were accompanied by an old man named Vlado who claimed he once worked the mines, and who demonstrated a vocabulary of a few Romany, German, and English words.

But he couldn't easily string those words together in any decipherable order, Flora soon realized. In the long ride to the Dubnik mine entrance, Vlado's communication was mainly about his name, his fee, and his joy that the war was over.

The second wagon rolled to a stop next to them, and the Major and the captain's man, Dieter, clambered off the barrels and jumped to the ground.

"Crikey, I thought we'd never reach here." Callaghan whacked the iron-rimmed wagon wheel with his cane. "Bloody wagons. Who would have guessed there would be no trucks in Presov?"

The Major directed Dieter to unload the barrels, boxes, and equipment, but when he started, Vlado began shouting in Slovakian and waving his arms.

"What's he saying?" Callaghan asked Flora.

"I don't know," Flora said. She tried to talk to him in Romany, but he continued to shout. She switched to German, then English, with the same results.

"Dieter, stop unloading for a minute," Callaghan said.

When Dieter stopped, Vlado went silent.

"We can't afford to attract any attention," Callaghan said. "What the devil is making him holler?"

Dieter cleared his throat. "Vlado say *verboten* to stay here, sir. Mine is haunted."

"You understand him?" Callaghan asked.

He nodded. "A little. I served with Slovak SS unit on Russian front. Good little fighters."

"Tell him we need to unload these bloody barrels and find a hidey hole in the bloody mine."

Dieter shook his head. "Sorry sir, I don't understand. Hidey hole?" He looked at Flora.

Flora translated for Dieter, who talked to the guide while they waited. After a few minutes Vlado spat on the ground and stalked off.

"Where's he going?" Flora asked Dieter.

"Home. He won't help us. He says to keep the fee."

"You can't let him go!" she said. "He'll just tell the others."

Dieter ran after Vlado and dragged him back. The old man shouted, and Dieter clamped his hand over his mouth.

"Everybody around here thinks the mines are haunted?" Callaghan asked Dieter.

Dieter asked Vlado, who nodded.

The Major turned to Flora and spoke softly. "Then it won't matter if he knows—nobody's going to go down there."

The Major was right. But maybe she could help spice up the story. She spoke to Dieter again. "Tell him we knew the place was haunted, and that's why we came."

He looked at her. "We did?"

She nodded. "The Major and I did. Tell him."

Dieter shrugged. He told Vlado, and the old man stopped struggling and opened his eyes wide. He said something to Dieter, who held up his hand and spoke to Flora. "He wants to know what you have in the barrels."

"Cognac, but you already knew that."

Dieter stared back. "Why are you putting cognac into a mine?"

She smiled. "Because of what's in the boxes."

Dieter translated for Vlado. Then he turned to Flora. "What's in the boxes?"

"*Strigoi morti*," she said.

At that, with no translation necessary, Vlado started shouting again, and he clawed at Dieter.

"I can't hold him much longer," Dieter said. He blocked the guide from biting his forearm.

"Tell him that I am their Gypsy servant," Flora said. "We've brought enough cognac to keep them calm for many years. But tell him that nobody should come here again, or the *strigoi* will become angry at the trespassers, and they will descend on them and their children."

Dieter relayed this to Vlado, who nodded his head vigorously. Dieter let him go, and the old man fell on his knees in front of Flora and spoke to her.

"What's he saying?" she asked Dieter.

"He promises on the graves of his wife and oldest son to tell everybody to stay away. But you must tell the *strigoi* that he is a good man."

Flora nodded and pulled out her purse from under her shirt. She gave Vlado triple his negotiated fee, and he took the money and shoved it in his pants.

"Tell him this—I will give the *strigoi* his name. Any mistakes…" she let her voice trail off and clasped her fist over her heart.

Dieter repeated this to Vlado, who shook his head, stood up, and shuffled out of the clearing without looking back.

Major Callaghan cleared his throat. "That was a sight to behold. What did you tell him?"

"That we're hiding cognac."

He shook his head. "I heard you say that. But what put the bee in his bonnet?"

She grinned "I told him about the *strigoi morti* in the boxes." At his blank look, she said, "Undead vampires."

The Major chuckled. "That'll keep anybody away—including me," he said. He pointed at the horizon. "The sun goes down early in the mountains. We ought to set up camp."

The men raised two tents, close to the mine's entrance, and Flora built a fire next to the abandoned ore carts. They heated their "K" ration meals in the coals and ate quickly.

"So this is where your grandfather worked before coming to Australia," the Major said.

Flora nodded. "Baba gave me his old map of the tunnels. I need your help choosing the best place to hide everything."

"I've seen his map," he said. "Raddy had it hanging on the wall in his front room before we went to war." He was silent for a moment. "Your grandfather told me a story of those ghosts Vlado was hollering about."

"Do you really believe in ghosts?" she asked.

"We miners are a superstitious lot, Flora. And every mine has its share of ghosts." The Major rummaged in his bag and pulled out a pocket knife.

"What did he tell you?" she asked.

He reached over to the firewood pile and selected a long and straight stick. He used the knife to strip the branches, tossing the shavings into the fire. "I reckon I shouldn't be scaring you with the story."

She shivered. "I can handle it."

Callaghan sharpened the end of the stick to a point and ran his finger over it. He cocked his head at the other man. "You listening, Dieter?"

"Yes, sir." He sat across the fire from Flora and Callaghan, as far away as possible from the boxes.

The Major smiled. "Good. Then I only have to tell this once," he said. He cleared his throat. "I'm reciting the story your grandfather told me, Flora. I cannot vouch for its accuracy."

She nodded.

The Major used the pointed end of his stick to stir up the fire's embers. "Raddy told me these mines have been active for a thousand years, and he reckoned even longer. Many generations of families spent their lives chasing the opals. And for most of that time, Dubnik was the only opal mine in the world."

He cleared his throat. "Flora, your grandfather told me that when he first came to Dubnik, he and three other miners were dropping a new shaft under the Viliam and Fedo galleries. They had sunk it down forty or fifty feet chasing an opal vein when bam!" He smacked the fire's embers with his stick, sending sparks flying in the air.

Both Flora and Dieter jumped.

The Major looked at them and chuckled. "Nervous Nellies, hey? Raddy and his mates fell right through the collapsed floor. The four of them tumbled down a steep and slippery chute that opened into a large cavern. They dropped twenty feet or so and landed in a small lake of water."

Callaghan drove the stick point-first into the ground and reached up with his hand to the top of it. "About this deep—halfway up their chests. Their torches and lamps and tools landed in the water, and it was pitch black in the cavern. The water was cold, and they didn't dare move for the fear of stepping in a hole and drowning."

He looked at Flora. "Your grandfather said they hollered for help, all the time getting colder. They heard nothing but the drip, drip, drip of water from above. They started poking around, and one of them found a ledge they could clamber on.

"Once on the ledge, they dove into the dark water and retrieved their lamps. They somehow got one lit, and looked around to see where they had fallen."

The Major used his stick to prod some red and orange embers out of the fire. "Look how these glow," he said. "That's what old Raddy and his mates saw in the cavern walls."

"*Die opale.*" Dieter said.

He nodded. "Aye. Opals, glistening in the walls, lit by the lamp. Opals the size of your fist, reflecting and amplifying the lamplight in grand swaths of green and red. And on the roof, around the stalactites, opals glinting back at them in deep purples and blues. A huge nest of the noble opals, guaranteed to make the four of them rich.

"There was a problem—the opals by rights belonged to their employer, Solomon Goldschmidt, the Viennese jeweler who had leased the mine," he said. "Another problem—and I reckon it was bigger than the first—was how Raddy and his mates were to get out of the cavern and return to the surface.

"But they didn't let either of these bother them. Instead, they dove for their picks and shovels, and they pulled the fattest, juiciest opals they had ever seen out of the wall behind the ledge. They filled their pockets, then they made a pile of the larger ones at their feet on the ledge."

The Major poked at the now-dim embers. "The lamp was low on fuel, and the glimmer from the opals was weak, just like this. They lit another lamp, and then their last one." He looked at Dieter. "And only then their opal lust died down enough for them to think about how they were going to get out.

"Your grandfather, Flora, was the scrawniest, smallest man among the four. After hours and maybe even days of arguing in the dark, they decided to send him up to get some ropes and buckets. The chute's opening was high over their heads, and the cavern's wall was slippery from the water and slime that oozed out of it.

"They were in a fine fettle, I reckon. To encourage him to return all the quicker, they made Raddy leave his pocketful of opals behind, and warned him not to tell anybody about the treasure. Then the biggest miner planted himself in the water up against the wall, and the next stood on his shoulders, and the next on his. Raddy climbed this human ladder, and he was able to touch the base of the chute.

"Raddy asked his mate to lift him up by his ankles, and after many tries and many tumbles back into the water, he was finally able to pull himself up and into the slippery tube."

Callaghan shook his head. "He told his mates he'd be back soon, and then Raddy shimmied up the chute in the dark. He was bone tired by the time he reached the shaft, but he made it to the ladder and pulled himself up.

"The gallery was deserted. Your grandfather had to drag himself in the dark out of the mine. When he finally reached the entrance, he collapsed on the ground." The Major looked around, then pointed at Dieter. "Probably right about where you're sitting, young man."

Dieter shuddered, and Callaghan smiled.

"Right before he passed out, Raddy told the foreman about the shaft and the chute and his three trapped mates, but he kept mum on the opals." The Major dropped his voice to a whisper. "He didn't wake up for a day and a half."

"Did they rescue the other miners?" Flora asked.

He sucked some air through his teeth. "The foreman told Raddy that he sent a boy down the chute with a rope tied around his waist, but after a few minutes they heard a piercing scream. They hauled on the rope, and found it had been cut, its end soaked red with blood. The screams continued for another hour, but the foreman refused to send anybody else down.

"Your grandfather told me he climbed down the shaft, but when he reached the bottom, he found the chute full of water. In it floated the cutoff piece of the rope, strung through the belt-loops of an empty pair of trousers."

A chill ran up Flora's spine.

Callaghan was silent for a long minute. Then he spoke in a soft voice. "They reckoned the other miners had gone crazy and had mistaken the lad for food, and God had drowned them for their cannibalism. The foreman had the shaft plugged, never knowing about the opal nest." Callaghan paused and then said, "Old Raddy told me that on the nights of the new moon, you could still hear that boy's scream echoing up from the shaft, pleading with the miners."

The three of them sat and stared at the fire. Then Dieter looked up. "Is it true, sir?"

Major Callaghan shrugged. "I don't rightly know. But I'd trade me arm and leg for an hour in that opal nest."

forty-one

JUST AS MADAME FLORA finished, George drove the van into the clearing and parked.

"Welcome to Dubnik Mine," George said. "Once the only known source of opals, and now an important refuge for five thousand Euro-bats."

Marie shuddered. "There will be bats flying around us?"

"They live in another section," George said. "We shouldn't see too many."

I shot a quick glance at Val, but the mention of the bats didn't seem to bother her.

George had parked halfway up the side of a tree-covered hill. A set of narrow gauge railroad tracks ran past a dilapidated wooden building and into an opening in the hill the size of a front door. Two rusted ore carts sat on the rails, close to the mine entrance.

Madame Flora was the last to climb out. She stood on the van door's threshold and looked around. "Nothing much has changed in the last six decades," she declared.

"This is where you camped?" Rose asked.

"Right by the entrance," she said. She pointed to the building. "That shack had a roof on it, and there's more trees on the hills, but the rest is pretty much the same."

Archie walked to the opening and turned back to face us. "This is where you buried the gold, Flora?"

She nodded. She had a grim look on her face.

Marie came up and put her arm on Madame Flora's shoulder. "We'll get it out for you, Grandma."

"If it is still in there," Archie said.

"It's in there," Madame Flora said. "I can smell it."

A small blue Skoda hatchback drove up and parked next to the van. A young man in jeans, boots, and a blue sweater got out. A blond ponytail hung halfway down his back. He popped his trunk, unloaded six large plastic cases, and stacked them close to the entrance.

George and Sue walked over and shook his hand. The air was chilly, and their breath came out in puffs as they talked.

Then George headed over to us. "Come and meet Cesar," he said. "We're renting the diving suits and rebreathers from him." He dropped his voice to a whisper. "I told him that Scott and Val are super-rich celebrities, here to have some very private fun."

Some cover story.

"Are you diving with us?" I asked Cesar.

He shook his head. "I'm only delivering the equipment. Mr. George paid extra money for your exclusive and private use of our site." He smiled, and with a jerk of his head, he flipped his ponytail over his shoulder. "It's beautiful diving in the mine."

"How many times have you been down there?" I asked.

"Not nearly enough," he said. Then he pursed his lips. "Normally we only allow cave-certified dive masters."

"Rose and I are certified," Marie said.

Cesar nodded. "Let's do the inspection."

While George and Sue set up camp, Cesar opened the cases and had Val, me, and the twins examine the equipment. We tested the regulators and monitors, checked the gas mixes, and verified the work-to-breathe levels. We examined the batteries and the bailouts, then checked the dry suits.

Once we were comfortable with the gear, we lugged the cases into the mine. It was a quarter-mile hike down from the mine's entrance to Viliam Gallery, but to get there, we had to crawl and drag our gear through three low spots. The mine was cold, damp, and dark.

"Why not fix the place up?" I asked Cesar.

He turned and shone his light in my face. "And let the rest of the world ruin it? We save it for serious divers."

And gold diggers like us.

He led us down a stone staircase carved out of the rock many centuries ago. We stepped off the stairs and onto a landing, and Cesar set two battery-powered lanterns on the floor. We were in a basketball court-sized cavern, standing on a ledge above a twenty foot wide shaft filled with water. Several nylon lines ran below the surface.

Val knelt down and dipped in her hand. "It's freezing!"

"Three degrees Celsius," Cesar said. "That's why you have dry suits and full face masks." He tied a dive light to a line and dropped it in the water. "Take a look at this."

The water was perfectly clear and very deep. I could see the shaft's brown walls, fading into a deep blue at the end of the light's reach. The nylon lines stretched down into the darkness below.

"Take small, short kicks as you descend," Cesar said. He dipped the end of a fin into the water by the light and sloshed it back and forth. Particles of silt broke free from the shaft's wall, and the water went dark as the light was blocked. "See what happens? Keep it calm, or you won't be able to see where you're going."

Another thing we'd have to worry about when we dove tomorrow.

Cesar pulled a laminated card out of his pocket. "I brought you a map of what we've explored," he said. He handed the card to me. "We've run nylon lines to all the areas in black, so you can't get lost. I'd advise you stay out of the red sections."

"Thanks," I said. We helped him shut off the lights, and we all climbed up to the entrance.

Back in the clearing, after Cesar drove off, I sat down with George, Archie, and Madame Flora. We clustered around a card table and studied the old map.

Madame Flora pointed to a section in the middle portion of Viliam Gallery. "This is where we hid it."

I held up Cesar's laminated card. The area she pointed to was marked in black. "I hate to be a spoil-sport," I said, "but this area has been well-explored by the divers."

She shook her head. "We didn't leave the gold in the open, Scott. Ned walled up the alcove."

I compared the two maps. It seemed that the back side of an alcove in the main gallery was missing from Cesar's map. "The gold's behind this wall?" I asked.

She nodded.

At least it wasn't in a red section. I turned to George. "How do we get through the false wall?"

"We'll have to pull it down," he said. "We can't use explosives—the mine could collapse."

I called over Val and the twins, and the four of us looked at the two maps.

"It's right around fifty feet deep," Marie said. "We'll have to schedule decompression time."

"Taking down that wall will make the water murky." Rose grabbed a pad. "We'll need three dives—explore, penetrate, and recover." She scribbled some numbers and looked up at George. "We should get a bit more oxygen, just in case. Can Cesar bring four more tanks?"

George nodded. "I'll call him tonight."

"How will we get the barrels out?" I asked him.

He smiled. "I've gotten my hands on an underwater sled a salvage buddy of mine suggested I use." He walked over to the back of the van and pulled out another large gray case. He unsnapped and lifted off the cover. Then he pulled back the top layer of egg crating. "Lend me a hand with this, and I'll show you how it works."

I helped George unfold the sled and attach a wire-enclosed propeller. It took only a few minutes for us to assemble it.

"The batteries should last you eight hours," George said. "And it's got an automatic buoyancy compensator—you attach a diving tank here along the side."

The sled was four feet long and two feet wide. We'd be able to put two or three small barrels on it at a time.

"You guys just have to bring the barrels to the bottom of the shaft, and I'll pull them up with my winch," George said.

We took the van into Presov for dinner, leaving George and Sue behind to keep an eye on the equipment. When we returned, George had a worried look on his face.

"Cesar brought the tanks while you guys were in town. But he says the local police chief is coming out tonight for an inspection."

"You cleared this trip with the authorities, did you not?" Archie asked.

"Of course, Mr. Morgan," George said.

Sue held up a manila folder. "I have the documentation here. For the next two days, the mine is ours."

I turned to George. "I think we should get the rest of our equipment underground. We don't want the cops to think we're about to tear up their mine."

"Good idea," he said.

We left Archie and Madame Flora above, and the rest of us hauled the winch, the sled, a bunch of communications gear, and the extra tanks below. We strung a pair of power lines for the winch and the radio. When we emerged an hour later, we saw the old couple sitting around a crackling campfire.

It looked like we had interrupted a serious discussion. Madame Flora sat with her arms crossed, and Archie was holding his head in his hands, his elbows on his knees. Both stared at the fire.

We joined them just as a set of headlights lit up the clearing. A white Skoda with blue lights on top parked next to the van, and a tall lady with short brown hair and wearing a gray uniform got out.

George and Sue walked over to her. After a minute, the three of them came over to the fire.

"This is everybody?" she asked.

George nodded. "All eight of us."

"Good." She looked around the fire at each of us. "Hello. I am Dara Sabol, Presov police chief." She spoke in a heavy accent.

We murmured our greetings.

She had a serious look on her face. "When I hear from Cesar your crew was to dive, I ask him why he not diving with you."

"Our team prefers to dive alone," George said.

Chief Sabol nodded. "That is same thing Cesar said." She stared at him. "But tell me your reason."

"Privacy." George pointed to me and Val. "These two are constantly hounded wherever they go. The last thing they need is a set of unflattering photographs of them in diving gear plastered over the gossip rags."

I wasn't sure if Chief Sabol understood or bought it, but after a minute she nodded. "I am making sure your team is safe, and I am being ready for all emergencies. This makes extra work for my men."

He nodded. "Thank you, Chief Sabol. We do appreciate it."

She shook her head. "The work will make my hands short. And holidays are coming."

George smiled. "We are so sorry to put you out."

She frowned at him.

Sue sighed. "Just a second, ma'am." She grabbed George's shoulder and whispered in his ear.

"Ah!" George patted Sue's hand and straightened up. "Chief Sabol, let me walk you back to your car."

The two headed away from the fire. I watched them stop at the car door. George pulled out his wallet, peeled off several bills, and handed them to her. She got in her cruiser, and he leaned in her window and talked for a few minutes.

After the chief left, George came back chuckling. "Sometimes I'm so dense. Thank you, my dear, for reminding me to tip her."

Sue rolled her eyes.

Then George let out a big rolling laugh. "Flora, you'll appreciate this—Chief Sabol told me to be careful, as these mines apparently are the home of three vicious vampires, and many people have disappeared over the years."

Rose giggled. "Grandma's story has become a legend."

Madame Flora snorted.

After we set up the tents, we gathered back at the fire. I held my hands toward the flames. "Was it this cold when you were here last time?" I asked Madame Flora.

"Colder, I should say. And our clothes and accommodations weren't as comfortable," she said. "I don't think I slept a wink that night."

"We've waited long enough," I said. "It's time to tell us how you hid the gold."

forty-two

FLORA SLEPT WRAPPED AROUND the barrels of gold and boxes of papers in her tent. Major Ned Callaghan and Dieter slept in the other. She had been listening to their snores for the past few hours.

It wasn't their snores keeping her awake; it was her own anticipation. By tomorrow night the gold would be safely stashed, out of the reach of Goering, the Nazis, and Soul Identity.

Dealing with the gold seemed to make some people happy. Goering was willing to swallow cyanide, thrilled that his next self would retrieve it from the depositary. Archibald was satisfied that its deposit into the Soul Identity vaults would boost his career. Baba had earned their move to America because of it. And by helping her steal it, Major Callaghan had settled his debt with her grandfather.

The gold didn't bring everybody happiness, of course. It had its victims. James certainly hadn't benefited from it, and neither did Flora's father, nor the other Jews and Gypsies killed in the camps.

And what about herself? Flora had thwarted its deposit into Goering's soul line collection, but the gold hadn't yet brought her any peace. She couldn't begin to imagine what damage she had done to her soul with the acts she had committed bringing it this far. The SS leader and his soldier, James, Private Lee and his girlfriend, Archibald—she had used and tricked and hurt them all.

And for what gain? Just to bury the gold? Would she ever be able to retrieve it? Would she be wise enough to return it to the victims? Would she be strong enough?

In the early hours of the morning, before Goering's barrels and boxes even went into the mine, while listening to the wood crackle in the fire and the men snore in their tent, Flora resolved that she would get the gold out. She would make sure it found its way into the hands of the victims' families. She would do this, or she would die trying.

When dawn finally broke and she heard the others stir, she crawled out of her tent. Major Callaghan sat in front of the fire. He had placed three tins on the coals. He looked up at her. "Eat all your tucker today, Flora. You'll need the energy."

Dieter came out, and the three of them finished the last of the "K" rations. Then while Dieter fed and watered the horses, Flora and Callaghan pored over the map. "It looks like Viliam Gallery is the best choice," she said.

"We'll have to see it ourselves to be sure." Callaghan rubbed his hands together. "Have you been underground before?"

"Baba and I hid in caves for years—first from the Nazis and then from the communists."

"So you know what to expect." Callaghan pulled out the lamps and a rope. "I'll get me a look-see while you and Dieter roll in the barrels."

Dieter tied a rope to one of the ore cars, and during the three hours while the Major scouted the mines, they used it to bring the barrels and the boxes to the top of a stone staircase. They had just hauled the ore car up for the last time and found Callaghan sitting inside of it.

"I have the perfect spot, Flora," he said. "It's a small alcove—easy for us to block up afterward."

"Dieter will like that part." She dropped her voice to a whisper. "He still thinks we have vampires in those boxes."

A grim smile broke out on Callaghan's face. "That'll do."

They spent another two hours maneuvering the twelve heavy barrels and three boxes down the staircase and into the alcove. When the last barrel stood against the wall, they rested for a few minutes.

Dieter eyed the boxes. He spoke in German to Flora. "Why do the *strigoi* want to be placed here?"

Flora shrugged. "I only do what they command," she said. She thought for a minute. "I suppose they seek a quiet place for a long rest. That's why they requested so much cognac."

The German nodded. "I had heard you should bury a bottle of whiskey next to a vampire to keep him calm. I did not know about cognac."

"It works even better," she assured him. "Especially among ancient vampires like these—ones who have chosen not to come back."

"The Slovak soldiers told me that any vampire who hasn't been killed after seven years can come back to another village and have a family of his own, sleeping in graves on the weekends. Is that true?"

"I have heard the same," Flora said. "Though some vampires, like my masters, choose a long sleep instead."

Dieter looked at the boxes. "Can they hear us?"

She shrugged. "Probably. But don't worry," she said, "they really do want to sleep, and as long as you don't threaten them, they'll leave you alone."

His eyes grew wide. "What could threaten the vampires?"

She pointed at the barrels. "Taking their cognac, or thinking about killing them."

He shook his head. "We shall not do that."

She smiled.

"Are you two talking about the vampires again?" Callaghan asked.

"Dieter wanted to know why they wished to come here."

"The buggers must have had their fill of German blood." He hefted a pick. "Me bones are aching. Let's get this corner closed up and give those bloody vampires a good rest."

"What will we use?" Flora asked.

He pointed further into the cavern. "I saw a wall over yonder. We can knock it down and use its stones."

Callaghan led them down the cavern to the old wall. Dieter swung the pick and broke it up, Flora carried the stones, and Callaghan built a new wall by fitting them back together.

"How can you do that without mortar?" Flora asked.

The Major chuckled. "Many years of practice," he said. He stood up and tapped the new wall with his cane. "The stones are well-shaped, and all it takes is a practiced eye to place them."

An hour later the wall was built and the alcove closed off.

Callaghan stood back and held up his lamp. "Looks like it's been there for a hundred years," he said. He turned to Dieter. "Where's my pick?"

Dieter pointed back in the cavern, and the Major limped over to the old alcove. When he didn't return right away, Flora called, "Major? Is everything okay?"

"Flora, come back here." Callaghan's voice was high-pitched.

Was he all right? She grabbed her light and hustled to the back of the cavern. "What's wrong?" she asked.

Callaghan stood inside the alcove where the old wall had been. He held his lantern close to the ground. The light shone on a wooden trap door built into the floor. "This is it," he said.

"This is what?" she asked.

"The shaft Raddy told me about."

She felt her stomach lurch. "Where they ate the little boy?"

"Where they found the opal nest." He knelt down and pulled on the ring attached to the door. "It's stuck. Where's the map?"

"In my tent."

He frowned. "I must see it straight away."

Back on the surface, Flora and Dieter stood looking over Callaghan's shoulder as he pointed on the map. "It's the shaft your grandfather told me about," the Major said.

"How can you be sure?" she asked.

"Because until the Great War came along, I listened to that bloody ghost story every Easter, Christmas, and Melbourne Cup." He stabbed at the map with his index finger. "And each time Raddy told it, he led me over to this map, tapped right here on this smudged spot, and swore he'd come back one day."

She said nothing, afraid of what he might suggest.

Callaghan looked at Dieter. "There's opals down there, me boy. Opals the size of apples, ripe for the picking."

Dieter smiled and nodded.

"Down there or not," she said, "we've got to leave first thing in the morning if we're going to make the Bratislava train and meet the captain."

"Flora, you can buy that train with your share of the eggs from our nest of opals," Callaghan said.

"It's a legend, Major. A story. You said so yourself." She said this slowly, and she tried to keep the emotion out of her voice.

He shrugged. "Legend or not, them opals are calling me. I can't leave here without at least seeing if old Raddy was right." He peered back at the map.

She took a deep breath. "I can't miss the train, or the boat, Major. Baba needs me, and I have to get back." She raised her voice just a little. "She's Raddy's wife—remember?"

Callaghan's head jerked up. "Of course I remember," he snapped. "It's just…" He paused for a moment. "Please, Flora. I need to look for that opal nest. I can't spend the rest of me days wondering if I missed the opportunity of a lifetime."

She knew the decision was hers; Ned Callaghan was duty-bound to help her get back to Paris. But Flora also knew she owed him, because she could never have gotten the gold this far without his help.

She needed to rendezvous with Baba, James, and Archibald Morgan in only five and a half days. No matter how important the opal nest was to the Major, she was determined to start their return in the morning.

That left only one solution. She stood up. "Okay, Major. Let's find your opal nest."

He got up. "You'll delay our return?"

"No." And when he frowned, she added, "We will look tonight—but we will leave in the morning."

He stared at her, then he slapped his hands on his knees and smiled. "I reckon we'll have to dig fast. Dieter, get the picks."

forty-three

IN LESS THAN HALF an hour, the three of them kneeled around the trap door in the alcove. Dieter stuck the pick's handle through the ring and forced the trap door open.

Callaghan held his lantern over the revealed shaft and peered inside. "I don't see any water," he said.

Flora saw a ladder attached to the side of the shaft. It disappeared into the darkness after a dozen rungs. She picked up a stone and dropped it down the hole. She listened, but couldn't hear a splash.

"I'll go first," Callaghan said. He shoved the pick into his belt, tied the end of a rope around his waist, and handed the coil to Dieter. "If I give a tug, both of you pull me out."

Dieter nodded.

The Major tied a thinner cord to his lantern and handed it to Flora. "Lower this down ahead of me." He sat down and swung his legs into the hole. He twisted his body around and tested a rung with his toes before planting his full weight on it.

Flora played out her line as he descended, keeping the lantern a rung ahead of the Major's feet. "Is it sturdy enough?" she asked.

"Sturdier than the ones your grandfather and I used in White Cliffs."

After she played out fifty feet of rope, Flora's lantern rested on the floor of the shaft. A few seconds later, Callaghan stepped off the ladder and picked it up. "Nothing's here," he called. "It's a bloody dead end."

They would make their train after all. Flora turned to hide her smile of relief from Dieter. "That's it, then," she called. "Come on up."

"Hang on a minute—what the devil is this?" The Major's voice echoed up from the shaft.

"Maybe he has found something?" Dieter asked.

Flora was afraid of the excitement in their voices.

They both peered into the shaft and watched Callaghan scrape his pick on the floor next to the ladder. A minute later he took a step back and stared at the ground.

"What is it?" Flora called.

"A bloody wooden plug, just like old Raddy said. It won't take but a minute to clear it. Come down here, Dieter!"

Flora looked up at Dieter and spoke in German. "If you go down there, come back quickly. We must catch that train to Bratislava in the morning."

"I will try, *fraulein*," he said. Then his eyes narrowed. "But if *die opale* live down there, we will be late."

She grabbed at his arm. "I must make that train, Dieter. If you're not here, I will—" she stopped.

"You will what?" He stepped toward her and stood with his face not six inches from hers.

She backed up and crossed her arms. "An hour before daybreak, if you have not returned, I will tear down the new wall, push the three *strigoi* boxes down this shaft, and seal the top."

His jaw dropped. "You wouldn't!"

"I would." She put her chin up. "But first I will tell them you are at fault for disturbing their rest."

Dieter stood still and stared at her. Then he swung around and scooped up a rope and a pick. "You will do no such thing, *fraulein*."

"Of course I will."

"No, you will not." He shoved the pick into his belt, tied the Major's rope to the top rung of the ladder, and swung his legs over the edge of the shaft.

"Why not?"

"I take with me the last pick. The vampires will remain asleep in their new home." And with that, he climbed down the rungs and disappeared into the shaft, leaving Flora alone.

She jerked awake. She sat wrapped in her coat, close to the edge of the shaft. She blew on her fingers then groped for the matches. She struck one and lit her lamp.

"Major?" she called.

No answer. Outside the lamp's glow the cave remained dark and silent. She wrapped her hands around its globe to warm them. This cast long shadows around the alcove.

She had watched first Dieter then Callaghan drop into the chute at the bottom of the shaft. The lamp they left at the bottom of the ladder sputtered out twenty minutes later.

She looked at her pocket watch. It had been five hours since the Major lifted out the wooden plug. Now it was four in the morning, and they needed to leave for Presov by six—seven at the very latest—if they were going to catch the train to Bratislava.

A faint scratching sound rose out of the shaft, and she realized this must have been what had woken her. She crawled to the edge and strained to hear.

"Flora." The voice was a whisper, distorted by the echoes from the shaft.

"Major?"

"Down here. Help me climb out."

She looked at the ladder disappearing into the blackness of the shaft. "Can't Dieter help?"

"No." Callaghan's voice was a whimper. "Please, Flora."

She pulled the cord and retrieved the extinguished lamp, then quickly attached her lit one and lowered it down to the bottom.

"Where are you?" she asked.

"At the top of the chute."

She peered down and thought she saw his hand in the gloom of the hole in the floor. "I'm coming, Major," she called.

She took a deep breath and climbed down the ladder. The rungs were cold and rusty and she had to squeeze them hard to keep her grip. She kept her gaze on the lamp under her and continued, hand over hand, until she stood on the bottom.

"In here," Callaghan whispered.

She knelt down, untied the lamp, and thrust it into the hole.

Callaghan's arm was up, blocking the light from his squinting eyes. "There you are," he breathed. "We found the nest, Flora. Old Raddy's story was true." His voice grew stronger, and a grin broke out on his dirty face.

"You found the opals?"

"The nest," he whispered. "The bloody nest is cursed."

"Cursed? Where's Dieter?"

His hand curled into a fist. "The Kraut tried to kill me."

"No!"

"Fair dinkum. We bundled up some opals, and then the bastard swung his pick at me head—he would have brained me if I hadn't ducked."

"Where is he now?"

"In the nest with the opals." He grimaced. "We must hurry, Flora. Help me out before it's too late."

"You'd leave him down there?"

"I can't get him up the chute." He coughed. "Besides, he has the company of the others."

"Others?"

"Raddy's mates. We found their bones." He winced. "The Kraut stuck his pick through me leg. I'm pretty much all bled out. Help pull me up."

She withdrew the lamp, placed a knee on either side of the hole, and reached down. "Grab my hand," she said.

He reached up and gripped her hand with his, but before she could pull, the Major grunted. "Hold on a minute," he said.

She let go and brought the lamp back. "Yes, Major?"

"When you do pull me out, we must hurry."

"I know. The train."

He shook his head. "Not the train. The water."

"Water?"

"Dieter's pick pierced the wall, and he hit a gusher. The bloody cave's flooded, and Dieter's drowned. I swam up to the chute as the water rose."

Flora looked past Callaghan's shoulders and saw his belly, knees, and one arm were jammed against the walls of the tunnel. "You're blocking the water?"

He smiled. "I'm acting like a big cork. The water's rising up the chute about a foot a minute, and it's bloody cold," he said. He looked down. "It's starting to leak around me, see?"

She saw his shirt was soaking wet. Water was flowing up through a gap between the Major's knees.

"So I pull you up, and then we'll plug the tunnel?" Her voice was rising.

"That's the idea," he said. "But we'll have to hurry."

She nodded and put the lamp back on the floor. She reached down past his hand and grasped his forearm and pulled as hard as she could.

He grunted and shifted a bit, but he didn't move. "Try it again," he said.

She pulled, squatting this time, wedging her feet against the sides of the hole and helping lift with her legs. She felt a vibration when something snapped.

He gasped. "You've dislocated me shoulder!"

"Oh my God." She looked into the gloom, and saw the water was rising. "We must stop the water."

Callaghan glanced down, then back at her. "Plug me up, Flora. Then get yourself back to Paris."

"I'm going to get you out, Major. Just give me a minute."

He shook his head. "Even if you pull me out of the chute, I'll never climb up that shaft. You have to leave me here."

"No!" she shouted. She stood up and took off her coat. "Use this to plug the gaps. It will buy some time."

He shook his head. "I can't move me arm."

"I'll do it." She dropped her coat into the hole, then pulled off her boots and slipped feet-first into the tunnel. She used her legs to jam the coat into the space between his knees.

"There's too many gaps to fill," he said. "And you'll need that coat."

"Major, I can't lose you." She reached up and grabbed her boots and wedged them in the gaps between his arm and belly.

"I can't breathe!"

"Sorry." She used her legs to rearrange the boots. "Is that better?"

"A bit. But the water's still sneaking up me back."

She bent down as far as she could and reached past his shoulders. Her fingertips touched the cold water, and she quickly stood up and looked around the shaft. There was nothing left to use.

Yes, there was. She stripped off her sweater and shirt, then bent back down and jammed them behind him. Then she used her pants, each leg filling the crack between the tunnel wall and his knees.

She grabbed the lamp and checked her work. "I think the leaks are plugged," she said. She climbed up and knelt at the edge of the chute.

He gave a faint smile. "You can't pull me out now."

"I'll go to town and get help."

He looked up at her somberly. "Flora, don't waste your time."

"But I can get help."

He shook his head. "Flora, I won't last much longer. The water is cold, I can't feel me legs, and I'm so sleepy." He closed his eyes.

"Major, wake up!" She struggled to keep the panic out of her voice.

His eyes opened, but soon they slid shut. "Can you do something for me?" he whispered.

"Anything," she sobbed. "Just hold on. I know we can figure something out."

"Come here."

She dropped into the tunnel and crouched next to him.

"Put the light out," he said. "Save it for when you leave."

The tears streamed down her face, but she wiped them away as she stood up and extinguished the lamp. Then she crouched down next to him again.

"Flora," he breathed.

"Yes, Major?"

"I'm cold."

So was she, but she wiggled around, found his head with her hands, and pressed his face into her bosom. She ran her fingers through his hair. They both shivered, and she squeezed him close. She decided to keep him talking. "Tell me about the opals," she said.

"The opals were bloody brilliant," he whispered so softly she had to bend her head down to hear him.

"So the nest was real," she whispered back.

"Just like old Raddy said." Callaghan's words slurred together. "I can see them now, Flora. The opals—they're beauties."

"Tell me about the prettiest one you see." She choked back her sobs, but she couldn't stop the tears from streaming down her face and dripping onto his cheeks.

"Bright red and green and blue—it's singing to me, Flora. Can you hear it?"

She squeezed her eyes shut and tried to focus on the red spots flashing across her vision. "I can almost see it."

"Listen to it, Flora. It's singing that I'll be right, and you'll make it back to Paris."

"I will?"

"Can't you hear it?"

She squeezed him even tighter. "I can through you, Major."

"Good. Now it's calling to me. I've got to go with it, Flora. Hold me as I go."

"I'll hold you." She stroked his hair. "Goodbye, Major," she whispered as he gave a long exhale. "Goodbye."

Flora stayed and held Major Ned Callaghan until his skin grew cold and the water seeped around her plugs and crept up to her waist. She forced herself to stand up, and with her teeth chattering and her body shivering almost uncontrollably, she climbed out of the tunnel, groped for the lamp in the dark, and headed up the ladder.

She reached the top, found the matches, and lit the lamp. She realized she didn't plug the hole, and she climbed down the ladder again.

Back at the bottom of the shaft, she failed to wedge the wooden plug into the hole in the floor because Dieter's rope prevented a snug fit. She pulled on the knot, but her fingers were too numb to untie it. So she jammed in the plug as tight as she could and climbed up the ladder. She closed the wooden trap door over the top of the shaft and stumbled her way out of the alcove, up through the tunnels, and back to the surface.

forty-four

ROSE AND MARIE FLANKED Madame Flora, each with an arm around her. The firelight sparkled in the tears running down the twins' cheeks.

"How'd you make it back to Paris, Grandma?" Marie asked.

"Most of the trip was a blur," Madame Flora said. "I dug through my belongings and got dressed. I found a sweater and some money in Old Ned's luggage. Then I cut the horses loose from their wagons and rode one of them, barefoot, to Presov. I just barely made that train."

George tossed a stick into the flames. "You know, if you had taken the time to plug that hole correctly, Flora, we wouldn't need diving gear tomorrow."

"If I had plugged that hole correctly, somebody else would have stolen the gold," Madame Flora said.

"Who would have gotten it?" I asked. "The Nazis?"

She nodded. "Back in the forties, before the Soviets took over, I got in contact with the mine's owners. I learned that the captain of the barge didn't buy my story of both Dieter and Major Callaghan having an accident in Bratislava."

"He was a Nazi?" Val asked.

"No, but he shared his suspicions with them, and they followed our trail to Presov. Then they found old Vlado. He brought them to the mine and told them my story about the vampires." She looked at George. "If the mine hadn't flooded, they would have found and taken the gold."

Archie had been sitting and staring into the camp fire. Suddenly he snapped his fingers. "Wait a minute—the journal in my desk drawer—it was yours!" he said.

I threw a glance at Val, and she gave me a tiny smile.

Archie pointed at me. "And that is how Scott figured out you stole the gold," he said.

"What are you talking about, Archibald?" Madame Flora's voice was sharp.

"The journal in Hermann Goering's soul line collection," he said. "It must have been yours—and Scott must have figured out how to read it."

"It was my journal." She glanced me. "But not anymore—I snuck in your office and burnt it up. Didn't you notice?"

"You destroyed Soul Identity property?" He stood up and shook his finger at her. "How dare you!"

She shrugged. "You had already left a copy for Scott, anyway. I wasted my time."

"What did you write in there, Flora? You need to tell me everything."

Madame Flora shook her head. "There is so much you don't understand."

Archie dropped his hand, but he remained standing, staring at her. After a minute, he said, "If I do not understand, I must request that you enlighten me, Flora. Enlighten us all."

Madame Flora's face flushed. "You can't handle the whole story."

"You could give me the chance!" His shout echoed off the hillside.

Val looked at her. "Maybe he's right, Flora," she said softly. "Maybe you shouldn't wait any longer."

Madame Flora let out a groan. She patted Rose and Marie's hands, then let go and stood up. She walked up to Archie and put her hands on her hips. "Sit back down," she told him. "Then we can trade secrets."

Archie returned to his chair. "I have hidden no secrets from you."

She sat between the twins and took their hands again. "I'll ask you one question, Archibald," she said. "And if you're honest with your answer, I'll tell you everything."

He nodded.

Madame Flora took a deep breath and glanced at Val, who smiled at her. Then she stared at Archie. "Do you ever wish things between us worked out differently?" she asked.

Archie broke her gaze and looked at the fire. "Why are you asking me this?" he whispered.

"It's the price of the whole story," she said.

Archie glanced at George and Sue, then at Val and me. He dropped his eyes back to the fire and grimaced. "Yes," he whispered.

Madame Flora leaned forward. "I couldn't hear you."

"Yes." He raised his eyes to meet hers.

"Yes what?" she asked.

"Yes," he said. "I wish things between us had worked out differently."

She nodded. Her features softened. "How?"

His eyes narrowed. "I answered your question honestly."

She shook her head. "I need more."

He looked down and let out a long sigh. "You understand that I have dedicated my current life to Soul Identity."

"You have put them before everything else," Madame Flora said.

He nodded. "Even ahead of my own needs. Every decision I ever made was factored against whether or not it aligned with the organization."

"But at what cost?" she asked.

"At all costs," Archie said. "I want the rest of your story, Flora. But as you suggested, first listen to mine."

forty-five

ARCHIBALD MORGAN KNOCKED ON Flora's guest house door. He smiled when he heard the sound of running feet.

The door swung open, and little Jamie grabbed Morgan's legs in a tight embrace. The boy looked up and gave him a big toothy grin.

Morgan reached down and tousled his dark curly hair. "Hello, Jamie," he said.

The boy reached up and grabbed his hand and led him into the guest room quarters.

Morgan reached into his pocket.

Jamie giggled and jumped up and down.

Morgan smiled and squatted next to him. He held out his fist and allowed Jamie to force it open.

The boy squealed and grabbed the three Tootsie Rolls lying in Morgan's palm. He ran through a door in the back of the room. "Mommy, candy!" he hollered.

Morgan heard a voice reply, "What did I say about candy before dinner?"

"It is only three pieces," Morgan called. "Besides, today is a special day."

Then Flora walked into the room. She untied her apron, unpinned her hair, and ran her fingers through her long, dark curls. She wore a white sleeveless evening gown, and a single ruby pendant dangled from a fine gold chain around her neck. "Mr. Morgan," she said, "how nice to see you."

She grew more beautiful every day. When she crossed the room and kissed his cheek, he caught a whiff of the Chanel No. 5 he bought her the previous Christmas.

"Happy birthday, Flora," he said.

She smiled and gave him a curtsy. "Thank you." She gestured toward the sofa. "I need another minute or two, and we'll have to wait for Mrs. Beasley before we can go."

Morgan sat and watched her sweep out of the room. He closed his eyes and brought to mind the image of the thin and ragged seventeen-year-old appearing in Nuremberg almost three years ago. She had blossomed since then.

He felt a tugging on his trousers, and he opened his eyes to Jamie's smile. He cupped the toddler's red cheeks in his palms. "Did you eat all that candy already?" he asked with a knowing smile.

Jamie nodded and beamed. Then Flora called, and the toddler ran out the back of the room.

Morgan sat back. Where had the time gone? Next month would be Jamie's second birthday; Flora said she was going to bake him a Howdy Doody cake.

The little boy brought joy to the whole office. Every weekday at three, when Mrs. Beasley marched him up to the second floor and into the overseer section, the ladies would gather around and fuss over him and pinch his rosy cheeks.

And Jamie soaked it up, flirting with each of them in turn. Freshly awake from his nap, he would giggle and laugh as the ladies played with him. Even Morgan would get in on the fun, putting the boy into his big overseer chair and spinning him around.

Yes, life in the Soul Identity office these days shone a lot brighter, now that Flora had accepted a position as his special assistant. She and her son had brought balance into the politically-charged halls.

And today was Flora's twentieth birthday. Her coming-of-age, as far as Soul Identity was concerned. She would now join the ancient organization as a full-fledged member.

It had not been an easy journey for Flora. After reaching America, she and her grandmother and soon Jamie kept to themselves in these same rooms. But then her grandmother passed away a little over a year ago, and with nowhere else to go, Flora turned to him for help.

Morgan was reluctant at first. Yes, he retained some twinges of residual guilt from the Nuremberg assignment, but he had paid her for her work, and he had brought her and her grandmother to America. Jamie too, for apparently Flora had gotten herself pregnant before they reached Boston.

In any case, it was only after he met the baby that he decided to see what he could do for Flora. Jamie captured his attention in ways he could not explain. Morgan had never asked Flora who the father was, and she had never volunteered. The rumor mill in the office had her in a love affair with a famous Croatian freedom fighter, and he hoped this was true.

He certainly didn't want Jamie to be the son of James Little the elevator man.

Not that he was jealous, but nobody needed a mental cripple for a father figure. Morgan had made sure Little had been well cared for upon their return to Sterling, and he was a good and dependable Soul Identity worker. His sacrifice to the organization was something all employees could point to and be proud of.

So Morgan decided to help Flora. He did owe her, after all, for her grudging assistance as he deposited the gold into Hermann Goering's soul line collection. And the letter of commendation she had Mr. Goering sign certainly helped his career: Morgan was now firmly next in line for executive overseer. Unless Isabella Vida, the old witch, managed to outlive him.

Enough of work. Today he was here to see Flora purely on a social level. For over a year now he had been watching her, biding his time until she turned twenty. He encouraged her education, helped her find child care, and augmented her meager lifestyle with a good job. He even was liberal with her time off when Jamie got sick, as he supposed all babies were wont to do.

But most of all, he was there for Flora. Morgan was delighted with the ladies' comments he overheard in the office. They all thought Flora was special, and they all encouraged him to court her.

At first he resisted the idea, mainly because he remembered how much Flora hated the work in Nuremberg. But after seeing her mature, and after falling under the spell of little Jamie, Morgan began catching himself dreaming about a life that included the three of them.

It was a good dream. Although Flora lost none of the passion that had filled her in Germany, she learned to harness it. Instead of losing her temper, he saw her become more determined. And instead of yelling at Jamie, he saw her laughing as she played with him. In Morgan's imagination, he saw her passion driving him as he guided Soul Identity and their family with his wisdom and vision.

Archibald Morgan, the most eligible bachelor at Soul Identity, was in love. And although he had never mentioned it to her, he was sure Flora knew, and he was confident she approved.

That confidence was why he was here today. Three weeks ago he worked up the courage to invite Flora to a birthday dinner and dance at

Worcester's Lakeside Ballroom. After considering his request for five long days, she accepted.

The last two weeks in the office had made him giddy with anticipation. The ladies swarmed around Flora, helping her choose the right dress and giving her advice on makeup and perfume. The fellows in the office, even crusty old Alexei Ivanov from the depositary, dropped by to congratulate him. Morgan felt like he was walking on clouds.

And at long last today had come, and here he sat in the guest house rooms of the most desirable woman he knew. He reached into his pocket and patted the red velvet-covered ring box. Tonight would mark the ending of their office courtship and the beginning of their engagement.

Marriage would follow. Not too soon, because the office girls would need time to plan the event. But not too late, as Jamie wasn't getting any younger, and Morgan had already detected some glimmers of character deficiencies that would only fester without a strong father figure in his life.

A knock on the front door woke him from his daydreams. He let Mrs. Beasley in and politely listened to her chatter. But his mind was on the evening ahead.

At last Flora was ready, and the two of them paused at the door for a final hug with Jamie. Morgan's heart skipped a beat as he and Flora kissed Jamie's cheeks simultaneously. And then they were off, Flora hanging onto his arm as they swept down the stairs, out the door, and into the back of the limousine.

"Please drive us to the Lakeside Ballroom, Mr. Hutchinson," Morgan said to the driver once they were under way.

"Yes, sir." The driver looked back in his mirror. "Ms. Drabarni, how are you this evening?"

Flora smiled. "I'm fine, Franklin."

"And little Jamie?"

"Into all kinds of mischief."

The driver chuckled as he pulled out of the Soul Identity gates. "As he should be, ma'am."

Morgan and Flora chatted about Jamie on the drive down to the ballroom on the shores of Lake Quinsigamond. In less than an hour they arrived.

He climbed out of the limousine in time to assist Flora. He was thrilled when she continued to hold his hand as they walked toward the entrance.

"Mr. Morgan, thank you so much for taking me out on my birthday," she said.

"The pleasure is all mine, Flora," he said. He dared a slight caress of her wrist with his fingertips. "But you must call me Archibald while we are out of the office."

"Archibald." She pointed at the pavilion. "Will you take me dancing?"

"Of course," he said, and after thirty minutes of whirling around the floor, they made their way into the restaurant. They sat on the outdoor terrace overlooking the lake. A waiter lit the candle on the table and gave him a hand-printed menu.

He peeked at Flora over the card. She was watching a couple walk along the shore in the late summer twilight. Her cheeks were flushed, and she was humming along with the music spilling out of the pavilion. A smile crossed her face, and he felt a wave of affection sweep over him. The evening could not be more perfect.

When the waiter returned, Morgan ordered for them both, then he chose to commence the serious conversation while they waited for its arrival.

He cleared his throat. "Flora, when we met three years ago in Germany, I would never have imagined we would be sitting here together."

She turned to face him and smiled. "Neither would I," she said softly.

"I have watched you grow from a girl into an enchanting lady."

She raised one eyebrow, but said nothing.

"You and little Jamie have brought a breath of fresh air onto our second floor."

"Jamie is my life. Especially now after Baba passed away," she said. "How I wish she was still here!"

He patted her hand. "Is it hard raising Jamie on your own?"

"I'm making it." This with her eyebrows lowered, just a little.

"You are making it, Flora," he said. "And we are all glad to help you however we can." He grabbed her hands with both of his.

Her fingers trailed over his palms. "You have been very good to us," she said. "I don't think we could have done it without you."

"It has been my pleasure." He leaned forward. "And it would be my pleasure to help even more."

She looked up at him. "You've done so much already."

The moment had come. He pulled one hand free from hers and reached into his jacket pocket. He grasped the ring box and took a deep breath. "Today is your twentieth birthday," he said, "and first thing Monday morning I can walk you through the membership process."

She tilted her head. "Membership process?"

"Soul Identity," he explained. "Now you are twenty years old, you may join."

"Ah." She pulled her hands free and ran her fingers around the base of the candlestick. "Archibald…" She looked up with a solemn expression on her face. "I'm not going to join."

He was afraid this might happen. "Flora, you have a great job at Soul Identity. You live on campus in our guest house. You are friends with all the ladies in the office. How can you not want to join?"

"I love the people—but not the organization." Her eyes narrowed. "I just can't bear the thought of joining the group that fought to protect the memories of the people who killed my father."

He sat back, astonished at the strength of the vehemence in her voice, surprised it was undiminished after three years.

She sighed and reached for his hand. "This is the one area where you and I do not agree."

He gave a wry smile. "I have been hoping for you to come around and see my side."

"And I have hoped the same of you." She leaned forward and smiled. "But this is only a small difference of opinion between us, Archibald. There are many things we have in common. Many joys we share."

"That is true." With great reluctance he pulled his hand out of his jacket pocket and abandoned the ring box. He forced his lips to lift in a nonchalant smile. And he said, with barely a tremor in his voice, "If you refuse to join us, what will you do for work?"

"I have a job."

He shook his head. "Once Soul Identity employees turn twenty, they either have to join or quit."

Her jaw dropped. "Are you sure?"

He nodded. "It is not my policy, but an ancient one. We will not have employees who will not believe."

She bit her lower lip. "Do you think you could bend this policy for me? At least until Jamie reaches school age?"

He pretended to think for a minute before he shook his head. "I cannot risk it, Flora. You know the politics—my career would be in jeopardy."

She withdrew her hands and looked at him in the eye. "It's that important to you, isn't it?"

"What?"

"Your career."

He looked away at the lake for a long minute. He reluctantly met her eyes and nodded.

"Then I had better find a new job as soon as possible," she said crisply. "I have no time to waste on frivolous meals." She stood up. "Take me home, Mr. Morgan."

"Please, Flora," he said, "let us first enjoy our dinner, and then Mr. Hutchinson can drive us home." Maybe by the end of the meal he could talk some sense into her and not let her throw her life away.

She pursed her lips. "Enjoy your dinner alone. I'll be waiting in the car with Franklin." She stomped off the terrace and back toward the pavilion, past the couple along the lake shore.

He carefully folded his napkin, stood up, and followed her. And along the shore of Lake Quinsigamond, Archibald Morgan, most eligible bachelor at Soul Identity, pulled the ring box out of his pocket and hurled it deep into the water.

forty-six

Present Day
Dubnik Mine, Slovakia

"MY ACTIONS SEEM silly and immature sixty years later," Madame Flora said to Archie.

He sat with his head bowed. "I was a fool."

"And I was too hotheaded," she said. "I'm truly sorry, Archibald."

He looked up at her. "I am too, Flora."

The fire had died down. Madame Flora got up and stood close to the glowing embers. "You want to know what was in that journal," she said to Archie. "It was my story. I wanted Goering's future carrier to read that instead of his hateful memories."

He stared at her for a minute without speaking. Then he chuckled. "Yesterday I would have scolded you for breaking the sanctity of the depositary. But today…" his voice trailed off.

"What will you do today?" she asked softly.

He looked up. "Today I just want to know the rest of your story."

She nodded and turned to me. "Bring your copy—I'm ready."

"Let me get it," I said.

Val and I walked over to the van. "She's actually going to tell Mr. Morgan," Val whispered, rubbing her hands together and blowing on them. "I wonder how he'll take it."

"I wonder how the twins will take it," I whispered back. I tried to imagine finding out that my great-grandfather was one of the richest people in the world. I opened the back of the van and dug for my bag. I pulled out the journal copy Archie had made and the translation Val and I had completed.

Madame Flora took the copied journal pages from me while Sue hung a battery-powered reading light on a pole over the old lady's chair.

Archie handed her his reading glasses. "Just in case."

"Thank you." She put on the glasses and looked at the pages for a few minutes while we waited. Then she spoke to Rose and Marie. "Girls, I wrote this in Nuremberg, during the trial. You should pay attention— maybe you'll learn something."

"Yes, Grandma," they said.

Madame Flora turned to Archie. "Let me read you everything before you ask any questions."

She cleared her throat. "I wrote this in an alphabet once common in Istria. It's called the Glagolitic script. My father taught it to me when I was a little girl. We used it for writing secret notes to each other, when we didn't want my mother reading them."

She pointed at the cover. "This says Flora Drabarni, 1946." She flipped to the next page. "The language is Romany, and I'll have to translate as I go. Bear with me."

Archie glanced at me. "You figured this out?" he asked.

"With Val's help. It's only a few pages," I said.

He nodded. "I am glad I left it for you."

Hopefully he'd still feel that way after he heard what it contained.

Madame Flora read us the fairy tale about the princess, her fairy godmother, the wolf, and the knight captain. When she was done, the princess's final dream hanging in the air, nobody spoke for a minute. She handed me the pages, and we all watched the fire's fading embers.

Finally Flora looked up at Archie. "There's a reason you felt so connected to Jamie. He's your son." She nodded toward the twins. "Rose and Marie are his granddaughters."

Archie stood up and walked over to her. He knelt down on the cold, hard ground at her feet and took her hand in both of his. He raised it to his lips and held it there. "Over the years I have had some very detailed and explicit dreams of us in Nuremberg," he murmured. "But I never once dared to think those dreams actually could be true."

Madame Flora reached out with her other hand and caressed Archie's white hair. Then she leaned forward and wrapped her arm around his shoulders and buried her face in his neck. Archie let go of her hand and embraced her.

After a minute of listening to them sniffle, George looked at the twins. "Better keep that diving gear ready, girls," he said loudly. "When we get back, you'll have to recover that ring from the bottom of Lake Quinsigamond."

That broke the tension, and Rose, Marie, Archie and Madame Flora were on all their feet, hugging each other and exclaiming in joy.

Val and I brought the journal back to the van. As I replaced my bag in the luggage compartment, its hook caught on the carpeted side and pulled a side panel loose.

Val tapped me on the shoulder and pointed at a small black box duct-taped to the wall where the carpet had been. "What's that?" she asked. The box had an extended antenna and a blinking red light on its side.

"Some kind of tracking device," I said. It looked low-tech. I stuck my head around the door and called for George and Sue to come over.

George stood with his hands on his hips and stared at the black box. "Somebody wants to know where we are," he said. "Let me disable it." He reached into the luggage compartment.

I grabbed his shoulder and said, "Maybe we should leave it."

He straightened up. "What's your plan?"

I shook my head. "I don't have one. But we don't know who's on the other end. Why let them know we're on to them?"

He eyed the device. "If it has a microphone, they already know."

"If it had a microphone, it wouldn't have been parked under the carpet in the luggage compartment," I said.

"Good point," he said. He scratched his head. "Well, as long as we're here and not moving, I guess it's not doing us any additional harm. But let's at least look for the listeners."

"You have tools to find them?" I asked.

"Of course I have tools," he said. He turned to Sue. "Let's break out the gadgets."

He and Sue lifted two yellow cases out of the luggage compartment and flipped them open. He removed the foam egg-crate packing and took out three antennas, a yellow box with a small video screen, and a bag of lithium batteries.

George inserted the batteries into the antennas and the box and flipped on their switches. "This is the best passive heartbeat scanner I could get my hands on," he said.

He reached into the case and pulled out three threaded spikes. He screwed them onto the base of each antenna, then handed two antennas to Sue. "Place them at least a hundred yards apart, darling," he said.

Sue took the antennas and headed across the clearing.

George handed me the other antenna. "Stick this into a tree about halfway up the hill."

Val and I climbed up about twenty feet over the mine's entrance. I reached up and jammed the spike into a tree trunk. Then we returned to the van.

George pressed some buttons on the yellow box. "Once the antennas synchronize with each other, we'll get a clear picture."

A minute later the box beeped, the screen flashed, and a daytime satellite image of the clearing appeared. A bunch of red dots lay superimposed over the picture.

George pressed a button, and the image zoomed in. "The antennas each have a GPS chip," he said. "This baby's got a 3G cellular card to connect to the Internet—the same as your mobile phone. That map is the latest and greatest satellite image, brought to you by your favorite search engine."

"How about the red dots?" I asked.

"That's us," He said. "The antennas listen for the electrical signature of a human heartbeat. When they find it, they broadcast its direction back to the box. The computer in here triangulates the position and mashes up the information with the map." He tapped the screen. "These four dots are us, and those four are the Morgan-Drabarni family reunion taking place by the fire."

"And these two in the corner?" Val asked.

"Those dots, my dear, are probably the local cops, sent by Dara Sabol," he said. He turned around and pointed toward the entrance to the clearing. "About fifty yards down our driveway."

"We can't have them watching us," Sue said. "Let's pay them a visit." She reached into the luggage compartment and pulled out a green carry-on duffel bag. She opened it up and removed two black balaclavas, two pairs of black gloves, and two black hooded sweatshirts. She tossed a set to George, and they both put them on.

George pulled down the balaclava so we could see his mouth. "If we're not back in ten minutes, call the cavalry," he said. He pulled two nightsticks out of the carry-on, handed one to Sue, and they jogged toward the entrance.

Val and I watched their red dots move away from the clearing and up the entrance road. They converged with the other two dots, and after a couple of minutes, two of the dots headed further down the road and out of range of the display.

George and Sue came jogging back. "Did you watch us on the box?" George asked.

I nodded. "Who were they?"

"Some local talent with badges. They didn't speak much English."

"You should have brought me with you," Val said. "My grandfather was from Lviv, just over the border in the Ukraine. I can speak a little Slovak."

"Maybe it's better if they don't know that," I said.

George slapped the nightstick into his gloved palm. "In any case, we reminded them that this is a private party, and it's time to go home to bed."

The twins had gone to their tent, and Archie and Madame Flora sat by the fire, holding hands and murmuring to each other.

I nudged Val. "Ready to get some sleep?"

She nodded, and we said good night. George held up the yellow box and told me he and Sue would keep an eye out for others.

Inside the tent, we zipped our sleeping bags together, laid them out on the air mattress, and climbed in.

Val snuggled into my arms. "Mr. Morgan made me cry when he knelt down in front of Flora," she whispered.

"You know, if we hadn't translated that journal, they'd still be thinking the worst about each other."

"Remember how upset I was the other day?"

"About how everybody's been doing the wrong things for all the right reasons?"

"Exactly," she said. "But now we're all doing the right things."

I flipped onto my back and pulled her on top of me. "Still, that's sixty years down the drain for those two." I reached up and ran my fingers through her hair. "If I got you pregnant, would you hide my child from me?"

She bent her neck and gave me a long kiss. "First show me how you'd get me pregnant."

forty-seven

I WOKE AT FIVE to the sounds of chopping wood. I slid out of bed and gasped when I planted my bare feet on the cold tent floor. I got dressed and unzipped the tent flap.

A thick layer of frost covered the ground. George and Sue stood under a lantern in front of a large stump. Sue swung the axe, and George placed, gathered, and stacked the wood. Their breath made puffs in the cold air.

I felt around for my jacket and climbed out. After I zipped up the tent, I headed over to the woodcutting couple. "Need any help?" I asked.

"We're just about done," Sue said. She took a swing at the log George had stood on its end. The axe bit into the wood, and she lifted it, flipped it over, and slammed the back of the axe into the stump. The axe head rang as the log halves fell to the ground.

George stacked the two halves on the stump, and Sue quartered them. Then she swung the axe into the stump and led me over to the van.

"The cops came back twenty minutes ago," George said as he showed me the yellow box.

"It looks like they brought friends." I pointed at the six red dots that formed an arc around the entrance to the clearing.

He nodded. "Last night Sue and I laid out a listening net. But we need Val to translate what they're saying."

"Let me get her," I said. I walked back to the tent and poked my head in. Val had gotten dressed and was slipping on her shoes. "Your translation services are required," I said.

"I heard." She grabbed her jacket and followed me to the van.

George handed her a pair of headphones plugged into another yellow box. She put them on and closed her eyes. After a few minutes she looked up. "They're complaining about how little they're getting paid to guard the celebrities," she said. "They're trying to figure out who we are. And they want to come over and get some coffee, but nobody knows enough English to ask for it."

"So they're friendlies?" George asked.

Val shrugged, and then she laughed. "Now they're discussing the mine's vampires. One of the guys just said that *strigoi* have blue eyes, ginger hair, and two hearts each."

"Maybe they've evolved to survive the wooden stakes," I said.

"Hold on—someone just asked how to kill them." She cupped her hands over the headphones and listened for another minute. "Here's the scoop," she said. "First you cut out their hearts, then you drive a nail into their foreheads, place garlic under their tongues, and smear their bodies in fat from a pig killed on St. Ignatius Day. Stuff them back in their coffins upside down, and they stay dead forever."

Sue poked George's belly. "You forgot the pig fat."

George was looking at the screen. "We'll have to figure out a plan for getting that gold out unseen," he said. "Friendly or not, if these guys see it, they'll want to share."

"We'll need to come up with a diversion," I said.

"What kind?" Sue asked.

I shrugged. "We'll think of something. But first let's get the gold."

After Rose and Marie planned their reconnaissance dive, Val and I headed into the mine shaft with them and helped them assemble their equipment.

Marie filled their dry suits with argon. "We'll keep this first dive to ten minutes," she said. "That limits the decompression, and it saves our residual nitrogen time for the recovery."

They ran through the dive checklists and slipped into the water. Rose slid her face mask on and bit into the mouthpiece. "Can you understand me?" she asked.

"You're garbled, but it works," I replied into the microphone. George had brought special ultrasonic audio and visual gear, but talking was difficult with rebreathers, as the closed-circuit full face masks had a bite mouthpiece.

I handed Rose a spool of nylon rope.

Marie switched on her wrist-attached camera, and Val held up her thumb. "The image is clear," she said. "I'll start recording now."

The twins waved and slid under the surface. I stood at the top of the shaft and watched their descent until they were out of sight, and then I joined Val at the screen.

"It's beautiful down there," she said. "I can't wait until we go."

I could wait.

"Marie, short strokes on your finning," we heard Rose say. "You're stirring up the silt." The twins had reached the bottom of the first shaft and were making their way through Viliam gallery.

"It should be another fifty feet or so, on your left," I told them. I watched as Marie swam the camera up to a walled-off portion. "That must be it."

Marie panned the camera around the edges, showing us well-joined stonework stretching from floor to ceiling. Rose drove a pin into a crack in the wall just before the stonework. She attached the nylon rope to the pin. This would let us find our way back through the churned-up muck after we tore the wall down.

I checked my watch. "You still have three minutes," I said. "Do you want to see if you can find the alcove your grandmother talked about?"

"Sure," said Rose. "Straight back?"

I checked the map. "Maybe another forty feet on the right. It might be hard to find—your grandmother said she covered the hole."

Marie panned her camera around the walls and floor, but none of us spotted anything.

Rose swam in front of Marie and waved to the camera. "We have to head up," she said. She shone her wrist light on the dive computer on her wrist. "We'll decompress at fifteen feet for three minutes."

After they surfaced, we helped the twins out of their suits, and the four of us headed out of the mine. Val gave George the video recording on a memory stick.

He plugged it into his screen and played it back. "I've worked out a plan to pull down that wall," he said.

"Where's Madame Flora?" I asked.

"Still in the tent with Mr. Morgan," Sue said.

"Are they all right?" Rose asked.

George laughed. "We heard them arguing a few minutes ago—I think they're fine."

Marie walked up to the tent and called, "Grandma, are you there?"

A second later, the tent flap opened, and Madame Flora stuck her head out.

"We need you to look at this video and verify the location," Val said, pointing to George's screen.

Madame Flora concentrated on a paused image on the video screen. "Can you rewind just a bit?" she asked.

George went back two seconds.

She clicked her fingernail on the screen. "That's the wall Ned built."

"And it's still intact," I said.

George hit the play button.

"Stop!" she shouted.

George paused again. The image showed the floor of the back alcove.

"That's the entrance to the opal nest." She ran her fingers around the bottom edge. "See the foundation of the old wall?"

The screen showed the jagged remnants of a wall rising an inch or two out of the silt on the floor.

"Where's the trap door?" Rose asked.

"Right in the middle, under these rocks." Madame Flora had a tremble in her voice. "Still hidden."

I looked at Val. "We have to go there."

Her eyebrows went up. "Are you sure?"

Tough question. The dark cave and tight spaces would put my panic attacks and Val's singing to the test. But if Madame Flora's story was true, Ned Callaghan's body was jammed in a tunnel at the bottom of the pit under that trap door.

"I'm sure," I said. How could I miss this opportunity?

"Let's get the gold, and if our nitrogen residuals are low enough, we'll all go," Marie said. She looked at George. "How are we pulling down the wall?"

George smiled. "I've got the perfect thing for you—spreader bars." He opened another green plastic container and pulled out a two-foot sharpened steel rod with a large swivel at its blunt end and six murderous-looking foot-long spikes attached below its point. "It's like an umbrella." He pressed a button near the swivel, and the spikes sprung out. "We'll pound three of these babies through cracks in the wall, attach a cable to each swivel, and spring them open. Then I'll crank up the winch from the surface and pull the wall down."

Rose hefted the spreading bar. "You have an underwater hammer?"

George nodded. "Right here in the case." He pulled out a short-handled bright yellow sledge hammer.

"Give us another hour to flush some more nitrogen," Marie said. She pointed at me. "This time you and Val can come and help."

forty-eight

THE FOUR OF US suited up and slid into the water. George handed the girls the three spreader bars and me the hammer. He held up a harness attached to a spool of steel cable and said, "I'll drop this down now—latch the three hooks to the swivels."

He tossed the harness into the water and fed out fifty feet of cable. Then the four of us slipped under the surface.

Rose led us through the descent. Val swam next, then me, and Marie came last. The water was clear, there was plenty of illumination from each of our lights, and I had no panic problems.

It took us a minute to drop down the shaft and reach the bottom of the gallery. The girls attached their spreader bars to the harness, I gripped the cable and pulled some slack, and Rose led us through a short tunnel and over to the wall that Ned had built.

"You two place yours at the bottom. I'll put mine at the top," Marie said.

The girls chose their locations, and I hammered their bars into the wall. It took a few minutes for each bar, and once I drove their ends through, I pressed the buttons and deployed the spikes. I tested each of them for a firm grip.

"We'll have to swim away from the cable," Rose said. We headed further down the tunnel, into the alcove that Madame Flora claimed held the trap door.

"George, you can pull it down," Marie said.

"Let me take up the slack," he said.

We waited, and a minute later he said, "Okay, I'm all set."

"Let her rip," Marie said.

Ten seconds later I heard a loud squeal. A jarring thud rumbled through my body. A series of loud clicks and pops followed this, then some angry scraping noises.

After a minute all went quiet. "Are you done?" Marie asked.

"I'm hauling out the harness and bars now," George said. "Give me five minutes."

Rose motioned to me. "We can look for Grandma's trap door while we wait."

I nodded, and we swam to the center of the alcove and pointed our wrist lights at the floor. I saw a straight edge, and I reached out and brushed away the dirt. Silt bloomed up and clouded the water around me, but I kept brushing, and soon I had an outline of a trap door, maybe two feet square. The girls removed some small rocks scattered on top, and after another minute the entire door lay in view. A large iron ring lay flush in the center of it.

We floated just above the door, shining our lights down at the ring. "Should we open it?" Val asked.

Rose shook her head. "We should get back to the wall." She and Marie turned and swam back the way we had come.

I looked at Val. "I still want to go down."

She nodded. "But not yet."

We swam behind Rose and Marie, and soon we reached a wall of murky water. It was impossible to see more than an inch or two in front of our lights.

"There's more silt than I thought," Marie said.

George's voice came over the wireless. "Can you show me?"

Rose had been holding out her arm, pointing the camera at the muddy water. "Aren't you getting this?" she asked.

"I see only brown."

"That's all there is," Rose said. She turned to face us. "Let's form a chain and head through."

"Can't we wait for it to settle down?" I asked. My heart had already started pounding, and I was struggling to control my breathing.

"It would take hours, and by then our residual nitrogen would be too high to recover the gold," she said.

Great. And although that was logical, a voice in my head screamed that it was okay to abandon the gold. I didn't think I could voluntarily swim into that cloud.

I turned to Val. "I need your help doing this." I tried to keep the panic out of my voice.

"You'll be fine. Just hold on tight." She waved to catch the twins' attention. "Scott needs me to sing to keep his panic down."

"Whatever it takes," Rose said.

Val held my hand and grabbed Rose's belt with her other. Marie grabbed Val's belt. "Just close your eyes, Scott," Val said. She started singing her Russian song.

I shut my eyes right before we entered the cloud of silt, and tried to do nothing but focus on Val's singing. It took a minute or so to calm my breathing, and just like in the Chesapeake, I let the music carry me through.

I took a chance and opened my eyes in the murky water. Our wrist lights hardly made a dent; I couldn't even see my fingers. We inched along the bottom of the cave. But then Rose found the nylon line on the right, and we were able to speed up. After twenty more feet of blind swimming we were back in clear water.

"Will the silt settle overnight?" I asked.

"It should," Rose said. "Let's go up to fifteen feet and decompress. We can get the gold tomorrow."

When we climbed out of the mine, we showed the video to Archie and Madame Flora. When she saw the trap door, Madame Flora shuddered. "What happens to bodies left in cave water?" she asked.

We all looked at each other and shook our heads. Then George cleared his throat. "You never saw any skeletons when they showed the pictures from the Titanic, did you? Just their shoes were left."

"The ocean has lots of scavengers," Sue said.

"So do caves." George looked at Madame Flora. "Anything leather will still be down there. Most of Ned's bones, too. The rest of him is either eaten or dissolved."

Madame Flora sighed.

I wanted to know our security state. "Are we still being watched?" I asked Sue.

She nodded. "Six of them, but they've stayed quiet."

"Did you have any more ideas about a diversion?" George asked me.

Actually, I had—something that would get us into the opal nest, too. "Vampires," I said. "Val said the guards were already scaring each other with stories about them."

"There are no vampires here," George said.

"We have Ned's skeleton," I said.

Rose touched my arm. "Do you really think you can swim through that tiny trap door?" she asked.

"I can do it." I had to.

Val frowned at me. "What's pushing you so hard?"

A good question. Although I didn't believe that I was a reincarnation of Ned, I still felt drawn to find out more about him. Ned had inserted himself into my life, and I had a duty to honor his request for relevancy.

"Ned's pushing me," I said. "How can I resist getting face to face with my previous carrier?"

She crossed her arms. "But then you're going to use his bones to trick the local cops. Isn't that almost sacrilegious?"

I pointed to Madame Flora. "From what you told us about Ned, I think he'd be tickled to help Raddy's granddaughter one last time."

"He would, Scott," Madame Flora said softly.

"I agree," Archie said. "It is our duty to honor and remember our former carriers. Perhaps you will discover something belonging to Ned which you can add to your soul line collection."

George scratched his head. "But how will Ned's skeleton scare away the cops?"

"Weren't they discussing how to defuse a vampire?" I asked Val.

She nodded. "What was it they said? Drive a nail into their foreheads, cut out their hearts, and put them upside-down in their coffins. You want to do this to Ned?"

"It could work," I said. "We'll show his skeleton to the cops, and then we'll tell them we need to perform some final rites to make sure the *strigoi* stay dead."

After a minute George said, "I like it. We can't have the cops watching us pull the gold out of the tunnel, and this bit of superstition just may scare them off."

Marie shivered. "I'm not going anywhere near that skeleton."

"Me neither," Rose said. "What if we start hauling out the gold while you two gather his bones?"

I looked at Val. "I can't do it without you."

She nodded. "I know you want this bad."

"I do. Thank you," I said. I stood up. "First thing tomorrow, we're getting Ned."

forty-nine

DISCUSSING THE RECOVERY OF a sixty-four-year-old skeleton sounded a lot less spooky on the surface than it did after we clambered into the mine the next morning. Especially when that skeleton once carried my same soul identity. I wondered if I would experience anything mystical when I encountered Ned Callaghan's remains.

But first we had to reach Old Ned. We needed to swim down the shaft and into the gallery, then head past the gold and back to the second alcove. Madame Flora said that under the trap door was a fifty foot ladder to the bottom, where we would pull up a not-quite-sealed plug in the floor. Last time she saw Ned, his body had been jammed in the chute three or four feet below the plug.

While Val and I recovered Ned's bones, the twins would use the underwater sled to move the barrels of gold from the near alcove to the base of the main shaft. We'd wait on winching up the gold until Ned's skeleton and our vampire tales had chased away the cops.

We checked our equipment and reloaded the rebreathers' scrubbers. Then we climbed into our suits and filled them with argon. George used the winch to lower the underwater sled, and the four of us descended. I carried a large mesh bag neatly folded into a small pouch dangling from my waist.

We swam the sled to the first alcove. The water was clear, I was calm, and our wrist lights illuminated the small room. Just as Madame Flora had claimed, we found the twelve small barrels stacked against the far wall. Three wooden boxes sat alongside them. An inch-thick layer of silt covered the tops of the boxes and barrels.

"That muck is going to fly up when we start shifting things," Rose said. "You two better go collect your bones—we'll hang the lights and get the boxes moved first."

Val and I swam back to the second alcove. Val attached a battery-powered light in the ceiling above, and I pulled the iron ring upright. I ran two yard-long nylon straps through the ring and when Val swam down, I handed her the ends to one of them.

"Wrap these around your hands and wrists." I demonstrated with my strap. I pulled myself into a crouch over the trap door, placing my fins on the sides.

Val followed suit.

We pulled together, and the trap door opened with a screech. We folded it over and peered into the hole. A rusting metal ladder, bolted to the side, crawled down the shaft and into the gloom outside the light's reach.

"You go first," Val said. "I'll be right behind you."

As I shone my light down the shaft, the same panic rose in me. I spun around and faced Val. "Maybe we don't need Ned's bones."

She stared at me. "Are you sure?"

I stared back, feeling the buzzing in my ears. I wasn't going to be able to do this.

Then Val started singing her song, and like a restless infant comforted by a lullaby, the panic subsided. I was able to swim headfirst into the shaft. I pulled myself down hand over hand. After thirty or so rungs I glanced at my dive computer and noted we were already at eighty feet. We were going to have to make it quick, or we'd be stuck decompressing for a long time.

"Let's check in with the girls," Val said. "Rose and Marie?"

No answer.

"Girls, are you there?" she asked.

Silence. Then I remembered our communications were ultrasonic, and we needed something close to line-of-sight to communicate. I began breathing hard, and I spun around. We had to get out of this hole.

Val rapped her knuckles on my faceplate. "Scott, calm down. We can do this." She sang a bit of her song.

I closed my eyes and forced myself to listen. I was calmed in less than a minute.

Val motioned with her hands. "We'd better hurry."

We pulled ourselves the rest of the way down. I saw the remains of an old rope tied to the bottom rung.

Val flashed her wrist light at the bottom and illuminated a large, silt-covered wooden plug about the size of a manhole cover jammed like a cork into a hole in the floor. The rope ran into a crack along one side. That loose seal explained why we were swimming and not walking.

I slid my fingers into the crack to test the plug's weight. It shifted, and I used both hands to lift it out of the hole.

I must have created a little current when I removed the plug, and that current must have sucked at the silt and mixed it up before spitting it back at us. The water grew murky, and we couldn't see more than a foot in front of us.

"Now what?" I asked.

"We either wait, or we swim into the plume," Val said.

I looked at my dive computer. We were down one hundred feet, only three minutes before we had to head up. I took a steadying breath. "I'll do it."

Val tethered me to her by tying a cord between the loops on each of our suit's hips.

"Wish me luck," I said. I swam blind toward the hole, stroking in sync to Val's song. My wrist light illuminated the silt particles, but I couldn't see ahead. I moved my arms to the sides and realized two things: My head and shoulders were at the top of a narrow tube, and the silt I stirred up made it even murkier.

I kicked my fins and propelled myself into the hole and down the chute. I kept my gloved hands in front of me and along the sides. Another foot in and I bumped into a blockage that felt a little squishy. Could this be what remained of Ned? It was hard to tell just by feel.

I unsnapped my mesh bag and slipped one of its handles onto my left wrist. I used both hands to pull at the lumpy object. After a minute of wiggling, parts of it broke off. I shoved the pieces into the mesh bag, then patted my hands on the floor of the chute and felt for more.

I grabbed quite a few pieces—whatever wasn't stuck. Then I propelled myself forward another foot and grabbed even more. Pretty soon my mesh bag was almost as wide as the chute, and it was blocking my forward progress.

"I've picked up all the loose pieces," I said.

"We're just about out of time," Val said. "Let's go."

I couldn't turn around because the chute was too narrow—my re-breather scraped along the top. And I couldn't seem to back out while carrying the mesh net.

"I'm stuck," I said. "Can you pull me loose?"

"Stop kicking," she said. I felt her hands on my legs. She pulled, and I pushed with my free arm, and after a minute I was floating free.

The water remained filled with silt. I brought my dive computer close to my face. The recovery had taken too long; we'd have to decompress at fifty feet for an hour before getting out of the cave. Good thing the twins were there—we could help them move the rest of the gold.

I felt around for the plug and sat it back on top of the chute's opening. Then I followed Val up the ladder. The mesh bag was ponderous, but I kept it from scraping too much silt off the walls.

We took our time ascending the fifty feet back to the alcove, resting each time our dive computers buzzed our arms to remind us to slow down. After ten minutes we reached the alcove and the light, and Val helped me fold back the trap door.

I took a quick look at the bag, but I couldn't recognize anything under all the silt. "Can you hear us, girls?" I called.

"We're here, Scott," Rose said. "What's up?"

"We've got Ned's bones, and we're heading your way. How's the gold moving coming along?"

"We've sledded all three boxes and eight of the twelve barrels over to the winching area," Marie said. She sounded out of breath.

"George has already winched up the boxes," Rose said.

George came on the intercom. "Do you want to send up the gold?" he asked.

"If the cops crawled down to the gallery, we'd have a hard time explaining it," I said.

"Good point," he said.

Val untethered me and turned off the light dangling from the alcove's ceiling. Then we swam toward the first alcove.

When we reached the twins, Rose pointed at the bag. "So that's Ned?" she asked.

"I hope so," I said. I held up the bag so everybody could see it under the light. Some of the silt had begun to flake off; I could make out a boot and what might have been a leg bone.

"That's just gross," Marie said.

I thought it was cool, but I let it go. I pointed to my dive computer. "We've got an hour of decompression—how can we help?"

"Let's get the rest of the gold moved," Marie said.

We joined the remaining four barrels with the other eight at the base of the main shaft. When we finished, George winched up the sled and my mesh bag. Then the twins headed up for the final fifteen foot decompression while Val and I waited the rest of our decompression hour.

Val pointed back at the rocks strewn on the floor in front of the first alcove. "What will the Slovak divers say when they see this?"

"That the vampires got frisky and made a mess," I said. "Let's start our ascent."

During our final decompression stop we discussed how to scare the guards outside our camp.

"It's the twenty-first century—they're not superstitious villagers chasing monsters with pitchforks," Val said.

"Their grandmas must have scared them with some Slovak folklore," I said. "We just need to wake up what's already there."

We'd have to wake it up enough that they wouldn't dare hang around to watch us haul out the gold.

fifty

VAL AND I FINALLY finished decompressing, and then we surfaced, unsuited, and dressed. Rose and Marie had already worked with George to clean the silt off the boxes, and Val and I went through the contents of my mesh bag.

I had grabbed over thirty bones, two pairs of boots, what looked like a leather overcoat, and a belt. It was definitely a body. But was it Ned's?

"Look at this," Val said. She brushed the silt off a block-shaped hunk of crud about half the size of a paperback book. "It could be a wallet."

I laid down the bit of rope I had cleaned off and took the block from Val. It looked like a standard bi-fold wallet. I found the crease and pulled the top layers apart. The leather was stiff, and it cracked as the two sides separated.

I used my thumb to force open the right inside pocket. A gold card, still shiny under some silt and about the size of a driver's license, lay inside. I pulled it out. "Ned Callaghan," I read out loud. "Member, Soul Identity. 1912."

"You found him, Scott." Val sounded choked up.

I stared at the card in my hands. I rubbed at some loose silt that obscured the logo. These bones truly did belong to Ned Callaghan, my soul line predecessor.

Val knelt next to me. "How do you feel?" she asked.

I tried to think of something apropos. "Overwhelmed," I said. That fit.

I picked up Ned's skull and held it in my hands. I closed my eyes and tried to remember what he had written in his soul line collection, and what Madame Flora had told me about him. I wished I had a picture of what he looked like.

The irony behind me and my soul line predecessor both helping an ethically challenged Gypsy lady walk away with some previously stolen gold didn't escape me. But we had work to do: I needed to stuff Ned's bones into one of the wooden boxes so he could come to the aid of Madame Flora one last time.

I tried to lay out Ned's bones in the proper order. Most of the larger pieces were easy to place, and I sprinkled the smaller bones by the hands and feet. Val helped, and soon Ned's skeleton took shape.

George and the twins stood to one side and watched. "You ready for a box?" George asked.

I nodded. "Did Goering's papers survive?" I asked.

He shook his head. "All three boxes were full of muck and what might once have been leather bindings," he said.

"That's probably for the better," Val said. "This way his future carrier won't have to deal with the drama of figuring out what to do with Nazi memories."

"Don't let Archie hear you talk that way," I said.

George brought over the boxes, and I placed the leather overcoat on the bottom of the first one. It was too long, so I folded its tails in. I put the larger pair of boots at one end, the belt in the middle, and Ned's skull, facing downward, at the top.

Val helped me place the other bones. We ran the vertebrae down the middle, slid what we guessed were the arm bones into the coat's sleeves, and jumbled the ribs and leg bones over each other. I slid the pelvis in backward, inside the belt, and placed the wallet, minus the card, next to it. Then we were done. George handed me the box's cover, and I gave Ned a lingering look before I set it on top.

I didn't know what to do with young Flora's old boots, so I tossed them in another box.

We all knelt by the water and washed the mud off our hands and arms. Then the five of us carried the three boxes up the tunnel.

George stopped us right before we reached the entrance. I squinted into the afternoon gray light, and I saw Dara Sabol, police chief, speaking with Sue, Archie, and Madame Flora.

"Leave the boxes here for now," I whispered.

We stacked the boxes in the shadows. Then we walked out of the cave and over to the fire to join the rest of our group.

Sabol stood up, hands on her hips. She looked at George for a minute before speaking. "How is diving?" she asked.

George smiled. "The kids are enjoying your beautiful mine."

"Tomorrow your two-day permit expires." The police chief looked at her watch. "Eight more hours."

George threw a glance at Sue, who raised her hands palm-sides-up. He turned back to Sabol. "Now Chief, you gave us two full days' access to the mines," he said. "We'll be out of here bright and early tomorrow morning."

She folded her arms low across her chest. "You come yesterday, and you here all day. Two days, as requested. Leave by midnight."

George sighed and looked at Archie. "I really thought we had a full forty-eight hours, Mr. Morgan."

Madame Flora cleared her throat, but Sue held up her hand and turned to the police chief. "Obviously this is just a misunderstanding between us. Can we please extend for another day?"

Sabol pursed her lips. "No extensions. Next group arrives at midnight."

"The next group?" Madame Flora's voice was sharp.

The police chief nodded. "Scientists study zooplankton in mine waters. They use our divers. One week, then you come back, okay?"

George pulled his wallet out of his pocket and started flipping through a large wad of bills. "If there's anything we can do…"

As soon as she saw the wallet, Chief Sabol turned and faced away and refused to meet his eyes again. "You must leave by midnight," she said as she stared at the ground.

Somebody was turning her screws. I pulled George off to the side. "Can we get everything out and away in eight hours?" I murmured.

He stuffed his wallet back into his pocket. "Only if we can lose our audience. Even then it'll be tight."

Ned would have to make an earlier-than-expected entrance. I walked around and stood in front of Dara. "Chief Sabol," I said, "would your guards like to help us and earn some extra money?"

She squinted at me. "Help you how?"

"Haul our gear up from the cave," I said. "And we need some help preparing a special ceremony."

She scratched her head. After a moment, she nodded. "You pay me. I pay them."

"How much?"

"One thousand two hundred dollars."

"For how many people?"

"Six."

I looked at George, and he pulled out his wallet. "I'll pay you half now, and half when we're done," he said. "Call your team."

The police chief pulled a handheld radio out of her jacket pocket and spoke into it. She put the radio away and smiled at me. "My men come in two minutes."

fifty-one

TEN MINUTES LATER, CHIEF Dara Sabol and five men in identical gray uniforms stood in front of me. "Tell us what to do," she said.

Sue handed me her intruder display. I saw fourteen red dots in the clearing, and no dots anywhere else. That was good.

I motioned to Val, and she and Madame Flora joined me. "Val will translate," I said.

Val spoke to the police in Slovakian, and they nodded. I noticed Dara give one of her men an uneasy look.

I pointed at Madame Flora. "Two men and this lady came to visit your mines in October 1946," I said.

Val translated, and the team turned to look at the old Gypsy.

"They brought three very special boxes to store in the mine," I said. "They hired a local guide named Vlado to help them."

After Val translated, one of the older men whispered something into Dara's ear. The chief looked at me. "Jan is son of Vlado," she said.

Talk about luck—maybe Jan could help me spin this story. "Did your father tell you about the boxes?" I asked him.

He nodded and spoke to Val.

"His father told the story many times," she translated.

I smiled at him, but I didn't say anything.

Jan looked at me, then at Val. I waited for him to think it through.

Then his eyes went wide, and he blurted something to Val, and his buddies gasped.

"He wants to know if we're here for the *strigoi morti*."

I nodded at Jan. "Tell me what your father told you," I said.

He spoke for two minutes, waving his hands and raising his voice a few times. When he finished, Val turned to me and Madame Flora.

"Jan says his father guided a beautiful Roma girl, a German soldier, and an old man on a cane to this entrance. They brought three *strigoi* in their coffins along with many barrels of cognac.

"Jan says they showed his father the three vampires. They slept fully dressed with their arms folded across their chests. Their skin was pure white, and their hair was fire-red. One of them had a long beard, and one was a woman."

Madame Flora snorted, and I glared at her.

Val continued. "Jan says his father helped place the vampires into the mine—"

"I wish he *had* helped," Madame Flora whispered.

"—but when they were finished," Val said, "the vampires burst out of their coffins and attacked the four of them. Jan says his father fought them off, saved the girl, and escaped."

Madame Flora opened her mouth, but I quickly grabbed her arm. "Ask him what happened to the vampires," I said to Val.

Val asked, and after Jan answered, she translated. "After he recovered from his injuries, his father returned with some German soldiers who were chasing the *strigoi*. The mine had half-flooded, the bodies had vanished, and the coffins and cognac had disappeared. The only thing anybody found was a ruined campsite here on the surface."

"And the girl?" I asked.

"I was about to translate that. Jan says his father talked about the beautiful dark-haired girl for the rest of his life. After they escaped, she thanked him and kissed him, but then she clapped her hands and vanished in a flash of blinding white light."

I leaned close to Madame Flora's ear. "Yet another admirer."

"The story sounds like it's been improved over the years," she whispered.

"It suits our purposes," I said. I turned to the police chief. "We are here to finish what was started sixty-four years ago."

Dara swallowed and looked away. Val translated, and the five men shuffled their feet and looked down at the ground. Jan spoke after a minute.

Val translated. "What do you want them to do?"

"The *strigoi morti* will soon awaken," Madame Flora said, "from the cognac we brought to keep them satisfied." She paused for Val to translate.

The six riveted their eyes on the old fortune teller.

Madame Flora sighed. "Unless we take care of them once and for all, they will start to hunt outside of the mine."

"How will you take care of them?" The police chief asked, shuddering.

"We must follow the old ways to kill them," I said. "Cut out both hearts, put garlic under their tongues, drive a nail in their skulls, and smear them in oil."

Val translated, and the police chief and her men stared at me with their mouths open.

"We have finished only one so far," I said. "The old man."

As Val translated, I motioned to George and Sue. "Bring the boxes," I called.

George signaled to Rose and Marie, and the four of them brought the three wooden boxes out of the cave. They laid them out by the entrance.

George came over to me. "Ned is on the far end," he said.

I pointed at Val. "Tell our friends that I wish to show them what a vampire looks like once we kill it."

Jan walked over and spoke to Dara. She shook her head, and Jan grabbed her arm and stared at her as he spoke again, this time more urgently.

"What's he saying?" I asked Val.

She watched them for a minute. "Jan wants to leave, right now," she said. "Dara is telling him he will be well paid. She just ordered him to stay."

Jan loosened his grip on the chief's arm and sighed.

I walked over to Ned's box and slid my fingers under the cover. "Tell them it's safe," I said. "They can come closer."

Val translated, and after looking at each other, the six of them gathered in a circle around the box.

I cleared my throat. "After we performed the procedure, we placed the vampire face-down in the coffin. He grew old before our eyes." I waited for Val to translate, and then I lifted the cover off the box.

All six of them flinched, and Jan gave a slight groan as he looked at Ned's bones.

"He's harmless now." I reached in and grabbed Ned's skull. "Even the nail disappeared—see for yourselves." I held it out to Jan, but he shrank back.

I offered the skull to the others as Val translated. Nobody seemed to want to touch it, so I placed it back in the box and put the cover on top. "The old one wasn't too difficult," I said, "but it took four of us to hold him down while we drove the nail into his head." I pointed to the other two boxes. "These two know what's coming, so it will be much harder. We need all of you to help us kill them properly."

The translation sparked off a loud and contentious conversation between the six of them. After a few minutes I asked Val to translate.

"They're almost ready to help," she said. She listened some more. "The chief told them they each would make two hundred bucks. That seems to have clinched it."

Another few minutes of discussion and the chief turned to me. "We are ready. What do we do?"

I pointed at the middle box. "When I lift off the top, hold her down."

George gave me a hammer and a long steel spike, and Sue handed Val a clove of garlic and a bottle of olive oil. I set the hammer on the ground, then got ready to lift the top.

"Ready?" I asked.

They each took a deep breath and nodded. Two of the men crossed themselves.

I pulled the top off as fast as I could and let out a yell. The six of them grunted and leaned forward, holding their hands out in front of them.

Except for the extra pair of women's boots we recovered, the box was empty.

Jan let out another moan, and I gave a loud gasp. Then I chewed on my bottom lip. "Let's check the other box," I said.

Val translated, and the six gathered around. When that box came up empty, they looked even more worried.

I swung around and pointed at the cave entrance. "They must have escaped—we must catch them before it's too late!" I yelled.

Dara motioned to her men. They huddled together and held a whispered conversation. After a minute, Dara came over.

"We go now," she said, chin up in the air.

I glared at her and tried to put on a big frown. "We need your help," I said.

"We are police, and I could arrest you for murder," she said. "Maybe even kidnapping." The police chief put her hands on her hips. "Clean up and leave by midnight, or your team goes to jail."

"So you're just going to leave us here?" I stuck out my lower lip and let it tremble just slightly. "With them?"

She shrugged. "Good luck," she said. She turned to George and stuck out her hand. "Give me rest of money."

George looked at me.

I scowled at her. "What are we paying you for? Give us the six hundred back."

She stared at me for a minute. Then she stalked off.

The six of them headed in a tight bunch to the edge of the clearing. Jan turned back and frowned, but then he waved his hand and walked away.

After five minutes of watching the intruder display, Sue smiled. "They're gone. That leaves just the eight of us."

George looked at his watch. "We'd better hurry."

fifty-two

SINCE WE HAD TO wait for more nitrogen to bleed out of our bodies before we dove again, we spent the next two hours packing our surface gear. Val and I helped George and Sue tear down the tents while the twins went into the mine, checked the diving gear, and replaced the scrubbers and tanks on the rebreathers.

When all we had left on the surface was the packed green van, the intruder gear, and the ashes from the fire, all eight of us went into the mine. Both Archie and Madame Flora insisted on being present when we pulled the gold out of the water, so we helped them negotiate the low spots in the tunnel, and we made our way to the top of the Viliam gallery.

"Are you sure it's okay to leave the outside unguarded?" I asked George.

He shrugged. "We don't really have a choice. We've only got five more hours, and I need Sue's help."

"Mr. Morgan and Flora are safer down here with us," Sue said.

I nodded. We were jammed for time.

George and Sue helped the four of us suit up. The twins descended, and Val and I stayed on the surface.

"Pull her up, George," Rose said over the intercom after a few minutes.

George turned the lever on the winch. Val and I waited for the first barrel to rise, and as soon as the top showed, we swam over and helped George maneuver it to the ledge.

Madame Flora walked over to the barrel and used her hands to wipe away the silt. She bowed her head and stood with both hands on its rim. Archie came and put his arm around her shoulders, and when she looked up and grinned, the six of us let out a cheer.

George lowered the cable back down, and in the next thirty minutes, we raised eight of the barrels.

"Okay, it's time to switch," Marie said. "We're heading up."

The reason we were switching was because our residual nitrogen level had climbed with all the diving. If Rose and Marie stayed down any longer, they'd be stuck in decompression for more time than we had left. As it was, they needed to hang out at fifteen feet for a half hour.

When their time was almost up, Val and I descended to the bottom of the shaft.

"Good luck," Rose called as we passed them.

We saw the remaining four barrels when we reached the bottom. Val tilted the first one, and I slid the cable loops underneath it. "Take her away, George," I called.

We watched the cable pull taut. The barrel slowly rose above us. A few minutes later the cable came back. We sent the other three barrels one by one to the surface.

I looked at Val when the last barrel went up. "That's it, then."

She nodded. "Should we retrieve our lights from the alcoves?"

I tapped my dive computer. "We barely have enough time for decompression." Our time was tighter than the twins' because we had retrieved Ned's bones from one hundred feet.

"Leave the lights," George said. "Come on up so we can get these barrels out of here."

So we made our final ascent through Viliam gallery. As we floated for our twenty minutes at fifteen feet, I thought about the mess we had made to the alcove, and I hoped it wouldn't come back to haunt Soul Identity.

My dive computer showed a minute left before we could return to the surface.

Then George's voice came over the intercom. "I'm sorry," he said. "We have a private permit to use this mine. You'll have to come back after midnight."

Who was he talking to? I grabbed Val's arm and switched off my wrist-mounted video camera.

Silence for a moment, and then I heard George again. "Hey buddy, you don't have to point that thing at me. Let me get—"

I heard what sounded like a car backfiring, followed by a woman's scream. Then a man's sharp voice, laced with a German accent. "You will do exactly what I say, or I will shoot the old man next."

"You son of a bitch—you shot my husband!" Sue yelled.

"And I will most assuredly shoot you as well if you do not follow my instructions."

Silence over the intercom. Val grabbed my hand. I looked at her wide eyes behind her mask and raised my finger toward my lips. She nodded.

"What do you want?" I heard Madame Flora ask.

"We want our gold back. All seventy-two bars."

"That gold is mine!" Madame Flora shouted.

"I am sorry you feel that way." Another sharp crack. Val gripped my arm.

"That was just a warning, old lady. The next bullet will surely land between your eyes."

Silence for what seemed forever. Then I heard Archie say in a wavering voice. "The gold is in the barrels. You may take it."

"*Danke*." And I heard in the background the faint sounds of orders. I imagined men hauling the barrels up the mine's tunnel.

I strained to hear anything over the intercom, but I couldn't make much out. Some labored breathing, some murmurs from what sounded like the twins, and every now and then a barked German command.

After what must have been thirty minutes, Sue's low voice came over the intercom. "Scott? Val? I don't know if you can hear me," she said. "But don't answer—just listen.

"The group is wearing uniforms with swastikas on their armbands. You heard the leader—he's the one who shot George." Her voice sounded choked up as she said that, and then she was silent for a minute.

"I think George is still alive, but I don't dare approach him. I whispered for him to lie still so they don't shoot him again.

"Six soldiers are hauling the barrels out of here. Every now and then only the leader's left guarding us. Next time that happens, I'm going to make my move. You guys need to wait this one out. Stir up the water so you can stay out of sight."

The line went silent. I stared at Val, and knew she felt as helpless and as powerless and as tension-filled as I was.

Sue wanted us to hide under a cloud of silt. A great idea, except that Val wouldn't be able to sing me through this one.

I took a deep breath and steeled myself for the panic attack that I knew would come. Then I reached out with both arms and scrubbed my hands against the wall.

The silt cloud blossomed and enveloped us. I gritted my teeth as the panic monster broke free within me. I clenched my fists and fought to control my breathing.

Val grabbed my arm and led me in a descent to just under the silt cloud. I felt the panic attack subside, and I squeezed her hand.

We waited. I glanced at my dive computer: it had been fifty minutes since George was shot.

Suddenly I heard Sue's yell, followed by a barrage of shots. Everybody seemed to be screaming. Then it was silent. Deathly silent.

I grabbed Val's hand and pointed upwards. She shook her head and signaled me to stop. I clenched my fists and tried to control my frustration.

Then I heard Sue call, "Watch out below!" I looked up and saw the winch falling toward us out of the silt cloud. I shoved Val at the wall and kicked hard to get away, and the winch passed between us on its way to the bottom.

The winch's cable dragged behind it. And then about thirty feet later, the cable was wrapped around the torso of a man in a green uniform, his eyes bulging and his mouth open as he passed us.

The man jerked to a stop five feet or so below where we floated. The winch must have reached the gallery's bottom. The end of the cable fell past him as the he twisted upward to face us. I pointed my light at him. The blood from cuts on his face made a red cloud form around his head, and it seemed his legs floated at unnatural angles. Sue had really messed him up.

The man reached into his boot and pulled out a small pistol. He pointed it at me, but at that moment the weight of the free end of the cable must have been enough to counteract his buoyancy, because he was jerked downward and out of the range of my wrist light.

Bullets wouldn't travel more than a few feet in the water, but just to be safe, I switched off my light and motioned Val to do the same.

Instead of responding, Val floated limp in the water.

I swam over to her. Her eyes were scrunched together, and her chest was heaving. I didn't think the winch had hit her. I reached out and spun her around. Her rebreather's status light flashed red—something must have malfunctioned when I pushed her; she wasn't getting any oxygen.

I spun her back around and cranked open her bail-out bottle and opened her regulator bypass. She kept breathing, and after a minute she opened her eyes and flailed her arms. She was alive.

At fifteen feet the five-pound tank would last fifteen minutes. Val could suck for another fifteen from my bail-out, but then we'd have to surface.

Sue came back on the intercom. "Scott? Val? I neutralized the leader and grabbed his pistol. The other six are heading back down this way. I've set up an ambush, but I only have four bullets. There's no time, or I'd ask to you to come up and help me. Sit tight, okay?"

So we waited. I wanted to get the small pistol from the leader floating below us, but I wasn't sure if he was done drowning.

We heard four shots over the intercom. Then we heard nothing. Did Sue get them all? I doubted it, because she would have said something.

"Hands in the air, or the old man dies!" Another German-accented voice yelled. Then silence. I gritted my teeth.

"Where is our *Rottenführer*?" the man asked.

"At the bottom," I heard Sue reply.

"That is unfortunate for you," he said. "Our orders were to take as many prisoners as we could, but you have eliminated five of our team."

"Only two more to go." Sue's voice sounded hard and flat.

I heard a short chuckle. "I don't think so." Another shot, and I heard the twins scream. Val's body was shaking violently.

"Silence!" the man roared. After the girls' screams stopped, he said, "The belly shot means you will have several days to remember how brave you were, until you die next to your husband."

"Damn you," Sue gasped.

"You have damned yourself," he replied. After a minute of silence, he continued. "The rest of you are to come with me."

"Where are you taking us?" I heard Archie ask.

"Back to the surface, to the *Untersturmführer*," he said. "Something tells me he will remember you older ones." He laughed. "And the two *frauleinen* will be a nice treat."

"Take us, but leave the girls," Madame Flora said.

"Ah, you prefer they die down here?" The voice sounded pleasant, as if he was about to tell the punch line of a joke.

"No!" Rose said. "We'll come."

"Perfect," the man said. "My partner will go first, then the four of you, and I will come behind. If anybody tries anything heroic, everybody dies. Is this understood?"

"We understand," Marie said.

And then we heard nothing more.

fifty-three

I WAITED UNTIL VAL had sucked her bail-out bottle dry and was half-way through mine. Then we headed up through the cloud of silt.

I fought the panic monster through the cloud. It wasn't as bad as before, probably because I was worried about what we would find waiting for us in the gallery.

When we finally surfaced, I helped Val pull off her facemask, and she took great, gasping breaths of air. I pushed from behind and helped roll her onto the ledge. I stripped off her rebreather, and she lay on her back and stared at the roof.

I quickly shrugged out of my suit and gloves. I helped Val get dressed so she could warm up. As soon as I got her lying down I hurried over to George and Sue.

They both lay next to where the winch had been. Sue's arms hugged her stomach. George lay face-up with his head turned away from me.

"They took Mr. Morgan," Sue breathed in my ear. "We have to get him back."

"You're not going anywhere yet," I said. I straightened her legs, unzipped her coat, and pulled up her shirt. The bullet had entered just below her navel, a couple inches to the right of center. It had left a hole less than a half-inch across. Blood seeped around its edges.

"I'm going to have to turn you," I said.

She nodded, then let out a cry as I rolled her toward me. I leaned over her and saw that the bullet had exited on her side, an inch below her left hip. There was just a trickle of bleeding from the quarter-sized hole.

"How bad is it?" Sue asked as I rolled her onto her back.

"Not as bad as it must feel," I said. "It looks like you twisted away just in time. The bullet exited cleanly."

She nodded and gave a big sigh. "Thank God," she said. "How about George?"

"Just a sec," I said. I used my dive knife to cut a strip off the bottom of Sue's shirt. I handed it to her. "Use this for the bleeding."

She took the cloth, and I knelt next to George and righted his head.

He was breathing, but not well. Bright red blood dripped from the corner of his mouth. His eyes were open and unfocused. I looked down at his chest, and I saw a small, bloody hole on the left side of his shirt, close to the bottom of his rib cage. I reached around him, but I could find no exit hole in his back.

I held his cheeks in my hands. "George, can you hear me?"

He blinked, opened his mouth, then closed it again.

"I can't sit up to see him—is he all right?" Sue asked.

"He's still breathing—but it looks like his lung was hit."

"What can we do?"

"We can treat him for shock." I turned Val's diving suit inside out and slid it under George to insulate his body from the cold ground. Then I dragged her broken rebreather over and put it under his feet so the blood flow to his vital organs would increase.

"We have to get him out of here," I said. "He needs more help." I rolled Val's empty bail-out bottle into my t-shirt and slid it under his neck.

Sue frowned. "What's wrong with Val?"

"Her rebreather conked out—and I didn't notice it fast enough. She needs a few minutes to recover."

She shuddered. "We're going to have to get out of here and rescue Mr. Morgan. Can you help me stand?"

I wasn't sure if Sue should be walking, but it would save time if I didn't have to drag her out. I placed my arms under hers and lifted.

"Wait!" She winced and lowered her head. After a minute she looked up. "Okay, the rest of the way now."

I lifted, Sue gasped and wrapped her arms around my neck, and then she was standing.

"Can you walk?" I asked.

"Give me a minute." Then she unwrapped herself from me and stood on her own. "It hurts like hell, but I can do this."

"Do you think you can help with George?"

She nodded. "Whatever it takes."

I helped her step over to him, and she reached out and grabbed his foot. "Hang on, Georgie." Then she turned to me. "How are we going to get him out of here?"

Good question. Then I thought about the carts outside of the mine entrance. "Maybe we can roll him up the tracks."

"Those carts are piles of rust."

"It'll be easier than carrying him." I said.

She twisted to grab George's hand, but then she let out a cry and grabbed my shoulder. "I need to sit down."

I lowered her to the floor right next to George. She reached out and caressed his face.

"I'll get the cart," I said. I headed toward the stone staircase leading up to the tunnel.

BOOM!

A shock wave came blasting out of the tunnel entrance and knocked me over. I banged my head on a rock, and it took me a minute to get my bearings and sit up. The air was full of dust, and this darkened the gallery. I couldn't see more than a couple feet.

"You guys all right?" I called.

"I'm here, and George is okay," Sue said.

"Val?"

No response. I crawled along the ground back to where I had left her.

Val lay face up. She was breathing, but she didn't open her eyes when I shook her.

"Did you find her?" Sue called.

"She's unconscious," I said.

"Bring her over here, and I'll keep an eye on her while you get the cart."

That sounded good, especially since the dust had settled enough for me to see Sue and George. I scooped up Val into my arms and carried her across the gallery. I set her down so Sue was between Val and George.

I looked up toward the tunnel and saw the lights were out, so I grabbed both Val's and my wrist lights before I headed up the stairs.

The dust was thicker in the tunnel, and I banged my head on the first low point. I crab-walked through the next two dips and avoided further injuries. Then I straightened up for the last section, and I slammed my shins into a large boulder.

As I pitched forward, I tried to contain the damage by landing on my hands. My wrist lights illuminated a pile of rocks just before I crashed into it.

I scrambled up and used my lights to trace the contours of the rock pile.

What I saw dashed my hopes: large boulders, the smallest at least two feet in diameter, filled the tunnel all the way to the ceiling. I scrambled my way up the pile and tugged at the top-most stones, but they were wedged in, and despite my efforts, they wouldn't budge.

I crept back the length of the tunnel, down the stairs, and into the gallery.

Sue looked up. "No cart?"

I shook my head. "They seem to have blasted the tunnel up close to the entrance, and it's now full of huge rocks. We can't get out that way."

"Can't get out…" Her eyes widened, and she reached out to George. "He needs medical attention, Scott—he's barely getting any air. He's got a tension pneumothorax."

"A what?"

"A collapsed lung. Every breath forces more air through the bullet hole into his chest cavity, and it's squeezing against his organs." She pointed to George's neck. "See how his veins are bulging? That's the pressure building up against his heart. He'll die, Scott, unless he gets immediate help."

fifty-four

I STARED AT GEORGE'S ashen face and bloated chest. "What can we do?" I asked Sue.

"Get him to a doctor now!"

That wasn't going to happen until we found another way out of the mine. I tried to remember anything from the first aid course I had taken as a teenager, but I drew a blank.

Maybe Sue knew. "What will the doctors do when we get him there?" I asked her.

She screwed up her face and clenched her fists, and I reached out and grabbed her arm. "I know you're in a lot of pain, Sue, but you've got to help me help George."

She stared at me and then back at her husband. It didn't seem I was getting through. I reached up and grabbed her cheeks in my hands, forcing her to look at me. "Sue?" I whispered. "How does a doctor fix a pneumothorax?"

She bit her lip and closed her eyes. Then she opened them, and I noticed her panic had subsided. "They put a tube in the chest," she said. "To let the air out and relieve the pressure."

Of course! Memories of that long-ago first aid class surged through my head, and I could see my teacher holding up a ballpoint pen and saying, "when all else fails, the barrel can be used as a tube." He had been talking about a tracheotomy, but that was close enough.

"Do you have a pen?" I asked.

She shook her head.

"How about George?"

She leaned over and felt through his pockets. "No pen."

Dammit. I glanced around the gallery, and I saw my discarded bail-out bottle. Maybe that would work.

I scrambled over to the bottle and used my dive knife to cut off a four inch section of the narrow-gauge hose. I rushed back to Sue. "Which lung do you think collapsed?"

She put her hand on his left side. "This one."

Her hand lay just above the bullet hole.

I decided to put the tube on the right side. I looked at Sue. "I'm going to cut a small slit with my knife, and then I'm going to shove in this tube. Are you okay with that?"

She looked at George, and then she reached out and stroked his cheek. She turned back to me, and I saw tears in her eyes. She nodded.

We unbuttoned George's shirt. I felt for a space between his ribs down at the bottom right side, across from the bullet hole. I placed the point of my diving knife on the spot I had chosen. Then I paused and looked at her. "Ready?"

She nodded, and I wiggled the knife back and forth as I pushed it downwards. It went through George's skin, but then stopped against something firm. I increased the pressure.

The knife broke through, and I wiggled it until I had a half-inch slit. I hesitated. "This is going to really hurt him."

"Do it!" she cried. Tears streamed down her cheeks.

I twisted the blade, and George let out a yell. His arms flew up and slammed into both of us, and his hands grabbed at the knife.

I jammed the section of tubing into the hole. Then I forced it downwards until I heard the hiss of air escaping. It sounded like a tire valve when the filling hose first detaches.

"You did it," Sue said.

I pulled out the knife, took a deep breath, and wiped my trembling, bloody hands on my pants. "Now we hope it works."

We watched George's bloated chest slowly subside. He seemed to be taking deeper breaths, and some color returned to his face.

Sue wiped his forehead and smiled at me. "What you did was amazing."

"You're the one who knew what to do." I pointed up the stairs. "George still needs help—we need to find a way out of here."

She grimaced. "The tunnel was the only way in. How big are those rocks?"

"I couldn't move them. We need some tools." I glanced around the cave. "But the winch is on the bottom, and we have no power, anyway."

I heard Val cough, so I crawled over to her. She looked at me and gave a faint smile. "What did I miss?" she asked.

I swallowed the huge lump in my throat and let out a chuckle. I slid my arm under her shoulder and pulled her into an embrace. "You had me so worried," I said.

"Where are we?" she asked.

Uh oh—how long was she without oxygen? "We're in Dubnik Mine, in Slovakia."

She turned her head toward me and kissed my cheek. "No, silly," she said. "Are we next to the water or next to the radio?"

Whew. "Next to where George had the winch."

She nodded. "Are the two power cables still there?"

I looked around. "Maybe, but the power's out. Only the battery LED lights are working."

"Good."

I pulled back and stared at her. "What makes that good?"

"We can use the cable as an antenna."

"For what? Your cell phone?"

She shook her head. "The impedance is all wrong for a cell phone. But I noticed that the base station for George's ultrasonic gear has a sixty kilohertz LF relay. All it needs is an antenna, and we should be able to communicate from this mine."

She grabbed my arm and pulled herself up. "George once told me that our communications centers scan many frequencies," she said to Sue.

Sue nodded. "They do—at least they used to, before we went digital. Maybe somebody is still listening, and they can get us out of here." Her hand flew to her mouth. "And Mr. Morgan too—I almost forgot about him!"

Val looked at me. "A sixty kilohertz signal has a five thousand meter wave."

"How do you know that?" I asked.

She shrugged. "I once did shortwave. Radio travels at three hundred million meters per second. Divide that by sixty thousand, and you get five thousand meters."

She definitely had recovered.

"Antennas have to be quarter, half, or full wavelength to work," she said. "A quarter-wavelength antenna would be twelve hundred fifty meters." Val scrunched up her face. "Where did you say the tunnel was blocked?"

"Close to the entrance."

"Do you think there's more than three hundred meters before the block?"

"Yes," I said. But what did that matter? Then I got it. Two pairs of power cables running up the tunnel meant there were four wires. "You want to string the wires together to make an antenna?"

She nodded. "A quarter-wavelength one."

"Let's find the cables." I passed her a wrist light, and we found the base station, its power cable, and the winch's power cable. I pulled out my dive knife, cut the ends off, and stripped the red and black wires inside each cable.

Val twisted the two red wires together. "When you get to the far end, just connect each pair of wires, red twisted to black," she said.

I needed to trust her on this. "How far up the cable do I go?" I asked.

"Three hundred and six meters, or three hundred and forty-six yards," she said. "Approximately. But try to get it as accurate as you can, because we don't have much battery power, and we can't afford much signal degradation."

Easier said than done. I knew my splayed hand spanned nine inches between thumb and pinky—it was my built-in ruler. I measured out four hand-spans on the bail-out bottle's tubing. Then I headed up the stairs, using the tubing to measure my way yard by yard along the cables.

I took my time, knowing I had to get it right. Once I was afraid I had lost track of my numbers, and twice I banged my head on the low overhangs. But after crawling my way up the tunnel, I found the three hundred and forty-sixth yard was about ten feet short of the rock pile.

I hesitated before I cut the cable. This was our last possible link to the outside. But we'd need to call for help if we couldn't force our way out, and George and Sue weren't capable of digging.

I sliced through the cables and stripped the wires down. I twisted together each pair, then cut two small sections off the tubing and shoved them over the bare wires. Then I crept back down the tunnel.

fifty-five

SUE LOOKED UP AS I came over. She had a big smile on her face. "He's awake," she said.

I knelt down next to George. "Hey, you really scared us," I said.

"I'm still scared." He gave me a tired smile. "Especially for Mr. Morgan. And Flora and the twins, of course."

"Me too," I said.

"Sue told me what you did, and I appreciate it, Scott."

I patted his shoulder. "You'd do the same for me."

"You betcha." He raised his hand and slowly flexed it. "Val says you two are rigging up an LF antenna."

I nodded. "Does anybody in Sterling still listen in on the low end of the spectrum, or did you guys go totally digital?"

"We have two offices who never upgraded—Tibet and Siberia," he said. "Sterling keeps the scanners on for the odd message coming from them." His voice had faded, and I had to lean in to catch his words.

"Low frequencies will reach all the way to Sterling?" I asked.

"They will," Val said. "That's why submarines, airplanes, and boats use them. They're even better than short wave, because their waves are ground-hugging."

"You're going with a quarter-wavelength antenna?" George asked her.

Val nodded. "That's all the wire we have. We'll have to use the ground to reflect the other quarter."

"Will that work?" I asked. I knew next to nothing about antennas.

"It will, but usually only when the antenna is vertical," George said. "Since we're underground, we'll have to hope there's not too much feedback."

"We can make a balun to cut out the noise," Val said.

She smiled when he saw my perplexed look. "You've seen the magnet rings on some computer cables, right?" she asked.

I nodded. "My old keyboard had one. That's a balun?"

She nodded. "Balun is short for balance-unbalance," she said. "The radio is expecting an unbalanced signal over coax, and that long monopole antenna you made is balanced. We can unbalance it by wrapping its close end around a magnet before we hook it up."

"Where will you get a magnet?" Sue asked.

I snapped my fingers. "Speakers have magnets—inside the underwater headphones."

Val nodded. "We can use the facemasks. Bring every magnet you can."

I retrieved the four facemasks and unsnapped the headphones. I sliced the speakers open with my dive knife and extracted a pill-shaped magnet from each earpiece. Then I brought the eight magnets to Val.

She stacked the magnets and wrapped eight loops of wire around the resulting cylinder. Then she pointed at the cart rails. "Attach the other end to the rails as a ground," she said.

I took my dive knife and slid the blade between one of the spikes and the rail's lip. I sawed it back and forth as I blew out the rust particles. Then I folded over the exposed black wire from the end of Val's makeshift antenna and jammed it into the de-rusted space.

Val shoved her end of the wire into the hole in the middle of the external antenna port on the base communicator. "We have an antenna," she said.

"Now let's hope the batteries last," George said. He still lay on his back with his feet propped on the rebreather. He motioned for the microphone, and Sue stretched the cord and handed it to him. He looked at each of us, and then he gave us a grin. "Relax—it'll work."

"That's my Georgie," Sue said. "Always positive."

Val turned on the communicator. A loud buzz came out of the speakers, and she frowned and turned it off.

"It's still too balanced," George said.

Val scratched her head. "I must have miscalculated. I think I need at least a meter of wire on the balun." She pulled on the antenna to make some slack, then replaced the existing eight loops with thirty new closely-spaced ones.

"That should do it," she said. She turned on the communicator. This time only a low hum came out. She smiled and gave a thumbs-up.

George pulled the microphone up to his mouth and keyed it on. "This is Soul Identity, identifier three-one-seven, calling over a temporary and insecure channel. Does anybody read me?" He released the microphone button.

We all strained to hear anything more than the low hum.

George pointed to the display. "The battery is low, so I hope they're not on a coffee break." After a minute, he repeated his message.

The line crackled, and then we heard a voice. "Go ahead, three-one-seven. Soul Identity HQ reads you loud and clear."

We all broke out big smiles. Sue reached out and rubbed George's arm, and Val and I hugged each other.

George keyed the microphone. "Three-one-seven, requesting remote authentication. Challenge is this—my first name." He closed his eyes and said to us, "we have to make sure these are the good guys."

After ten seconds the voice returned. "Three-one-seven, your first name is George. What can we do for you?"

"We have a level five emergency. A team of unfriendlies attacked us with deadly force. The EO and the three non-members are now hostages, and eight-oh-four, two others, and I are trapped in a mine. We are wounded, and we need medical assistance as soon as you get the EO to safety."

Silence except for the hum. George let his microphone hand fall to his chest. "We just sent them into hyperdrive," he whispered.

A minute later the voice came back. "Three-one-seven, I escalated to Mr. Berringer and Ms. Blake. They are headed to the communications center, and I'll patch you through in ninety seconds."

"Thanks, HQ," George said. He keyed the microphone again. "While we wait, can you pull up an infrared sat image of our location?"

"I'll get it ready, but I'll need the DEO's authorization before pointing the bird."

"You'll have it." George turned his head to look at Sue. "Anything else?" he asked her.

"Activate Mr. Morgan's tracking device," she said.

George nodded. "You catch that, Sterling?"

"Affirmative. Stand by for the patch. It should be less than sixty seconds. You hang in there, three-one-seven."

"Thanks."

I thought I could clear something up while we waited for Berry and Ann. "Are you two ex-CIA?" I asked.

Sue smiled. "No, Scott. We cross-trained with the FBI and NSA, but never with the CIA."

"That we know of, at least," George said.

The radio crackled. "George? Sue? Ann and I are here," Berry said. "What's going on?"

Sue grabbed the microphone from George. "A hostile group of what we think are neo-Nazis kidnapped Mr. Morgan, Flora, and the twins, and trapped the rest of us inside the mine. We neutralized five of them. We need your authorization to grab some satellite images, and to enable Mr. Morgan's tracking device."

"Authorization granted."

"HQ, point the bird," Sue said.

"Roger that," the voice from the communications center said. "We're acquiring the site now. We're using the coordinates from your last tracked position at one eight hundred Zulu."

"Patch the image up to the communications center," Ann said.

"Should be just a minute, ma'am."

Berry came back on. "Sue, are you okay? How are Scott and Val?"

"George and I were both in the line of fire, but we're stabilized, sir. Val and Scott are shaken but operative. Get Mr. Morgan and then worry about us."

"Image coming through now, Mr. Berry."

"What are we looking at?" Ann asked.

"Let me zoom in…there. It appears there are seven people. Four are inside a vehicle. Mr. Morgan's transmitter has been activated…give me a second to overlay…there. He's the one with the blinking green dot."

"He's in the vehicle," Berry said.

"Affirmative. Those white spots on your screen appear to be some sort of campfire."

"So they're right outside the mine?" George asked.

"At least Mr. Morgan is. And I can confirm he's still alive, with a slightly above-normal heart rate, and a body temperature of ninety-nine point five."

"Do we have any other assets in the area?" Sue asked.

"Checking, eight-oh-four," said the operator. After a minute he returned. "The closest team is four hours away. In Budapest."

"Mr. Berringer, I recommend authorizing their deployment," Sue said. "We don't know the hostiles' intentions."

"I agree, Sue," Berry said. "Ann?"

"I concur," Ann said.

"Authorized," Berry said. "Get them out there, and keep us informed."

"Roger that, Mr. Berringer, we will—"

"Hold on, what's happening?" Ann cried. "What are they doing to him?"

"What do you see, Ms. Blake?" Sue asked.

Berry jumped in. "It looks like they've pulled the four out of the car and toward the fire. Now they're, oh God, somebody hit Mr. Morgan, and he's fallen down."

Val came and stood by me, and I put my arm around her.

"Those bastards are still hitting him!" Ann said. "Operator, how is he?"

"Increased heart rate, rapid breathing—"

"They stopped," Berry said. "Now somebody's picking him up and…"

We waited.

"The four are back in the car," Berry said. "Mr. Morgan is slumped over."

"Is he okay?" Sue asked.

"He's alive, but it seems he's fallen unconscious, eight-oh-four. His heart rate and breathing have dropped to low levels, and—"

The voice was cut off, and I noticed that the hum in the line was gone.

Val walked over to the radio. "The battery is dead," she said after a minute.

"We're cut off." Sue slumped back on the ground. "It's up to the Budapest team now."

"I hope they hurry," George whispered.

fifty-six

Present Day
Dubnik Mine, Slovakia

AFTER SITTING FOR TEN minutes with my arms around Val and listening to George moan in his pain and Sue weep in her frustration, I stood up and walked around the gallery. I pointed my wrist light into the shadows by the stairs and walls.

"Are you looking for something?" Val asked.

"Yeah. The four dead guys. Where could they be?"

Sue blew her nose and said, "I shot them as they reached the top of the stairs. They fell over the side, close to where you are. Can't you see them?"

I walked over into the shadowed corner and found them. I played the beam of my light over the twisted bodies of four young men. They each lay face down. Their hair was cropped short. Each of their green uniforms had a large blood-rimmed exit hole in the middle of the back. "Found them," I called.

"Are they all dead?" Sue asked.

"They're not moving."

"Could you make sure?"

Great. I dropped to my knees and felt the neck of the one on the bottom of the pile. His skin felt cold, and I could detect no pulse. Same with the two middle ones.

But the guy on top felt warmer. And when I grabbed his shoulders and turned him over, his blue eyes caught mine and darted away. I looked down. He held a pistol, and he had it pointed at my head.

I dove to the right just as he fired. Then I kicked at where I hoped his chest was.

The soldier let out a faint cry, and I spun around and grabbed at the pistol. The barrel was hot, and I struggled to hang on to it and point it up and not at me.

He fired again, and I winced as the flame from the barrel burned my hands. But the bullet whined over my head, and I climbed on top of him and forced his arm further back, pushing as hard as I could.

His other hand grabbed at my face, and I bit his thumb. He yelled and tried to pull back, but I had become a bulldog. I ground down until I felt my teeth slice through his knuckle.

He screamed and jerked his hand away, leaving me with the top joint of his thumb and a mouthful of blood. I spat it onto his face and pushed harder on his arm. He fired again, but I had his arm back far enough that the bullet slammed into one of the bodies with a thud.

One last push, but somehow he jerked free and swung his arm back. I tried to twist the pistol before he could shoot, and then I felt a third pair of hands grab at it. I pulled, but it slipped out of my grasp, leaving me holding the man's empty hands.

Another shot, and the body beneath me convulsed once, twice, and then went still. I swung my wrist light around. Its beam caught Val dropping the pistol.

"I thought you were dead," she said. She wrapped her arms around me and kissed me hard.

"You saved me," I said. "Again." I squeezed her tightly, and we rocked back and forth on the pile of bodies.

After a minute we helped each other stand up. I flicked on my wrist light and cringed when I saw the bullet hole in the man's forehead.

"How'd you know you weren't shooting me?" I asked.

"His hair," she said. "It's a buzz cut, and it's much thicker than yours." She picked up the pistol and stuck it in the waist of her jeans.

I searched through the bodies and pulled out a knife and two more pistols. We walked back to George and Sue with our arms around each other.

George looked up. "Val flew like a bat out of hell when that first shot was fired."

"She saved my life." Then something hit me. "Wait a minute…did you say bat?"

George gave me a blank look. Then he smiled. "Bats." He let out a chuckle, then grimaced. "Don't make me laugh," he said.

"What's so funny?" Sue asked.

He turned to her. "Where are the bats, Sue?"

She shrugged. "Far away, I hope. I hate bats."

He smiled. "I'll ask you again, my dear. Where are those lovely, beautiful, friendly Euro-bats?"

Then Val snapped her fingers. "If we find the bats—"

"Then we'll find our way out," Sue finished. "I guess I don't hate Slovakian bats."

"The diving rentals guy told me they bricked up the end of the tunnel to keep the bats out of the gallery," George said. "Right past the staircase."

"So we can break through that wall and fly out," Sue said.

"There's only one problem," Val said. "We have no tools."

"Let's go and look," I said as I got to my feet. "Maybe a brick is loose."

Val and I climbed the stairs, and instead of turning left and up the tunnel to the blockage, we turned right and faced a bricked-up wall.

Val traced the edges with her light. "It looks pretty solid."

I ran my fingers over the wall, looking for either a loose stone or a crack in the mortar. The joints were tight. I planted my foot against the bottom center of the wall. "Let's see how strong it is," I said. I stepped back and kicked, but the wall didn't budge. I kicked again and again, not stopping until pains shot up my leg.

Then we tried slamming our bodies into the wall a few times, but when nothing happened, we slumped down and caught our breaths.

"We're so close," Val said.

I closed my eyes. "I wonder if this is how Old Ned felt when he was stuck in the chute."

She reached out and grabbed my hand. "You really connected with him, didn't you?"

"I did," I said. "And I can't wait to get the rest of his story into my soul line collection. He needs more than that letter."

"He had more than a letter—we read his story about the cave-in."

That triggered something, and I looked up and smiled. "We sure did—Ned told us how he and Raddy escaped!"

Val straightened up. "They dug to another tunnel, didn't they?" She banged on the wall with her fist. "Just like we need to do."

"But they had picks," I pointed out.

"And we don't."

I smiled.

She looked at me. "You have a pick?"

I shook my head. "Ned only left me a hammer."

She stared at me as if she thought I had gone off the deep end. "You left it in your soul line collection, Scott."

"Not the hammer—he took his pick into the opal nest."

She slumped back. "You're going to go there after all."

I nodded. "We need the pick, and we need to help everybody else."

"Nobody but Flora's grandfather has survived that nest, Scott," she said. She grabbed both of my hands. "We just have to wait the four hours until we're rescued."

"George may not last four hours without medical assistance," I said. "And from what we heard on the radio, Archie, Madame Flora, and the girls won't either."

She sighed. "Is this your fight, Scott? Do you care enough for them that you would die to save them?"

That brought me up short. "Of course I do—don't you?"

After staring at me for a long minute, she spoke with measured words. "I do. I'm over helping Flora save her damn gold, but certainly I would die trying to save Rose and Marie. It's not our fight, but it's not theirs, either."

That summed up exactly how I felt. "And they need our help," I added.

"They do," she said. "I'll come with you."

"Are you sure?" I asked.

"I'm sure." She stood up and offered me her hand. "Besides, we both know you'll never get down that chute without me."

fifty-seven

OVER GEORGE AND SUE'S protests, Val and I suited up for yet another dive. Val used Marie's suit and Rose's rebreather.

We checked and rechecked our equipment. I knew we needed to be quick—our tanks were almost empty and the rebreathers' scrubbers were almost full, so we didn't have enough oxygen for a long decompression. We walked through our dive sequence several times. Val and I agreed that if we didn't find the picks right away, we'd return and sit with George and Sue and wait to be rescued by the Budapest team.

And then, right after we filled our suits with the remaining argon, I froze as I remembered we had yanked out the headphones to make our balun. Val wasn't going to be able to sing me through the tight spots. I turned to her and frowned. "The headphones are gone."

She grabbed my hand. "You'll have to remember what I sound like when you need it."

I nodded. I already knew how bad the panic attacks got. I'd make it.

Our facemasks felt a little funny with the earphones cut out, but the fit seemed tight, and we slid underwater.

This final dive was no scenic trip. We descended quickly down the shaft. Val's gloved hand gripped mine as we passed the body of the drowned soldier in a gruesome embrace with the winch cables.

Then we reached the tunnel. We swam into the alcove where the gold had lain. Val grabbed the light we had left, and we swam over the stonework strewn on the floor from where we had pulled down the wall.

We reached the second alcove, and I grabbed the other light from the ceiling. Val helped me open the trap door, and we pulled ourselves hand over hand down the fifty foot ladder.

I wrestled out the wooden plug at the bottom of the shaft. Then I looked at Val. She gave me a thumbs-up, tethered me to her with a nylon leash, and followed me into the chute.

Once again it was tight and full of silt. I scrunched my eyes shut and gritted my teeth and rode my way through the panic. I scraped myself against the sides, but after the first twenty feet, the chute widened out and the silt settled down. I could see both Val behind me and the walls for a few feet in front of me.

We followed the chute a hundred yards or so. My dive computer said we had descended to 150 feet. We had only another two minutes to find the picks.

The chute ended in a gaping hole on the wall of another gallery. The water was crystal clear, undisturbed for sixty-four years. From the entrance we could peer into the opal nest that first Raddy and then Ned and Dieter had found. It was a beauty: twenty feet high and twice as deep. The opals embedded in the walls caught our light's beams and threw back shimmering greens, blues, and reds. I could see what had driven the men crazy.

But this was no time for opal hunting. Val and I pointed our lights at the floor. We were hesitant to descend the twenty feet to the bottom, so we floated around close to the ceiling and searched below us.

Val grabbed my arm and pointed with her light. I added my own beam, and we saw a skeleton crumpled in the corner. That would be Dieter, I guessed: the flood he had caused would have scattered the older bones of Raddy's fellow miners.

We descended to the skeleton. I brushed back some decayed clothing, and there it was: the pick-axe. The handle had snapped and come loose, but the metal head seemed solid. Mission accomplished—I grabbed the head and pointed Val toward the surface.

She shook her head and pointed to the far wall, where the largest opals shone. Some of them were set neatly in a pile.

Was she crazy? We had neither the time nor the oxygen to retrieve the opals. I pointed to the tube and pumped my arm for emphasis.

She unleashed herself and swam to the corner. But she brushed the opals aside and picked up a hammer that must have been lying there for a century. Then she grabbed two golf ball-sized opals and pointed upward.

We ascended through the dive computer's beeps. I re-plugged the hole to the chute, followed the ladder up, folded down the trap door, and swam up the tunnel, past the stonework, around the drowned neo-Nazi, and up the shaft to fifteen feet.

We had ten minutes of decompression time remaining when we checked the rebreathers. Val's was fine, but when she saw mine she spun me around and ripped loose the bail-out bottle strapped to her leg.

My tank must have been empty. I plugged the hose into the bypass and switched over. After ten more minutes we ascended to the surface.

We climbed out of the water and helped each other remove the rebreathers.

Val started to unzip her suit, but then she stopped. "I'm just about worn out," she said. "Can you help with this?"

I knew how she felt. My muscles ached, and my knees and hips felt like somebody had pounded knitting needles through them. "We're almost done," I said as I tugged on her zipper.

We peeled off our suits and got dressed. Val put the two opals in her pocket. I gathered up the pick-axe head and the hammer, and we headed over to George and Sue.

Sue looked up. "Any luck?"

I nodded. "We found the old tools. How's George?"

"He's out again." She stared at me and bit her lip. "He needs help soon, or else…"

Val reached out to her, and the two shared a quick hug. "We'll make it, Sue," she said, "Just hang on."

fifty-eight

VAL WEDGED THE BLADE of the pick-axe into a hairline crack she had found in the wall. I swung the hammer at the pick, but instead of widening the crack, the blade turned, and Val yelped as her fingers smashed into the wall for the eighth or ninth time.

This was supposed to be the easy part. We were tired and making stupid mistakes.

Val repositioned the pick-axe head, I swung the hammer, and again the axe head bounced out of the crack and twisted.

I dropped the hammer and took the pick-axe head from her. Something wasn't right, and we weren't getting it. I let the axe head drop, and I slid down the wall to the ground.

Val joined me. We slumped together in silence.

Then she looked up. "We busted down the alcove wall yesterday. What's different about this?"

"Our tools," I said. "We had George's hooks."

"But at least they went into the wall when you hammered on them." She picked up the pick-axe head. "This just bounces right out."

I watched as she hefted it. The way the metal was arced between the pick and the blade wasn't helping; most of the force of my swings was deflected downward into Val's hands.

Val sighed. "Too bad old Ned didn't leave you more detailed instructions."

"Too bad he left his hammer and not his mining genes," I said.

Then I thought about that hammer. "If we had a handle on the pick," I said, "we could swing it at the wall instead of making puny little whacks on it with the hammer."

"Maybe you can just swing the hammer into the wall."

I picked up the hammer. Its head was too broad and its handle too short to cause any damage.

But maybe we could do something else. I cleared out the hole in the pick-axe head with my finger. Then I slid the bottom of the hammer's slender handle through the top of the hole, all the way down until the hammer's head sat snug against the top of the axe head.

"Now I can swing the pick-axe," I said.

Val smiled, and we stood up. I held the hammer like it was a tiny baseball bat, and I took a practice swing.

"Hit with the pick side, and not with the axe," she said.

That made sense. I spun the handle around and aimed at a brick at my shoulder height. The pick hit the center of the brick and made a piercing ringing tone, and my hands stung from the handle's vibration. But the brick cracked, and Val and I let out a whoop.

After two more solid strikes, the first wedge of the brick came loose. Val teased it out by wiggling it back and forth, and the next hit sent the rest of the brick's fragments flying.

In only ten minutes we cleared an opening big enough for us to enter. I pulled the hammer and pick apart, shoved the pieces into my belt, and stuck my arm with its wrist light into the hole.

We both peered inside. The tunnel ran straight ahead at a slight incline, and our lights petered out before reaching the end.

"Let's get going," Val said.

"You have the pistols?"

She handed one to me, and I stuck it in my waistband. Then we climbed through the opening and headed up the tunnel.

After fifty yards I stopped. I could hear the bats.

The chirping sounded like a flock of baby birds. We followed it around a corner where the tunnel forked. We took the branch sloping up, toward the chirping.

We climbed a flight of stairs and stood at an opening to a large gallery. Here the bats were much louder. The floor was covered with bat guano.

I aimed my light up toward the roof, and we both cringed when it bounced off hundreds of tiny red eyes. "Let's find the exit," I said.

We walked into the gallery. Our boots sunk through at least six inches of guano and slid along the floor, and I caught Val from falling into the muck. The stench slammed into us, and we both breathed through our mouths. Every now and then a bat would whir around the gallery, and we'd instinctively duck.

We reached a wall at the far end of the gallery. We searched, but we couldn't find an opening.

"There's got to be a way out," I said.

"I don't see it."

"Let's get the bats to help us." I pulled out the pistol.

She screwed up her face. "What are they going to do when you fire?"

"Hopefully fly away, so we can follow them."

She shivered. "What if they attack us?"

"You have a better idea?"

She shook her head and stared at me wide-eyed.

I flipped the safety and glanced at her. She scrunched her eyes closed. Then I fired, and we were engulfed in a maelstrom of flying hairy bodies, leathery wings, and harsh screeches.

fifty-nine

VAL SCREAMED AND CLUTCHED at her hair as the bats whirled around us. My light caught little snapshots of them flying by, their tiny mouths snarling at us, their red eyes turning them into demons. I pulled Val into my arms and shielded her with my body. I ducked my head down next to hers and shouted, "Maybe shooting that pistol was a mistake."

"Can you see the exit?"

I flashed my light around and saw bats disappearing into a hole in the wall, maybe ten feet in front of us and three feet up. A place we had missed. I led Val forward and stopped just to the side of the gap. I marked the edges with my light. The hole was round and three feet wide.

I gave Val a boost and followed her up the tube. The floor was slick with guano, and we crawled up as fast as we could, all the time with the bats screeching and bumping into us in their frenzied dash to exit the gallery.

I felt a warm breeze after a hundred feet, and the beam from my wrist light caught the fog in the air. Another minute later we tumbled out of the tube and onto the side of a hill.

We collapsed on the ground and lay on our backs and gasped for fresh air. We stared up at the black sky. The almost-full moon and some bright stars shone through gaps in the trees above us, and the bats continued to stream out of the hole, screeching as they flew away into the night.

Val turned to me. "Do we go back and get George and Sue first?" she asked.

Good question. If something happened to us as we tried to rescue Archie, Madame Flora, and the twins, the Budapest team would never find their way into the cave in time. George and Sue would die in the gallery.

But spending time rescuing them could give the Nazis a chance to kill their four hostages.

George and Sue were too weak to help us, and getting them first would tire us out and make it even harder to rescue the other four. This meant that our only chance of saving all six was to stop the Nazis on the surface first.

We had to try to save everybody. "First we get the Nazis, and if we survive that, we go back for George and Sue," I said.

She looked at me for a minute before nodding. "I think George and Sue would agree," she said slowly. "They'd insist that we rescue Mr. Morgan before we worry about them."

I felt every muscle ache as we got to our feet.

"Where's the camp?" Val asked.

I pointed up the hill. "Hopefully on the other side of this ridge."

We scrambled up a couple hundred feet to the top. Sticks and leaves stuck to our guano-covered clothes and shoes.

I peeked over the ridge. Our clearing, I could see through gaps in the trees, was only a hundred yards below us.

We headed down the slope, trying our best to move silently. After a few minutes we were above the mine entrance, right behind the tree where Val and I had placed the heartbeat sensor.

We now had an unobstructed view into the clearing. A large black truck stood near the entrance, and George's green van sat parked in the middle. A guard in a soldier's uniform stood by the van's open door and pointed a rifle inside. That meant at least one hostage was alive.

A fire burned in the campfire pit, and next to that stood a boxy but sturdy steel structure. It was two feet tall, and it had a ten foot chimney attached. Another soldier poked a metal rod into a slit on one side of the box. He then worked a set of bellows attached to the opposite side. On top of the box sat a large round pot, its shape reminding me of a dome on an Orthodox church. The twelve barrels were open, scattered around the fire.

The structure resembled a small furnace. "They must be melting the gold bars into something unidentifiable," I said.

Sterling told us there were three bad guys, but we had spotted only two. Then I saw him: a man in a chair on the far side of the fire.

We crept to the edge of the tree line so we could see him better. He sat in a wheelchair, and a blanket covered his lap and hands. Like the others, he wore a green uniform with a large swastika on its shoulder. His head drooped toward his chest, showing sparse and trimmed white hair rimming a large and freckled bald spot.

"That must be the *Untersturmführer*," Val whispered.

I nodded. "I wonder if he's the same one from Madame Flora's story."

"The one with the receipts?"

"It would explain the wheelchair."

Val shook her head. "If it's him, he must be feeling really good right about now—he's finally got his gold back."

Like Madame Flora felt an hour ago. I turned to face Val. "Let's grab him and trade him for our guys."

She wrinkled her nose. "The way we stink? We'll have to stay upwind to catch him."

We crept toward the old man, stopping each time the furnace man turned our way. The guard had his back to us, his rifle still pointed into the green van.

When we drew within twenty feet, we pulled out our weapons and dashed to the man in the wheelchair. Val put her pistol to his temple, and I yanked the blanket off his lap.

The old man jerked awake, but I grabbed the gun from his spotted hands before he could react. I caught his eye and held my finger to my lips. He nodded and threw a glance at his men.

While Val guarded him, I crept around the fire and snuck up on the furnace man. I jumped up and shoved my pistol into his back.

He let out a cry and twisted around. When he saw my weapon, he dropped his poker and put up his hands. I reached into his holster and removed his pistol, and then I motioned Val forward.

Val pushed the wheelchair around the fire and next to me at the furnace.

I looked at the old SS officer. "Do you understand my English?"

He nodded.

"You are the *Untersturmführer*?"

He nodded again.

"You shot two of our team?"

"And I lost five *sturmannen* doing that." His voice was sharp and his accent heavy.

"You blew up the tunnel to trap us inside?"

He nodded. "I see it did not work."

"Apparently not," I said. "You took the gold we just recovered?"

"It is not your gold. It is mine." The words came out in a hiss.

"Hold that thought." I pointed at the van. "Let's make a trade. You for your hostages."

His eyes narrowed. "I will not give up my gold."

"We can talk about the gold later. I want my team back."

He stared at me for a minute. "You should take the gold instead. Your team is weak and not worth the trade."

I tilted my head. "Are they weaker than you?"

His eyes narrowed, but after a moment he called out to the remaining guard.

When the man saw us, he swung his rifle around and pointed it at Val. The *Untersturmführer* shouted instructions at him, and the man lowered the rifle, turned back to the van, and gestured to those inside.

The old man looked at me. "He brings your team."

I nodded, and soon the guard led Archie, Madame Flora, and the twins over to the fire. Their wrists were bound in front of them, their faces were puffy and red, and Archie dragged his right leg behind him. But they smiled when they saw Val's pistol at the old man's head and mine on the furnace man.

The guard stood back and pointed his rifle at Archie.

"You guys okay?" I asked.

Rose nodded. "Did George and Sue…" She swallowed.

"They're hurt, but if we hurry, they'll survive." I looked at the SS officer. "How do you want to do this?"

"All three must lower their weapons at the same time," he said.

"You give your word that you will not harm us?" I asked.

"I do," he said. He looked at me with a steady gaze. "My men follow every order without question."

"Show me," I said.

He spoke to them in German. When they nodded back, he turned to me. "They are ready," he said.

Val and I glanced at each other, then lowered our pistols at the same time the guard lowered his rifle.

Archie let out a groan. "I must sit down, Scott," he said, "before I collapse."

I shoved my pistol into my pocket, then I walked over to him. I put my arm around his shoulder and let him rest against me.

I motioned to the twins. "Can you get some chairs?"

Val untied their arms, and the girls ran to the van. After a minute they returned with two folding chairs. I helped Archie sink into one, and they assisted their grandmother into the other.

As the twins untied Archie and Madame Flora's arms, I watched the old lady shoot glares at the SS officer.

"This is the same man you told us about?" I asked her.

She hissed, "He was supposed to die sixty-four years ago."

The old man smiled. "I almost did, *fraulein*," he said. "But in your haste to escape the barn, you did not finish me off."

"I got the gold," she said. "Even without your papers."

"Now that gold is mine."

"Let's talk about that," I said to him. "Tonight you took it from us." I pointed at Madame Flora. "But she stole it from Soul Identity. Goering stole it from you, and before that, you stole it from your prisoners." I scratched my head. "Now how does that make it yours?"

He stiffened when I mentioned Goering. "The Reichsmarschall, that fat pig—his greed ruined our plans."

"Plans?" I asked. "The war was all but over when he swiped it from you."

"Martin Bormann himself delivered my final assignment," he said. "I was to melt down this gold into unidentifiable bars and deliver them to Spain. And now I intend to complete that mission."

I had read how after the war, a trail of Nazi gold blazed through Spain and Argentina and into the US. "That path's been exposed since the seventies," I said.

He smiled. "My path still awaits my delivery."

It was hard to think of a bunch of octogenarian Nazis patiently waiting to receive this shipment of gold. On the other hand, it wasn't that different from Madame Flora's wait.

I pointed to the furnace. "Why melt the gold?"

"My orders still stand—I must immediately eliminate the swastikas and the Reichsbank serial numbers."

Five iron forms lay halfway between the furnace and the black truck. "You're re-casting it?" I asked.

He nodded. "We shall make twenty-five golden Buddhas, each weighing thirty-six kilograms."

"And you'll smuggle the Buddhas to Spain?" I asked.

"No smuggling is necessary." He smiled. "I have a license to deliver gold-painted religious artifacts anywhere in the E.U."

They had certainly thought things through.

George and Sue were jammed for time. I turned to Archie and said, "We have to get George to a hospital—he won't last much longer." I pointed at the guards. "These two could help us get them out."

The old man looked at me. "Your teammates survived?"

I nodded.

"They told me they killed them." He spat on the ground. "These young *sturmannen* make me miss the efficiency of the old days."

I suppressed a shudder.

He shot a frown at his guards. "My men can help you."

In exchange for what? I looked at him and raised my eyebrows.

He pointed at the furnace. "I help you, and you leave me the gold."

I looked over and saw Archie biting his lip. "Are you fine with this?" I asked.

Archie stared at me for a minute. Then he nodded. "George and Sue are worth more than any gold," he said.

I turned to Madame Flora. She sat with her head bowed, and she clenched and unclenched her hands. She grimaced, but then she nodded.

I waited for her to speak.

"Get George and Sue," she muttered. "My quest is over, and I did my best. Now save our friends." She smiled and wiped her eyes.

She had grown. At that moment I was insanely proud of Madame Flora. I fought a lump forming in my throat as I faced the *Untersturmführer.* "You have a deal. Help us rescue our team, and you can take the gold."

He seemed to struggle to hide his smile. He barked another order to his men, listened to their reply, and turned to us.

"My *sturmannen* are ready to help," he said.

Now for the delicate part.

I knelt down between Archie and Madame Flora. "The four of you are going to have to remain his hostages for a little longer," I said.

"Why is that?" Madame Flora asked sharply.

"So he knows his own men are safe," Archie said. He reached out and grabbed her hand. "He will not shoot us."

Archie was partially right. The old man would need both of his men to get the gold out. But the real reason I was giving him the gun was to prevent Madame Flora from killing him. "You'll be safe until his men are back on the surface," I said.

Madame Flora sighed.

I glanced at the SS officer and dropped my voice so only Archie and Madame Flora could hear me. "We got through to Ann and Berry," I said. "Whether or not we make it back, the Budapest team will be here in less than three hours."

Archie let a thin smile cross his lips.

I turned to the twins. "Girls, can you keep your grandparents out of trouble?"

"Of course," Marie said.

I looked for Val, and saw her sitting on the ground. Her knees were drawn to her chest, and she rocked back and forth with her eyes closed. I went over and put my arm around her. "Are you okay?" I asked.

She shivered. "I keep thinking about how I shot that soldier in his forehead."

"He would have killed me if you didn't," I said. I pulled her into an embrace and held her as she buried her face in my chest. "You want to stay here on top?"

She shook her head. "And think about what I did? I'd rather keep myself busy. And you need my protection from the Nazis."

The *Untersturmführer* would hold our four teammates hostage, and Val and I would hold his two soldiers hostage. A truce balanced with threats.

I returned the pistol to the *Untersturmführer*. "If anybody up here is harmed, your men die," I said loud enough for everybody to hear.

The old man took the gun from me and pointed it at Archie. "Hurry back and your team will live."

Rose handed me a small knapsack. "Take this with you," she said. "That's water, chocolate, granola bars, four flashlights, and some serious painkillers. Good luck down there."

I hoisted the knapsack onto my back, then led Val and the two Nazis up the ridge.

sixty

WE SPENT A HALF hour climbing back over the ridge and to the bat entrance. We stopped for water and granola bars outside the entrance, and I explained the tunnel's layout to the Nazis.

The guard spoke a little English. "Why do you go back for your team?" he asked. "Isn't it a sign of weakness to save the fallen?"

"Not all of us come from your good, strong Aryan stock," I said.

The thought seemed to cheer him up, which was good, as he was about to see his four buddies, all prime examples of Aryan stock, lying dead in the Viliam gallery.

Val led the way down the chute and into the bat room. The soldiers came next, and I pulled up the rear. We walked down the sloping tunnel, then we squeezed through the hole Val and I had smashed through the brick wall.

The stairs were dark, and our flashlights didn't carry far. I turned to the rifle guard. "Your men's bodies lie in that corner," I said.

He nodded. "We were here when the bitch shot them." He spoke in German to his companion. Neither of them even looked in that direction.

Val and I hurried over to where we had left George and Sue. We shook them awake and helped them drink some water and eat some chocolate. I gave them each two hydrocodone tablets.

"We traded away the gold to get the Nazis to help us carry you out," I said.

"Flora let you give away her gold?" George's skin was gray again, and his voice was faint.

"She was almost happy to do it," Val said.

He smiled. "You hear that, Sue? They think we're worth at least twenty-five million bucks."

"Maybe you can ask for a pay raise," Sue said, and they both chuckled.

I motioned the two soldiers over. "We need your help carrying our teammates," I said.

The rifle guard nodded. "We make a sling with the diving suit, *ja?*"

"Good idea," I said. We tied each of my suit's arms to its corresponding leg. This made two loops. Then we slid one loop over George's shoulders and slipped his arms through it.

We lifted George to a sitting position. The rifle guard squatted behind him, back to back, and positioned the other loop under his arms. He stood up with a grunt and lifted George onto his back. The other guard grabbed George's legs and set them on his shoulders. Then they turned and carried George up the stairs.

"Do you think you can ride piggy-back?" I asked Sue.

She nodded.

I handed the knapsack to Val, and I backed over to Val's rebreather. Val helped Sue climb on top of it, and then Sue got onto my back. She gasped as I grabbed her legs and wrapped them around me.

We stumbled our way out of the cave for the last time. Val lit the path and guided us when we couldn't see, and we all helped pass George and Sue through the small hole in the brick wall. The final guano-filled chute was tough, but with one person pushing and another pulling, we got everybody out of the bat hole and onto the ridge in less than an hour.

We took a break and ate the rest of the chocolate and granola bars. Then we carried George and Sue over the ridge and down into the clearing.

Rose and Marie met us at the bottom of the hill, right next to the now-blocked mine entrance. "We called for an ambulance, but they said it would be two more hours," Rose said.

"The hospital suggested we drive ourselves—it's only twenty minutes away." Marie pointed to the green van. "We've already got the directions, so if you can help us load George and Sue into the back, we'll take them down straightaway."

"Is everybody going?" Val asked.

They shook their heads. "Grandma's not leaving the gold," Rose said, "and Mr. Morgan's not leaving Grandma."

"Damn right I'm not leaving," Madame Flora said. She and Archie had walked over to see George and Sue.

"Then we'll stay with you," I said to her. I took the pistol back from the *Untersturmführer* and carried Sue over to the green van. I grabbed my mobile phone from the luggage, and I put the pistol in the glove compartment. Then we helped buckle in George and Sue. The twins sped out of the clearing, leaving Val and me with Archie, Madame Flora, and the three Nazis.

I powered up my mobile phone and called Berry and Ann.

"When your radio conked out, we thought the worst had happened," Berry said. "But the twins called us an hour ago, and now we see the van is on the way to the hospital."

"You're still watching us on satellite?" I asked, looking up.

Ann laughed. "We had front row seats when you and Val climbed the ridge and surprised the men around the fire."

"Of course, we didn't know it was you and Val," Berry said. "Not until the girls called and we spoke to Mr. Morgan."

"How far away is the Budapest team?" I asked.

"Another hour or so. They can help you liberate Flora's gold."

"It's not hers anymore," I said. "I traded that gold for the Nazi's help carrying George and Sue out of the mine."

Silence for a moment. Then Ann said, "Scott, it's worth a lot of money. You traded all of it?"

"All of it." I said firmly. "George and Sue saved our lives, killed five of the bad guys, and helped us build a radio so we could contact you. We all would have died without their sacrifice."

Silence again. Then I heard Berry clearing his throat. "We weren't arguing about George and Sue's value, Scott. We're just wondering if we could renegotiate once our Budapest team arrives."

"I gave them my word, dammit."

"Scott, they're Nazis," Ann said. "They'll use that gold to promote hate, even kill people with it."

I thought about that. I sure didn't want to help spread racism and hatred, but I had needed to save George and Sue, and giving up the gold for their lives made sense.

In hindsight, my decision looked like yet another example of making the wrong decision for the right reasons. Was I entitled to trade the gold for others' lives? And even if I was entitled, was I obligated to keep my word to a bunch of killers?

It was my word I had given, and not anybody else's. I had told the old Nazi officer that he could take the gold, and reneging on my word, no matter how rashly given, was not an option.

I hung up the phone and stuck it in my pocket. Somebody—maybe even everybody—would be unhappy with this decision.

sixty-one

Present Day
Dubnik Mine, Slovakia

GOLD IS HEAVY: A tiny half-gallon milk jug full of the stuff weighs eighty pounds. That was about the size of each of the million dollar Buddhas the old Nazi planned to make.

Gold melts at a thousand degrees Centigrade, and that was why the soldier had been stoking the furnace, and why the furnace had a ten foot stovepipe attached: it takes the combination of a high density carbon charcoal and a draft-inducing tall stovepipe to coax a furnace to produce that temperature.

The old SS officer explained all this to us while we waited for the gold to finish melting. He showed how he had attached the crucible to the furnace's frame with a set of ratcheted hinges, allowing the gold to be poured into the cast-iron Buddha molds.

"Won't the molds melt?" Val asked.

"Iron doesn't melt until fifteen hundred degrees," the old man said. He motioned the furnace man to get one of the molds, and he showed us the built-in funnel at the top. "We fill the mold with molten gold, and then we immerse it in water to cool."

The soldier inserted a large wooden handle into the side of the furnace's frame. He cranked the handle around three times, and the crucible tilted a half-inch toward the old Nazi's wheelchair.

"Each crank will pour out fifty-one milliliters of gold. That's one kilogram per crank," the SS officer said. "Thirty-six turns for each Buddha."

The guard stepped forward. He wore what looked like a pair of silvery oven mitts. He grasped the Buddha mold in his hands and set it on the edge of the furnace. Then he nodded at the furnace man.

The furnace man cranked the handle, and we could see the molten gold glowing bright orange and red.

"No swastikas left now," I said.

Archie and Madame Flora came over to watch as the soldier turned the crank enough to bring the molten gold right to the crucible's edge. A nod from the Nazi captain in the wheelchair, another turn of the crank, and the first few tablespoons of gold dribbled through a slot in crucible's lip and fell into the Buddha mold.

The old Nazi let out a cackle, and the soldier turned the crank another thirty-five times. The Buddha mold was full, and the rifle man wrapped a pair of sturdy tongs around its funnel. The two hefted the mold off the furnace and over to the barrel of water. They dropped it in, and we heard a loud hiss. A small cloud of steam roiled off the surface. The guard grabbed the next Buddha mold and brought it to the furnace.

It took ten minutes for the two men to fill the five molds and drop them into the barrel. When they were finished, they climbed in the black truck and backed it close to the furnace.

Val pointed at the barrel. "Why isn't the water boiling?"

"Specific heat," the old man said. He glanced at his watch. "Gold cools thirty-three times faster than water heats. They will reach equilibrium at fifty degrees in nine more minutes."

Fifty degrees Centigrade was one hundred twenty-two degrees Fahrenheit. The men would be able to reach into the barrel and pull out the molds without burning their hands.

"You know an awful lot about gold," I said.

"I've had sixty-four years to learn everything there is to know about gold." He stared at me. "Do you know a single ounce of gold can be stretched into a wire over eleven kilometers long?"

"If you know so much, then you know where that gold came from." Madame Flora stepped next to me. She held her hands behind her back.

The old man turned to her. "Of course I do."

"Yet you dare abscond with it?" she asked.

He straightened his shoulders and barked, "It is my duty!"

"That's all I've ever heard you men say about this gold—it's your *duty* to take it from me." She swung out her arms and pointed a pistol at him. "That gold belonged to victims you had no right to kill. You have no valid claim to it."

Madame Flora must have pulled the pistol out of the glove compartment in the van before the twins left. The Nazis were still inside the black truck: she had timed this well.

The old man sneered at her. "That gold, *fraulein*, was stripped from our enemies by me and my men to keep the Third Reich afloat during the war."

"One of those enemies you stripped was my father," Madame Flora said. She flipped off the pistol's safety. "You may have ripped the gold from his body, but you lost it to me over sixty years ago." Her voice rose to a scream "I will not let you take it back!"

"We had a deal," he said to me.

"We did," I replied. I turned to Madame Flora. "What are you trying to do?"

"Recover my gold." Her voice was firm, and the pistol didn't quiver in her hands.

I watched out of the corner of my eye as Val grabbed Archie's arm and led him back toward the tree line. "You're going to get us killed," I said. I pointed to the black truck, backed up at the furnace. "What about the other two Nazis?"

"You'll have to stop them before they shoot us," she said.

I sighed and reached into my pocket. "Damn it, Madame Flora, why—"

Just as I pulled out my pistol, the two men hopped out of the truck and aimed their rifles at Madame Flora and me.

I pointed my pistol at the soldier aiming at me. "I've got this weird sense of déjà vu," I said to the Nazi captain.

"I have it too," he said. He called in German to his men, and they walked our way, keeping their rifles trained on us. In a minute they stood next to the furnace, about three feet away from their captain. Their rifles stayed pointed at me and Madame Flora.

I locked eyes with my soldier, and I spoke to the old man. "It takes two men to pour the gold—you can't afford to lose another soldier." It wasn't much in the way of bargaining power, but it was all I had.

He looked at me and sighed. "*Ja*, we are at an impasse."

I was happy he recognized that.

I shifted my aim to the other soldier as I spoke to Madame Flora. "You agreed to let the Nazis have the gold if they helped us save George and Sue."

"But we can't let them take it, Scott," she said. "I'd rather die than give it up."

"But you already gave it up," I said. "An hour ago." I took a deep breath and risked a glance at her. "Even if you're willing to die for it, I'm not," I said.

Silence for a minute. Then, with a cry, she swung her pistol away from the old man and pointed it at my chest. "You promised to help me recover my gold!"

"I did," I said quietly.

"And you dare give it away?" she snarled.

With her pistol pointing at me, we were in serious danger of the Nazis shooting both of us. I swung my pistol and pointed it at the *Untersturmführer* to dampen their enthusiasm. "We spent the gold to save George and Sue," I told her, "because people are more important than things."

Out of the corner of my eye, I watched Val and Archie creep from the woods and head for the black truck. Nobody else noticed; they were focused on Madame Flora.

She kept her pistol trained on my chest, a tear forming in the corner of each eye. "How could you betray me?" she cried.

I took a step backward, hoping to keep everybody looking at us and not at Val and Archie, who I could see climbing into the truck's open doors. "Is it really your sense of justice that's driving you right now?" I asked Madame Flora.

Her face tightened. "What else would it be?"

I shrugged. "Maybe it's guilt. Or regret."

She raised the pistol from my chest to my head. "Guilt from what? I didn't steal the gold—they did."

It's not easy staying rational around a crazy old lady who's pointing a pistol at your head. "Maybe you're sorry that you couldn't save your father," I said. "Or your grandmother. Or Ned. Or James. Maybe you're thinking little Jamie would have enjoyed getting to know his father."

"How dare you presume to understand my motives?" Her voice trembled.

"I'd like to understand," I said. "Do you really think if you get your gold trust established, it will somehow make up for your past mistakes?"

Her eyes flashed. "Stick with your day job, Scott, and stop trying to analyze me. I'm warning you."

I pointed at her pistol. "Why are you aiming that thing at me?"

"Because you turned against me—you tricked me out of my gold."

"We spent your gold to save the lives of those willing to die for your cause—who were shot through no fault of their own," I said. "Isn't that exactly how you said you wanted to spend it?"

We stood silently for another minute, glaring at each other.

I pointed with my free hand at the old SS officer. "These miserable old Nazis are not worth dying for."

We stood for what seemed forever. Finally she nodded and lowered her pistol. "You're right, Scott. They're not worth dying for." She wiped her eyes and put on a small smile. "I am so sorry."

I took a step toward her, and she half fell, half collapsed into me. I hugged her with my free arm while I kept my pistol trained on the old man.

She squeezed me back fiercely. "Thank you," she whispered.

I kissed her old wrinkled cheek. "You're a tough old bird."

The two soldiers and I lowered our weapons, and they started talking very fast German with the *Untersturmführer*. I patted Madame Flora on the back.

Just then the truck's engine roared. I turned and saw it jerk back and come to rest with its rear bumper against the furnace. Then Val gunned the engine, and the furnace and crucible tilted toward us.

Everything seemed to move in slow motion. I waltzed Madame Flora out of the way. The two soldiers dropped their rifles and pulled back on the old Nazi's wheelchair. When the furnace fell over with a crash and a shower of sparks, we all managed to avoid its path.

The remaining ten gallons of molten gold flowed out of the crucible like red-hot lava out of a volcano. It blazed a path to the center of the fire pit and formed a four foot wide puddle. The fire pit's ashes floated on its orange surface and glowed like hot embers.

The two soldiers scrambled over to the truck doors, but Val and Archie hopped out and pointed their pistols at them. The soldiers raised their hands.

The old Nazi gave a hoarse cry and wheeled himself to the edge of the fire pit. He stared at the glowing gold puddle with his mouth wide open.

I unwrapped my arm from around Madame Flora's waist, and she and I walked to the opposite edge of the fire pit.

I looked toward the truck. The two guards lay face down on the ground. Val and Archie stood over them and trained their pistols at their backs.

The old man glared at Madame Flora, his face twisted in anger. "You people are no more than clumsy animals," he screamed. "The only value you have is your dirty bodies. I remember at Dachau how we froze your kind and then tried to thaw them out. Our leaders thought that intercourse with Gypsy girls was the best way to revive a frozen man, but they were wrong—you people were clumsy even in bed."

Madame Flora stiffened. "You worked on the freezing experiments at Dachau?"

He nodded and spat onto the gold puddle, where it evaporated with a sizzle. "We used our prisoners to our Fuhrer's glory," he said. "Their hands built our weapons. Their bodies taught us how to save our pilots downed in the North Sea. And when we killed them, we sold their clothes, tanned their skins, and extracted their gold to pay for our Reich's food and oil."

Madame Flora marched around the fire pit, turned his wheelchair toward her, and put her hands on the chair's arms. "You tortured men in medical experiments to save your own pilots?" she asked. "You ripped the gold out of their mouths to feed your soldiers?"

"Not men, *fraulein*. Animals." He spat this out. "We exterminated you vermin to purify our country. I made sure we benefited as much as possible."

Madame Flora stared at the old SS officer with wide-open eyes. She shook her finger not six inches from his nose. "Your extermination left me fatherless. My grandmother died of a broken heart because of you."

He pointed right back at her. "You people are all the same. No matter how humanely we treated our inmates, they kept messing things up. They sabotaged the weapons, fooled the guards, and devised countless ways to escape." He spat in her face. "You are one of them, *fraulein*—a good for nothing Gypsy animal who messes up any well-ordered plan."

"I am proud to be one of them!" She let out a cry of fury and launched herself on top of him, her hands wrapped around his neck. The old Nazi fought back by pounding his arms on her back, but his blows seemed weak and ineffectual.

When she finally pulled back, the SS officer took a few heaving breaths. "I hope it was I who killed your father," he hissed, and he spat at her again.

Madame Flora howled. She hooked the arm of the wheelchair and spun it around. She grabbed the handles and shoved the chair right at the puddle of molten gold.

Archie cried, "Flora, no!"

I tried to reach the chair but I wasn't fast enough. The wheels hit the stones surrounding the fire pit, and the chair came to a sudden stop.

The old man must have reached out and grabbed Madame Flora's arm as he was launched out of the chair, because they tumbled together toward the red-hot puddle. They let out wild screams when they landed in it, and their hands sunk in past their wrists. Their clothes burst into flames, and they collapsed face down into the gold. Their bodies writhed for a minute, and then they lay still to our stunned silence.

sixty-two

THE TWO SOLDIERS, ARCHIE, Val, and I stood in a ring around the fire pit as we watched the gold puddle dull from orange to yellow. We had retrieved Madame Flora and the *Untersturmführer* and covered what was left of them with blankets from the back of the black truck. Somehow by mutual consent we all had placed our weapons in a pile next to the fire pit.

Val grabbed my hand. "I was only trying to cause a distraction," she said. "I didn't mean to hurt anybody."

"They hurt themselves," I said. Then I turned to the soldier who spoke some English. "Our friends will arrive soon. You two need to leave now."

He looked at the now-solid puddle of gold and then back at me.

I shook my head. "My deal was with your boss."

He glanced at the barrel containing the five golden Buddhas and let out a sigh.

"Take your furnace and your *Untersturmführer*," I said. "He's got plenty of gold on him."

He spoke in German to the other soldier, and the two loaded the old man's body into their truck. They took their furnace and the iron molds, then they climbed up front and drove out of the clearing.

As soon as they were gone, Archie knelt down next to Madame Flora's body and peeled back the blanket. A thick layer of gold coated her front side, and her bare back was charred where her clothes had burned off.

Archie reached up and stroked her gold-coated face. He mumbled something I couldn't hear.

I knelt down next to him and put my hand on his shoulder. "Are you okay?" I asked gently.

He turned to me and smiled. "I loved her, you know. I always did, right from the first time I saw her."

I nodded and swallowed the lump in my throat.

He traced her cheek with his fingertips. "At least we had the last two days together."

I squeezed his shoulder.

"She killed herself chasing this gold," he said.

"I suppose that chasing it gave her life meaning," I said. "And she showed the strength to give it up at the end."

He nodded.

We knelt in silence for another minute. Then Archie gave another caress to her cheek and pulled the blanket over her body. "Good-bye, my love," he whispered.

Soul Identity's Budapest team arrived in two green vans thirty minutes later. They were efficient in cleaning up the site. Val and I gave them directions to the bat hole, and they retrieved our equipment and the bodies of the five Nazi soldiers. They chopped the now-solid puddle of gold into smaller pieces, and they loaded them and four of the five golden Buddhas into the first van.

We placed Madame Flora's remains into the back of that van. Archie sat next to her body, and Val and I got in front. We left the Budapest team and drove with the gold down to the hospital to see George, Sue, and the twins. I used my mobile phone to call Chief Dara Sabol. I told her to get her police officers to the clearing and recover the five dead Nazis. She stopped questioning me when I mentioned the million dollar golden Buddha we had left as payment for her troubles.

We headed up to the hospital's recovery room. George and Sue had both survived surgery, and both their prognoses were good.

Rose and Marie were understandably shocked at the news of their grandmother's death. Archie, Val, and I spent the next several hours sitting quietly with them, reliving moments from Madame Flora's life.

The girls cried when I told them how she finally relinquished her claim on the gold, then cheered when I related how she stood up to the SS officer's vile comments.

Rose looked at Marie. "Grandma died exactly the way she lived."

Marie nodded back. "Passionate to the end."

epilogue

ARCHIBALD MORGAN, EXECUTIVE OVERSEER of Soul Identity, walked to the podium and adjusted the microphone. "We, the friends and family of Flora Drabarni," he said, "are here to celebrate her life in this memorial service." He gave Rose and Marie a sad smile.

Val and I sat in the front row of the Soul Identity headquarters auditorium in Sterling, Massachusetts. The twins and their mother sat across the aisle on our right. George and Sue sat next to us on our left.

George rested his new cane against his leg and caught my eye. "A little bird told me that Mr. Morgan is making a big announcement," he whispered a little too loudly.

Ann Blake reached forward and swatted him with her program. "Don't ruin the surprise, George."

I turned around to smile at her and Berry, and I saw the auditorium jam-packed with people—more than had come to Bob's centuriat party the year before.

Val and I had just returned from my and Ned's soul line collection in the depositary, where I had placed one of the opals, Ned's Soul Identity card, and my rendering of the story Madame Flora had told. Val decided to keep the other opal as a souvenir of our adventure in Slovakia.

I grabbed her hand as Archie unfolded a small stack of papers, laid them on the podium, and adjusted his glasses. The auditorium went silent, and he cleared his throat and began to read aloud.

"On April 15, 1929, Matko and Anja Drabarni celebrated the birth of their only child, Flora," he said. "This was in the Istrian peninsula of what was then Italy, and is now Croatia. In 1943, Flora and her grandmother Violca, one of our Soul Identity readers, went into hiding after the Nazis sent the rest of their family to a concentration camp. They scavenged in the woods until the war's end, and in 1946 they came at our bidding to Nuremberg. After Flora and Violca helped us conclude a delicate mission, they moved to Sterling."

Val leaned over and whispered in my ear. "Delicate mission?"

"The understatement of the year," I whispered back.

Archie looked around the auditorium. "I see several of you who can remember working here with Flora. She stayed full-time until 1949, and then left to start her own business and become a recruiter for us."

I looked behind me and saw a few older people nod their heads and smile.

Archie cleared his throat. "In 1947, Flora's only child Jamie was born. Some of you may remember Jamie running around our office, and you may even know that Jamie was killed in Vietnam."

More heads nodded. Archie pulled out a handkerchief, then took off and polished his glasses. He resettled them on his face and leaned forward on his elbows. "What you may not know," he said gravely, "is that I am Jamie's father."

For a moment you could have heard a pin drop in the auditorium, but then the air filled with the buzzing of excited whispers.

Archie waited for a moment, his face beaming. Then he chuckled and said, "I was surprised to find out as well, but when Flora broke the news to me last week, I was pleased as punch to meet my new family."

That triggered another round of whispering. He picked up and shuffled his papers. "If I had to pick a single word to describe Flora," he said, "I would choose 'passionate'. Throughout her life, she always knew what she wanted, she was filled with conviction that she was right, and she used her passion to push until she got it."

Archie looked up, and two tears spilled out from under his glasses and ran down his cheeks. "Last month in Slovakia, Flora helped us fix a problem which, to what will be my everlasting shame, I should have prevented six decades ago," he said. He dabbed the tears with his handkerchief. "At the end of the mission, Flora suffered a fatal accident. She was eighty years old. She is survived by her—I mean our—granddaughter Lily and our twin great-granddaughters Rose and Marie."

Archie turned and faced a movie screen behind him. The lights darkened in the auditorium, and pictures from a slide show were projected. We saw photographs of a young Flora with her grandmother, then with Jamie. When a picture of her and the twins came up, George grunted and said, "I took that one in Venice last year. After she shot Andre Feret."

The slide show ended with a picture of Madame Flora standing outside of her palm reading business on Kent Island. She looked exactly like the first time I met her: a stern expression, sparkly eyes, her jaw set in determination.

The image faded, the lights came on, and Archie turned back to face the audience. "When Flora was helping us in Nuremberg, she kept a diary in the form of a fairy tale." He picked up a small stack of papers. "Here is our seventeen-year-old Flora in her own words."

Archie used the translation Val and I had made to read from Flora's short diary. He read the story of the young princess and her fairy godmother, and how her family was killed by evil wolves. He read about the brave knight and how the princess almost got him killed.

Archie's voice cracked, and he stood silently for a moment. Then he read to us how the princess drugged the captain and learned of his love for her.

When Archie broke down in sobs, Rose and Marie came up to the podium and stood on either side of him. Rose took over and read how the princess seduced the wolf's guard, then how the princess and the captain consummated their love for each other.

Marie read the final entry: how the princess planned to trick the captain and divert the treasure. She read about the princess's dreams to live happily ever after in a castle with her captain.

When she finished, Archie gave each twin a hug and returned to the microphone. "Flora deposited this story in a soul line collection back in 1946," he said. "Last month we helped our beautiful princess finish her quest. I have penned an addendum to her unfinished story." He took out another piece of paper and read it to us.

And the beautiful princess succeeded: she tricked the captain and stole the magical teeth. She and her fairy godmother's friend hid them far away in a distant land. The captain took the princess and her fairy godmother to a new castle in the land of the eagles.

But the beautiful princess was not happy. The magical teeth smoldered in their hiding place, and she could find no peace. She ached to tell the captain, but he spent his time with the other knights, choosing to become their general. When she bore their son, she hid him from the general.

Many years passed. The magical teeth remained hidden, and the beautiful princess and the captain-turned-general remained apart. And one day, when they both were old and gray, the general discovered the magical teeth were missing.

When confronted, the princess confessed to the general that she had tricked him. She led him to place where she hid the magical teeth, and she begged him to help her destroy them for once and for all. He agreed, and they declared their love for each other. Then, with the help of their friends and family, they recovered the magical teeth.

But the teeth were cursed, and a lesser wolf appeared and attacked the beautiful princess. She fought hard, but as she killed the wolf and destroyed the teeth, she suffered her own mortal blow.

Archie paused again and wiped his eyes. Rose and Marie put their arms around his shoulders. He murmured something to them, and then he read us the rest of his story.

The general mourned the loss of his beautiful princess. He promised their family that he, and indeed all the knights, would remember her sacrifice and fight to defeat all future wolves. And he waited for the day when he and the beautiful princess would finally be reunited.

The audience remained silent as Archie folded the papers and put them in his pocket. He grabbed the microphone with both hands.

"Flora spent her life on a quest against injustice," he said. "I have decided to continue her battle by personally funding and helping to direct her foundation for the Roma people. This morning I notified my good friend and fellow overseer Mr. Berringer that I would be resigning my position as the executive overseer of Soul Identity, effective in six months."

A gasp from the crowd, and Archie reached out and grabbed the twins' hands. "I also have a lot of catching up to do with my family," he said with a grin.

Val started to clap, and we all joined in a prolonged applause. George struggled to his feet, and the rest of us jumped up to give the overseer a standing ovation.

At the end of the service, as we were exiting, Val grabbed my arm. "He did the right thing," she said.

I smiled and replied, "And, finally, for all the right reasons."

Acknowledgements

Reviewing what seems like countless drafts is hard work, and I'd like to thank the many people who helped me through this: Shameless authors Bill Flynn, Mike Monahan, Don Fowler, Ellen George, Keith Knapp, and Lila Pinord; co-workers and friends Ken Ray, Angie Williams, Jason Chen, Mat Dickson, Alan Packer, Bob Kennedy, Jamie Dexter, Brian Thomas, Rodney Abelev, Amnon Horowitz, and Efim Hudis; and family members Mom, Dad, Kristin, Alison, and Holly. Your comments, questions, edits, and suggestions were exactly the motivation and help I needed.

Fred Brisard and Brad Wright helped me use proper diving terminology. David Hansen gave me a first-hand account of dealing with panic attacks. Any mistakes I made in relaying this information are mine alone.

Christian Nielsen and Nipoon Malhatra made generous bids at two charity auctions, and they each received the right to name a Soul Intent character and embed a cherished personality trait. Christian and Nipoon: I hope Justin Nielsen and Mukesh Rana Malhatra met your expectations—they certainly brought depth to their scenes.

Lastly, a great big thank you to my wife Irina for giving me the most precious gifts of all: time, understanding, and unending support and encouragement. I love you with all my heart, darling!

About the Author

Dennis Batchelder is a computer security architect. He lives with his family in Bellevue, Washington, and spends his off-hours working on the next Soul Identity novel.

Visit Dennis on the Web at **dennisbatchelder.com**.

CPSIA information can be obtained at www.ICGtesting.com
Printed in the USA
LVOW062224031211

257677LV00001B/148/P

9 780979 805622